W9-CYH-214

Dear Readers,

The last rose of summer may be fading, but Bouquet romances bloom all year long! And for this back-to-school month—which often means more reading time for Mom—we've got four delightful, heartwarming stories to enhance those late-summer afternoons in the hammock, the porch swing, or even the rocking chair.

After 25 Harlequin novels, it's high time for Vanessa Grant to grace Zebra with **If You Loved Me.** When Emma's 18-year-old son goes missing on a kayaking trip in the Northwest wilderness, Emma has no choice but to put herself at the mercy of onetime lover Gray McKenzie—an outdoorsman with his own plane. He knows every inch of the territory—but can he find his way back into Emma's heart?

It's a long way from high society Boston to Little Fork, Wyoming, but Caitlyn makes the trip when she inherits half a ranch, never dreaming that a sinfully handsome partner will be part of the deal. And who would have dreamed that **Caitlyn's Cowboy** would melt the ice around her heart? Gina Jackson makes her Bouquet debut with this captivating tale of magical love.

Newcomer Susan Hardy sweeps her readers into the breathtaking North Carolina mountains, where free-spirited Clementine "Clem" Harper is reluctantly swept into the arms of city slicker Will Fletcher. Will soon discovers that it's not easy to win the heart of a mountain gal . . . until he learns the secrets of **Mountain Magic.**

Veteran romance writer Judy Gill's **All in the Family** features two meddling daughters who can't resist "fixing up" newly divorced Dad Jet Cotts with one of their teachers. Karen Anderson is reluctant at first, but somehow this handsome, athletic, warmhearted man makes her feel cherished for the first time in ages. Maybe matchmaking isn't such a bad idea after all!

Kick back, slip off your shoes, and settle down for a nice, long read. Let your eyes follow your heart into these four enthralling romances . . . and before you know it, it will be next month—and time for four more. Enjoy!

The Editors

COWBOY'S KISS

"Just try to relax and remember where you are," Dane said. "You're home in your own bed. Everything turned out all right. You're safe."

"I'd feel a lot safer if you'd hold me."

Caitlyn looked up at Dane with pleading eyes and he couldn't stand it any longer. He pulled her into his arms and nestled her against his chest. "Is that better?"

"Oh, yes." She gave a soft sigh that made the blood in his veins start to sing. "It's much better. But I'm still cold. Can we . . . can we get under the covers?"

He should go. Right now. She was too tempting and he wasn't made of steel. How much longer could he resist her? The feel of her soft curves against him was driving him crazy.

"Please?"

He groaned and fell back on the pillows, holding her full length against him.

"What are you thinking about?"

Her voice was soft, a whisper against his ear, and he shivered with longing. "Nothing. I'm not thinking about anything at all."

"That's impossible." She flicked out her tongue and licked his ear. "I know what you're thinking about. I'm thinking about it, too. Please kiss me, Dane. I want you to kiss me again."

Dane groaned in surrender. It was impossible to resist her when she was right here, in his arms. He reached out to brush back her glorious hair, nuzzled the side of her smooth silken neck, and then he claimed her lips with his own. . . .

CAITLYN'S COWBOY

GINA JACKSON

ZEBRA BOOKS
KENSINGTON PUBLISHING CORP.

http://www.zebrabooks.com

ZEBRA BOOKS are published by

Kensington Publishing Corp.
850 Third Avenue
New York, NY 10022

First Printing: September, 1999
10 9 8 7 6 5 4 3 2 1

Printed in the United States of America

*This one's for Jill D'Andrea and Hans Fischmann,
our perfect bride and groom.*

ONE

As far as Caitlyn Bradford was concerned, it was a perfect day for a garden wedding. The thermometer had dipped below fifty degrees, a record low for the middle of June, and low gray clouds gathered on the horizon, heavy with rain. The biting wind fluttered the paper airline tags attached to her luggage, tugging at them like invisible fingers and threatening to rip them off before she reached the terminal. Caitlyn pushed her rented baggage cart with one hand and reached up with the other to make sure her long auburn hair was still caught neatly in the twist she wore at the nape of her neck. Her ex-husband was getting married today, in what the society pages called, "an intimate affair for three hundred of the couple's closest friends." Caitlyn knew it wasn't very charitable of her, but she hoped the sky would open up in a downpour.

There were only four people waiting at curbside check-in. It was obvious that saner travelers preferred the long lines inside the terminal to the prospect of being buffeted by the wind or drenched by the impending rain. Caitlyn decided to chance that the storm would hold off long enough for her to check her bags. If she checked in now, at curbside, she'd have time to enjoy a steaming cup of cappuccino at the airport restaurant before she boarded her flight.

As she took her place in line, the heavyset older woman in front of her noticed Caitlyn's heavily loaded luggage cart. "Excuse me, hon, but don't you know that you're only allowed two suitcases and a carryon?"

"Yes, I know." Caitlyn smiled politely. She hated being called *hon* by perfect strangers, but the woman probably meant well.

"I called and they told me they'd take my extra luggage if I paid for the additional weight."

The line was moving fast. No one wanted to be out in the elements for long, and that included the two male employees assigned to curbside check-in duties. The younger of the two, a fresh-faced kid who didn't look old enough to be out of high school, hefted the heavyset woman's suitcases onto the wheeled platform while the older employee stapled the baggage claim stubs to her ticket. And then it was Caitlyn's turn.

"You're only allowed two suitcases and a carryon, miss." The older man frowned.

"I know." Caitlyn sighed. She hated to repeat herself. "I called and they told me they'd take my extra luggage if I paid for the additional weight."

The older man nodded. "That's right, but you can't do it here. You have to take it inside and get it weighed."

"Is there any way that you could take care of it for me?" Caitlyn drew out the folded bill she kept for precisely this purpose. She'd learned early on that a tip could do wonders to bend the rules. "I'd be happy to pay you for your trouble."

The older man grinned as he accepted the bill. "Well . . . my partner's pretty good at judging weight. What do you say, Bobby?"

"Sure." The younger man grinned at her. "You already went through our line. It wouldn't be right to make you stand in another one."

"That's really nice of you." Caitlyn drew out another bill and passed it to him as he reached for her first extra suitcase.

"This one's pretty light." He hefted the heavy suitcase and placed it on the cart. He did the same for the other three and then he winked at her. "I'd say that ten dollars ought to cover the extra weight."

Caitlyn nodded and handed him two fives, very pleased with the way she'd handled the problem. When the taxi driver who'd brought her to the airport had loaded the baggage for her, he'd joked that her suitcases must be loaded with bricks. She'd expected that her extra luggage would cost her at least fifty dollars, perhaps even more, but she'd spent less than half of that by tipping the curbside employees.

Once the claim stubs for her luggage had been stapled to her ticket, Caitlyn picked up her shoulder-bag carryon and headed toward the terminal. When she reached the door, she turned back for one last look at the six large Louis Vuitton suitcases that sat on the top of the baggage cart and sighed. All her worldly possessions were packed inside. It wasn't much to show for three-and-a-half years of marriage to Spencer Sinclair, but at least she wouldn't have to listen to his mother's constant criticism of her any longer.

The terminal was crowded with fellow travelers, and Caitlyn gave a satisfied smile as she passed the long, snaking line of people at the check-in counter. Not only had she saved herself money, she'd also bought herself some time. A glance at the bank of computer monitors flashing departure and arrival schedules confirmed that she had almost an hour before she was due to board her flight. She would spend that time in a cushioned booth at the airport restaurant, planning out precisely what to do once she got to Little Fork, Wyoming.

The summons from her aunt's lawyer had come only yesterday. Aunt Bella was dead. Caitlyn hadn't known her father's sister well, but three months ago, Aunt Bella had called to ask her if she would be the executor of her will. Naturally, Caitlyn had agreed. Her parents had died several years ago and Aunt Bella had been the only other family member she'd had left. Her aunt hadn't sounded ill the last time they spoke. But now, barely twelve weeks later, Aunt Bella was gone, too.

Caitlyn selected a small booth in the corner of the restaurant and placed her order for cappuccino. While she was waiting, she thought of the last conversation she'd had with her aunt. Aunt Bella had asked about Spencer and the floodgates had opened. Caitlyn had found herself crying on the phone and telling her aunt that she'd filed for divorce. She'd even gone into the sordid details and admitted that she'd come home early from the office to find Spencer in bed with Ardis Pelton, the daughter of his mother's best friend.

Aunt Bella hadn't seemed shocked by the news. She'd just offered her brand of good-sense advice. It was a fact of life that some husbands strayed, and it was up to Caitlyn to decide what she wanted to do about it. Divorce was one solution; forgiveness was another. Was Caitlyn sure that her marriage wasn't worth saving?

Caitlyn was sure and she'd told Aunt Bella why. Instead of putting Ardis into a cab when Caitlyn had walked in on them, Spencer had dressed and driven her home. Then he'd gone to his club and called her. He'd apologized; he hadn't meant for her to find out that way, but perhaps it was best that the truth about his affair with Ardis had come out. If Caitlyn wanted to file for divorce, that was agreeable to him. As a matter of fact, it would be best if she did. Ardis had just learned that she was pregnant and they wanted to marry as soon as possible.

The waitress was here with her cappuccino. Caitlyn stirred it with her cinnamon stick, took a sip of the sweet coffee, and sighed. What had gone wrong with her marriage? Were there warning signs that she'd missed? They'd been in love at the beginning. Caitlyn was sure of that; but they'd both been busy professionals and they hadn't had that much time together.

Caitlyn had explained all that to Aunt Bella. There was no use in denying that they'd grown apart, that they'd turned into friendly strangers living under a common roof. She'd thought it was natural. Didn't most marriages settle down eventually into a companionable groove? Aunt Bella had laughed. A companionable groove was just another name for a rut, and that wasn't good. She'd agreed that there was no reason for Caitlyn to fight to preserve her marriage with Spencer, not if she felt that way about him. They had no children and it was clear that he wanted out. And didn't Caitlyn want out, too?

Caitlyn had admitted that she did. She was tired of working hard all day and then coming home to be the perfect society wife. She had felt, for some time now, that there had to be more to life than that.

Aunt Bella had agreed that she'd made the right decision. And then she'd said something very surprising. Caitlyn should do her best to regard her divorce as a door opening instead of a door closing. After her divorce was final, Caitlyn could test her wings and discover what *she* really wanted to do with her life.

Caitlyn sighed. She'd grown accustomed to being Mrs. Spencer Sinclair and the thought of being on her own again was just a bit frightening. The divorce process itself had been easy.

The Sinclair family lawyers had taken care of everything and Caitlyn hadn't argued over the details. She'd agreed that the divorce should be accomplished as quickly and as quietly as possible. Yesterday morning, she'd gone to their office to finalize the whole thing. She signed where they'd told her to sign, initialed where they'd told her to initial, and gone straight back to the house she'd shared with Spencer to pack up her things.

Bitsy Beauchamp, one of Caitlyn's friends from the Boston Hospital Ladies' Auxiliary, had been waiting for her in the driveway. She'd said that there was no way that Caitlyn should be alone at a time like this, and she'd helped her pack her things. When that had been accomplished, Bitsy had declared that she was taking Caitlyn out for lunch to celebrate her new freedom.

On the way out, they'd met the mailman, who had arrived with a special-delivery letter for Caitlyn. It was from Jeremy Campbell, her aunt's attorney, and it had informed her of Aunt Bella's death. Mr. Campbell had requested that Caitlyn fly to Wyoming, her expenses to be paid by Aunt Bella's estate, to fulfill her responsibility as the executor of her aunt's will.

Over their warm scallop salad at Pietre's, Bitsy's favorite restaurant, Caitlyn had come to a decision. There was no way she wanted to stay in Boston and continue her career in the Sinclair Advertising firm. It would be much too painful to face Spencer every day. She had the cash settlement from her divorce. Spencer had been generous about that. She'd fly out to Wyoming, settle her aunt's affairs, and then she'd start a new life for herself.

"Will there be anything else, ma'am?"

The question from the waitress brought Caitlyn back to the present with a jolt, and she glanced at her watch. "No, just the check, please. It's almost time for me to board my flight."

Caitlyn smiled as she reached into her purse to leave enough money to cover the bill and provide a tip for the waitress. Then she rose to her feet, straightened the jacket of the seafoam-green designer knit suit that she'd worn to the last Junior League luncheon, and set off for the plane that would carry her to her new life.

* * *

Twenty-six hours later, Caitlyn felt like a new woman. She'd accomplished a lot the preceding day. She'd arrived in Denver in the early afternoon, taken a room at the historic Brown Palace Hotel, and spent the remainder of the afternoon shopping for some authentic Western wear. She'd eaten dinner in the hotel restaurant, gone back up to her room, and enjoyed her first restful night's sleep since she'd filed for divorce. This morning, she'd boarded a plane to Cheyenne, taken a taxi to the local Ford dealership, and used part of the cash settlement that Spencer's lawyers had given her to buy something she felt was appropriate for her new life in the West—a truck.

Of course it wasn't really a truck, not exactly. It was an all-wheel-drive Explorer. But the salesman had assured her that it could do anything that a truck could do, and Caitlyn grinned as she drove down the freeway. She'd stopped at a local drive-in to get a giant-sized soft drink, and now she was sipping a diet cola from a plastic straw that was inserted in a the cover of a Styrofoam cup and her long auburn hair was blowing in the wind from the partially open window. What would Spencer say if he could see her now? Caitlyn laughed out loud as she imagined his horrified expression. For the past three-and-a-half years, she had been the perfect society wife. Every article of her clothing had been especially designed for her; her jewelry had been chosen from the Spencer family heirlooms, and her hair had been styled in Boston's most exclusive salon. She had been elegant, proper, and excruciatingly tasteful, just as a Sinclair wife should be. Her picture had appeared on the society pages; their home had been featured in the Sunday supplement, and the guest lists for their parties could have been taken directly from the pages of the social register.

Would things have turned out differently if she had given up her career? Caitlyn thought about it for a moment, and then she shrugged. Spencer's mother had objected to what she'd called Caitlyn's "little job." No Sinclair wife had ever worked. It simply wasn't done. Certain unenlightened persons might incorrectly assume that Spencer wasn't able to provide for her.

Caitlyn had stood her ground. She had worked too long and too hard to give up her career simply because she was marrying the boss. And surprisingly, Spencer had supported her. He had told his mother that he had no objection if Caitlyn continued in her position as a senior marketing executive at his agency, as long as she agreed to give up her job when they had children.

But there hadn't been children, not even a false alarm in three-and-a-half years of marriage. Caitlyn had wanted a baby, but it just hadn't happened. And when she'd suggested that they both go in for testing, Spencer had vetoed the idea. If she eventually got pregnant, that was fine. And if she didn't, that was fine, too.

And now Ardis was pregnant with the baby that should have been hers. Caitlyn forced her fingers to relax their death grip on the wheel. She was starting a new life. It was foolish to dwell on the past. She made a random selection from the stack of country-western CDs that she'd bought at the music store in Cheyenne and slipped one into the carrier. She had never listened to country-western music before, but it seemed appropriate. She was in Wyoming, and that was in the West.

As LeAnn Rimes sang of unfaithful husbands, lost loves, and lonely beds, Caitlyn's full lips turned up in a smile. She was free, for the first time in her life. She was twenty-seven years old, on her own, and accountable to no one except herself. Once she had driven to Little Fork and discharged her duties as the executor of Aunt Bella's will, she could go wherever she wished and do exactly as she pleased.

Where would she go? Caitlyn's smile grew even wider as she considered the possibilities. She wouldn't really have to *do* anything, at least for a while. If she stuck to a budget and used her reserves wisely, money shouldn't be a problem for at least a year. That was enough time to decide on a place to live and an occupation that pleased her. She might even go back to college to get another degree, and moonlight as a freelancer at an ad agency to support herself.

A loud blast from an air horn roused Caitlyn from her thoughts and she glanced in her rearview mirror. The driver of a huge semi was blinking his lights, signaling that he wanted to pass. Caitlyn eased up on the accelerator and slowed, allowing the truck to pull out into the adjoining lane.

As the semi paced her, Caitlyn glanced over at the driver.

He was handsome, in what Spencer would have termed a "blue-collar" way, and she smiled politely. But her smile soon changed to a frown as she realized that he was gesturing at her to roll down her window. Was something wrong with her new Explorer?

Caitlyn turned down the volume of her stereo and pushed the button to lower her window all the way. Through the rushing wind and the noise of the other traffic, she made out the words "truck stop," "next exit," and "coffee." Realizing that the handsome trucker was attempting to pick her up, Caitlyn shook her head and raised her window again. It took a few minutes for him to get the message, but at last he dropped back and took the exit without her.

A grin spread over Caitlyn's face. Of course she wouldn't have stopped for coffee with the trucker, but the fact that he'd attempted to pick her up was a compliment of sorts. He'd found her attractive, even though her hair was windblown and she was wearing no makeup. Would other men also find her attractive?

Caitlyn supposed she'd have to be careful, now that she was single again. She certainly didn't want to give anyone the wrong impression. She wasn't some love-starved divorcée searching for a new man. As a matter of fact, Caitlyn didn't really want a man.

Was she bitter about men, now that Spencer had betrayed her? Caitlyn thought about it for several moments, and then she shook her head. She didn't hate men. That wasn't it at all. And she didn't think that she was depressed about her divorce. She was simply numb and she felt as if someone had given her a shot of Novocain that had affected her whole body. She needed time to get back to normal again, to get in touch with her feelings, and to discover how she felt now that she was no longer Mrs. Spencer Sinclair.

Caitlyn put a determined smile on her face. She was on her own, and she intended to enjoy her new freedom. She'd married Spencer and it had ended badly. Other women had gone through the same thing, and most of them had managed to pick up the threads of their lives. She wasn't foolish enough to believe that she would never fall in love again; but for the first couple of years, at least, romance was simply off her agenda.

TWO

"Hey, Dane. You heard anything yet?"

Dane Morrison swung out of the saddle and handed the reins to one of the stable hands. He gave Warrior, his big black stallion, an affectionate slap on the rump and then he turned to Gibby, the red-whiskered cowboy who ran the chuck wagon and the ranch kitchens. "I dropped by Jerry's office and his dad said she was due sometime this afternoon. Jerry's supposed to show her the paperwork and then bring her on out."

"How about the will? Bella left her the ranch, didn't she?"

Dane's blue eyes narrowed slightly. "Jerry's dad wouldn't tell me one way or the other. He said the will had to stay confidential until she arrived. But it stands to reason that she got the ranch. As far as I know, she's Bella's only living relative."

"Think she'll sell it out from under us?"

"Maybe, maybe not." Dane shrugged, his red Double B shirt stretching tautly over his well-muscled chest. "We're turning a good profit, so that should impress her. And it won't be that easy finding the right buyer. If she's as smart as Bella told me she was, she'll wait until the end of the season to make up her mind."

Gibby looked worried and Dane didn't blame him. Gibby had been the head cook at the Double B ever since Bella had bought the land that surrounded her little bed-and-breakfast and turned it into a dude ranch. "What are we gonna do if she decides to sell?"

"Hope that the new owner will hire the lot of us, I guess." Dane sighed, stretching out his long legs. "But maybe it won't come to that. The way I see it, it's up to us to convince her not to sell."

"And just how are we supposed to do that?"

Dane shrugged again, leaning against the weathered rail of the corral and slouching a bit so that Gibby didn't have to crane his neck to look up at him. "I don't know, exactly. I guess we could try to make her fall in love with the place, the way Bella did."

"Fall in love?" Gibby's eyebrows shot up at the suggestion. "Maybe you've got something there. She's young and she's divorced, ain't she? And you're not half bad-looking. Maybe you can romance her a little and bring her around to our way of thinking."

Dane laughed, pulling off the baseball cap he wore when their guests weren't around and letting his dark wavy hair blow in the breeze. "You can put that idea right out of your head, Gibby. She's a big-city gal, a regular blue-blooded society lady from *Baaston.*"

"So what?" Gibby grinned, showing the gap in his front teeth. "You got along fine with the group of society gals that just left. Every one of 'em was making sheep's eyes at you."

"They were just having a little fun on their vacation. Not one of them was serious and you know it. They just liked the idea of flirting with a real cowboy, that's all."

"Well, maybe *she'll* like the idea of flirting with a real cowboy, too." It was clear that Gibby wasn't willing to give up just yet. "What does she look like?"

Dane began to frown slightly. He didn't like the calculating grin on Gibby's face. "How would I know? The only picture I've ever seen of her was the one Bella kept on her mantel. And that was taken when she was twelve years old!"

"I seen it." Gibby nodded. "She was a right pretty gal and I bet she grew up to be a real beauty. As I recollect, she had nice red hair. I've always been partial to red hair."

Dane grinned, his teeth flashing whitely in his tanned face. "That wouldn't have anything to do with the color of your own hair, would it, Gibby?"

"Maybe it would at that." Gibby grinned right back. "But mine's barn red and hers is the color of cinnamon. Do you think she still has those pretty green eyes?"

Dane remembered the remarkable color of her eyes in the

photograph, the exact shade of the water in the Atlantic Ocean right before a gale blew in. "Sure, she does. People's eyes don't change color when they grow up."

"Right pretty, they were. It seems to me that a man might tumble hard for a pretty little thing like that. And she might come to feel the same way about him. If things worked out right, they might even get married and settle down right here on the ranch."

"I'm not looking for a wife, Gibby." Dane's blue eyes turned cold. "And I'm willing to bet that she's not looking for a husband. She just got divorced."

Gibby nodded. "I suppose you're right, but it's too bad. Still, she could be mighty lonely, out here in a strange place by herself. If you're dead set against it, maybe Jake wouldn't mind romancing her a bit."

"Leave Jake out of this!" Dane's brow furrowed as he thought about Jake Wheeler, the wrangler that Bella had hired at the beginning of the season. "Bella would spin in her grave if she thought that rodeo bum was after her niece! Haven't we had enough trouble with him?"

Gibby shrugged. "He's been real good since Bill Perkins threatened to break his neck if he ever caught him near Dorothy again. He's been ridin' all the way over to Cripplecreek to do his drinkin' and such."

"Let's keep it that way." Dane sighed. "I'll do what I can about making her feel at home here, but let's not count on romance to tip the scales in our favor. We'll just show her how good our operation is and leave it at that."

Gibby nodded. "Okay. You're the boss . . . at least for now. We'll do it your way. Now I got to get moving. There's biscuits to mix up for tonight's barbecue."

Dane shook his head as the cook walked away. If he didn't miss his guess, Gibby wasn't through with his plan to make Bella's niece fall in love with a cowboy. It really wasn't such a bad idea, but he'd make sure that Jake wouldn't be that cowboy. And it wouldn't be him, either. He'd enjoyed the love of one good woman, and that was enough for any man. And now that she was gone and he'd finally learned to deal with the pain, he wasn't about to let another female into his life.

* * *

Caitlyn smiled as she took the exit for Little Fork, Wyoming. The Explorer had been a pleasure to drive and she'd enjoyed sitting up so high. It had been very different from driving the low-slung silver Jaguar that Spencer had leased for her. On several occasions, while driving to the office, Caitlyn had worried that the Boston city buses, with tires that loomed taller than her Jag, were going to squash her like a bug.

As she drove down the main street, Caitlyn's smile grew wider. Little Fork, with its quaint, false-front buildings, looked like the set of a Western movie. There were hitching posts outside every store, and several had real horses tethered to them. She half expected to see John Wayne swaggering down the street or Gary Cooper riding by.

Since there was only one long street, it was a simple matter to find Mr. Campbell's law office. Caitlyn parked in front of the tree-shaded wooden building and opened the door of her car. She had styled her hair and done her makeup in the immaculate restroom of the service station and she knew that she looked every inch a professional in her camel-colored cashmere suit. Her blouse was made of ivory-colored silk with a loose tie at the neck; and her purse, a medium-sized shoulder bag, matched the ivory leather of her stylish strapped shoes.

As she walked toward the office door, Caitlyn was pleased by her reflection in the dusty plate-glass window. She looked smart and businesslike, exactly the way she wanted to look. Caitlyn took a deep breath, pushed open the door, and heard a bell tinkle somewhere in the rear of the small building. A moment later, a young man emerged from the back, polishing his glasses on his shirttail.

Caitlyn stared at him in shock. He couldn't possibly be Jeremy Campbell. A lawyer would never greet a client in worn blue jeans and a denim shirt with a ragged hole in the elbow!

"You made great time. We didn't expect you for at least another hour." The young man gestured toward a chair facing an antique wooden desk and Caitlyn sat down obediently. He'd known she was coming, and that meant Mr. Campbell must have told him. Perhaps he was here to do odd jobs. But that idea dissipated into thin air when he pulled out the chair behind the desk and sat down, leaning forward to smile at her. "I'm Jerry Campbell."

Caitlyn's green eyes widened with surprise. *"You're* the Jeremy Campbell who wrote to me?"

"Nope. That was my father. I'm Jeremy the second, but folks around here call me Jerry. I wouldn't let 'em call me Junior. Dad retired right after he wrote you that letter about your aunt's death."

"I see." Caitlyn nodded, although she didn't see at all. "Perhaps we had a bad connection, but you sounded a lot older when I spoke to you on the phone this morning."

"You talked to Dad, not me. He still comes in every morning to take a few calls. Likes to keep his hand in, you know? He's never come right out and said so, but I know half of the reason he comes in is to keep his eye on me."

"Oh." Caitlyn couldn't think of any appropriate reply. She really wasn't accustomed to dealing with lawyers who were so candid.

Jerry Campbell gave her a disarming grin. "I just graduated from law school and Dad doesn't completely trust me yet. He's been here for thirty years and he built up the practice from scratch. He just wants to make sure that he's leaving it in good hands."

Caitlyn nodded, smiling at him. "I guess I can understand that. But it must be hard on you."

"Nope. I like it. Dad's a crack lawyer and he keeps me on my toes. Once he's satisfied with the way I'm handling things, he'll start spending less time in here and more time fishing. That's his first love, fishing. Do you go by Bradford or Sinclair?"

It took a moment for Caitlyn to switch gears, but she managed. "Bradford. I took my maiden name back after the divorce."

"Okay." He flipped open the file. "Bella's got you down as Bradford in her will. Not that it would make any real difference, but it'll save us some paperwork. Did you bring a copy of your divorce papers with your name-change?"

Caitlyn nodded and pulled the divorce decree from her bag. She started to hand him the packet, but she hesitated. She really didn't want any strangers to know the particulars of her divorce. "This will be confidential, won't it, Mr. Campbell?"

"Jerry. And it sure will be." The young lawyer nodded. "Your ex-husband played hardball?"

It took a moment for Caitlyn to catch his meaning; but when she did, she shook her head. "Not exactly. Ours was what they call a friendly divorce."

"Maybe, but I never heard of any that really were." He took a moment to skim over the papers and then he looked up to meet her eyes. "You used his law firm?"

Caitlyn nodded. "Yes, it was more expedient that way."

"I've heard of them. They're tough and they're good. I'd say it's a miracle that you walked away with more than the clothes on your back. I assume that in addition to the cash settlement, you also put something away for a rainy day?"

"What do you mean?"

"You know. Things like expensive presents to friends that you could collect later? Or an envelope full of hidden cash that couldn't be traced?"

Caitlyn stared at him in shock. "I had no idea our marriage was in trouble. And even if I'd sensed that it was, I wouldn't have . . . have *cheated* like that!"

"You're Bella's niece, all right!" He beamed at her and Caitlyn felt like a student who'd just turned in an "A" paper. But then his expression turned somber. "We all loved Bella, you know. She was as tough as nails on the outside, but she had a soft heart."

Caitlyn nodded, pleased at his description of her aunt. "I only met her once. She came back east for my twelfth birthday and stayed with my parents for a week. I liked her a lot and I always wanted to come out here to visit her, but I just never got around to it. And now . . . it's too late."

"I know." He seemed to sense her regret and he gave her a moment of privacy as he paged through the will. When he looked up, he was grinning. "It's all pretty straightforward. Your aunt made some cash bequests to her long-term employees, but she left half of her remaining estate to you."

Caitlyn was shocked. "To *me?* But . . . but I barely knew her!"

"She didn't tell you that you'd inherit?"

"No! Aunt Bella called me three months ago to ask me if I'd

be the executor of her will. I agreed to do it, but I really had no idea that she meant to leave me anything. She didn't mention it, and your father certainly didn't tell me in his letter. He just asked me to come out here to settle Aunt Bella's affairs and enclosed a check to cover my expenses."

"It's not like Dad to leave out an important fact like that, unless . . ." Caitlyn watched as he paged through the documents and drew out a handwritten note. "Ah! This explains it! Bella had a meeting with Dad the week before she died and she asked him not to mention the terms of her will until you arrived. At that same meeting, she changed those terms so that you would inherit, instead of her favorite charity."

"But . . . why?"

"Her reason's right here, in Dad's note. She told him about your divorce, and she said she thought you could use a change of scene. Dad's a real stickler about writing everything down. Says it's saved him a lot of trouble over the years. He marks those notes 'C.Y.A.' That stands for 'Cover Your . . .' Well, you probably know what the 'A' stands for. Don't you want to know who gets the other half of her estate?"

Caitlyn blinked. He'd switched gears again. "Yes, of course I do. Is it the charity she mentioned?"

"Nope." He chuckled, grinning at her. "It's Dane."

Caitlyn wracked her brain, but she knew she'd never heard the name before. "Who's Dane?"

"Your new partner. You own the Double B, fifty-fifty. That's the name of your aunt's place, the Double B. Her brand is two B's, back to back. You do know what a brand is, don't you?"

Caitlyn blinked again. This young lawyer kept throwing her curves. "I think so. Would that be like the brand they put on cattle?"

"Right you are. I wasn't sure you'd know, coming from the big city and all; but I guess you've seen a few cowboy movies. They used our main street for a location, a few years back. It was great for business and we got new paint jobs on all the buildings. Do you have any questions or are you ready to go?"

This time Caitlyn was ready for the abrupt change of subject. "Go where?"

"To the Double B. They're waiting to give you a tour of the place. Do you want to change here or wait until you get there?"

"Change." Caitlyn repeated the word. "As in clothes?"

The young lawyer nodded. "You'll stick out like a bull in a flock of sheep wearing that fancy suit. Not that it isn't pretty, of course; but it'd be a real shame to get it all dirty."

Caitlyn didn't bother to ask why her suit would get dirty at her aunt's bed-and-breakfast. She just rolled with the punches and smiled. "I'll change here if you don't mind. What should I wear?"

"Jeans and something. That's what everybody wears around here. Did you stop for dinner on the road?"

"Dinner?" Caitlyn glanced down at her watch and saw that it was only noon. "Do you mean last night's dinner?"

Jerry Campbell stared at her for a moment and then he chuckled. "Sorry, I forgot that you were from the East. Dinner out here is what you call lunch. And supper is what you call dinner. Our lunch is the snack you have in the middle of the afternoon."

"I'll try to remember that." Caitlyn felt her mind spinning again. "And what do you call breakfast?"

"Breakfast. You can never go wrong ordering breakfast. Now you go on in the back and change, and I'll run down to Millie's and rustle us up some sandwiches and coffee for the road. What do you take in yours?"

"The sandwich or the coffee?" Caitlyn was proud of herself when he laughed.

"Both of 'em. Millie makes a mean smoked ham."

Caitlyn nodded. "Then that's what I'll have. And I like my coffee black."

"You should have it with cream and sugar." He shrugged, grinning at her. "We get some fierce winds around here in the winter, and one of 'em's likely to blow you away."

Caitlyn smiled because that was what he seemed to expect; but the moment he was gone, her smile disappeared. If Mr. Jerry Campbell thought that she was staying in Little Fork, Wyoming, one minute longer than it took her to sell her half of Aunt Bella's bed-and-breakfast, he was crazy!

THREE

"Lordy!" Gibby stood by the chuck wagon, a wooden spoon in his hand, staring at the two vehicles that were pulling up to park in the spaces at the front of the ranch house. "It's her, all right. I can see the sun glittering off of that pretty cinnamon hair of hers."

Dane nodded. "Don't know who else it would be, since that's Jerry's truck. Looks like she's driving a brand-new car. She must have made out okay in the divorce."

"That's a good sign, ain't it?" Gibby turned to him anxiously. "If she got a lot of money from her ex, she won't need to sell."

"You could be right." Dane half listened as Gibby chattered on about the reasons why she might want to keep the ranch. He was much more interested in watching Caitlyn Bradford climb out of her car. Gibby was right. Her hair *was* the color of cinnamon, and it was too bad she'd slicked it all back in a bun. He found himself imagining what it would be like if she let it fall loose around her shoulders and he sighed.

Gibby grinned and poked his arm with an elbow. "She's awful skinny; but she sure is pretty, ain't she?"

"Not bad." Dane gave his best nonchalant reply and went back to his assessment of her. She had a nice trim little figure, and it would be even better if she'd gain a little weight. She was much too thin, but she probably believed the trendy slogan that a woman couldn't be too thin or too rich.

Dane turned away slightly so that Gibby couldn't see the pain in his eyes. They'd joked about that when Beth had first started losing weight. He'd accused her of dieting to be fashionable; but she'd denied it, insisting that her weight loss was the result of the new exercise class she was taking.

Dane sighed. She must have suspected that something was wrong, but she hadn't shared her worries with him. Maybe if he hadn't been so busy, if he'd spent more time with her, he would have seen the warning signs earlier. But he hadn't. And Beth hadn't been the type to complain.

Gibby poked him again, rousing him from his guilty memories. "So? What do you think of her?"

"Looks okay, I guess." Dane nodded and resumed his scrutiny of Bella's niece. At least she was wearing blue jeans. That was one point in her favor. But they were brand new and she looked so uncomfortable in them, Dane was sure that they weren't her usual style of dress. Her cream-colored blouse was pretty, but it would get trashed in a hurry if she intended to do any real work. As he watched, the breeze blew the soft material against her body, outlining her breasts, and Dane swallowed hard. He'd been on the ranch for too long. If Bella's niece was planning to stay on at the Double B, he might just have to drive over to Cripplecreek some night with Jake.

"So, what do you say I ring the gong and get everybody together to meet her?"

"Okay." While Jerry unloaded her luggage and carried it up to the porch of the ranch house, she leaned over, her back to them, to pet one of the ranch dogs. Dane tore his eyes away from the enticing sight and turned back to Gibby. "That's a real good idea. Round up everybody who's not out with the guests."

"What's he doing now?" Gibby gestured toward Jerry, who had come back to take her arm. "Can't she walk on her own?"

"I'm sure she can. Go on, Gibby. Get the guys together and tell them that the new owner's here."

"Me?" Gibby looked surprised. "I thought maybe you'd want to tell them. You could give them a pep talk, tell them to be polite and all."

"You do it. You know what to say. I'm going up there to meet her."

Gibby nodded, and then he started to grin. "You think Jerry's gonna try something with her?"

"None of my business if he does."

Dane turned and strode off toward the main house with a worried frown on his face. Gibby was right to be concerned and it *was* his business, in a way. Caitlyn Bradford was the new gal in town, and Jerry was young and single. Everyone in Little Fork expected him to get engaged to Nancy Hooper, but it hadn't happened yet. It was up to Dane to keep Jerry out of trouble. Nancy's dad had a hair-trigger temper, and there was no telling what he'd do if Jerry ended up disappointing his youngest daughter.

Her suitcases were piled up by the door and Dane picked them up and carried them inside. Once he'd stashed them in Bella's private quarters, he walked down the hallway, listening for the sound of their voices. He heard a laugh from the ranch house living room and he breathed a deep sigh of relief. Jerry was probably just giving her the five-cent tour.

He stopped outside the arched doorway and drew a long, deep breath as he spotted her. Caitlyn Bradford was even more beautiful than he'd thought. She was standing in the center of the room, staring at the massive river-rock fireplace. There was an almost childlike expression of awe on her face, and her deep-green eyes were sparkling with excitement.

As Dane stared at her, he wondered what she'd do if he barged right in, pulled her into his arms without a word, and kissed her. Would she scream? Faint? Slap his face? Or would she kiss him right back? The thought was tantalizing, and he forced it out of his mind with difficulty. He couldn't forget that he was here on a mission. Caitlyn Bradford had the power to sell the ranch that had been his home for the past four years, and he was determined to stop her from doing it.

"I had no idea that Aunt Bella had turned her bed-and-breakfast into a dude ranch!" Caitlyn looked around her in awe. "Where are the . . . uh . . . dudes?"

"Guests. We never call them 'dudes.' Your aunt insisted on that."

Caitlyn whirled to see a tall, lanky man leaning against the door frame. His hair was dark and curly; his skin was tanned the color of the leather seats in her Explorer, and his startling blue eyes were regarding her impassively.

"Oh." Caitlyn gave him a polite smile. "Thank you for telling me. Where are the . . . guests?"

"They're all out on a day trip, riding the fence line and rounding up strays."

He didn't respond to her polite smile, and Caitlyn began to frown. "The guests actually *work* on the ranch?"

"Nope. We let them think they're helping out because that's what they come for. They want to go home and tell everybody that they were cowboys for a week."

"I see." Caitlyn nodded. He was obviously a ranch employee, but he certainly wasn't very friendly! And he wasn't working, either. He seemed quite content to just stand there, staring at her. "Why aren't you out on the day trip with the guests?"

"That's not part of my job. I'm the head wrangler."

He was leaning against the door frame as if he owned the place, and his casual pose irked her. Caitlyn squelched the insane urge to reach out and touch his arm to see if his muscles were as hard as they looked, and glared at him. There was no denying that he was handsome in his faded blue jeans and his tight red shirt.

Without really intending to, Caitlyn thought about Bitsy Beauchamp. Bitsy had talked about the "Sex Quotient," and she'd rated everyone's husband on a scale from one to ten. Spencer had gotten a five. Bitsy had judged him handsome enough, but she'd said Spencer lacked that extra dose of sexiness that would make a perfect stranger drag him home for a wild night in her bedroom. Caitlyn hadn't really understood Bitsy's rating at the time, but she did now. Aunt Bella's head wrangler would have blown the top right off Bitsy's scale.

It was difficult, but Caitlyn forced herself to step closer to him. If he thought he could intimidate her by his sexy masculinity, he had another thought coming. "You'll have to excuse my ignorance, but I've never been on a dude ranch before. Exactly what does a head wrangler do?"

"Basically, I run the place." He smiled, his teeth flashing

whitely in his tanned face. "I handle the books, order supplies, pay the bills, book the guests, arrange for their transportation and entertainment, and supervise the ranch staff. And when the season's over, I manage the real ranching that goes on around here."

"I see." Caitlyn felt the color rise to her cheeks. He was staring at her boldly, almost as if he were undressing her with his eyes. She had to put a stop to this immediately by letting him know that she was his new boss. Assuming her sternest expression, Caitlyn faced him squarely. "What's your name?"

"Caitlyn Bradford meet Dane Morrison."

Caitlyn whirled around, startled by the sound of Jerry's voice. She'd almost forgotten that he was in the room! As her eyes darted to the lawyer's face, she noticed that there was a hint of laughter in his eyes. What was so funny? She was about to demand an explanation when the name he'd called Aunt Bella's head wrangler finally registered in her brain.

"Dane Morrison?" Caitlyn turned back to him with utter disbelief. "You're *Dane?*"

The tall cowboy nodded. "That's what my friends call me."

Caitlyn drew a deep breath for courage and faced him square on. She wasn't his friend and there was no way she'd call him by his first name. "I'm glad to meet you, Mr. Morrison. It appears that you're my new partner."

"Your new *partner?*"

This time it was his turn to be surprised. Caitlyn felt a rush of triumph as his hand slid from the door frame and he straightened up to his full height. At least she'd managed to rattle him. Then she turned back to Jerry, still glowing from her minor success, and gave him her coolest smile. "You're the lawyer. You explain it. I'm going to take a shower and change. I'll expect to see both of you here in exactly twenty minutes to discuss the details of dissolving the partnership and selling this place."

FOUR

"What do you mean, I can't sell?" Caitlyn straightened her shoulders in the black pin-striped business suit she'd donned for their meeting and leaned forward aggressively, the way she'd seen Spencer do when he was confronted by a problem. She'd insisted that they sit at the round oak table on the ladder-back chairs in the corner of the huge living room rather than lounging on the leather-covered sofas that were arranged in a casual grouping near the fireplace.

Jerry didn't seem at all intimidated by her pose, even though it had always worked when Spencer had done it. He just grinned at her and shrugged. "It's pretty clear your aunt didn't want you to sell. I'd wager to say that's the reason she divided it up."

"I know Aunt Bella gave *him* half." Caitlyn turned to glare at Dane, who had somehow managed to slouch comfortably despite the straight-backed chairs. "But why can't I sell my share?"

Jerry handed her the section of the will that was highlighted in yellow marker. "Because your aunt set it up that way. It's right there on page four. She checkerboarded the Double B before she died."

"Checkerboarded?" Caitlyn tried not to look puzzled. For all she knew, this country lawyer was trying to pull a fast one on her.

"It means that she divided the land into small square sections. Your sections touch only at the corners. They alternate like the squares on a checkerboard. I'll give you a couple of examples. The ranch house is on one of your sections, but the building that houses the kitchens is on one of Dane's. He's got the horse barns, but you have the corrals and the feed shed. Are you beginning to get the idea?"

Caitlyn sighed. "I'm getting it. But what prevents me from selling my sections?"

"Nothing, provided you can find someone who wants to buy fifty isolated sections of land. They're practically worthless. Nobody in their right mind would buy only alternating squares on a checkerboard."

"I see." Caitlyn sighed, picturing a huge checkerboard superimposed over the Double B Ranch. Though her situation was frustrating, it did tickle her sense of humor. "Did I get the red or the black?"

Jerry looked puzzled at her question, but Dane laughed. "You got the red. Mine are black, just like Bella's heart for thinking up this scheme."

"Very appropriate." Caitlyn couldn't help it; her lips twitched up in a grin. At least her adversary had a sense of humor. As she turned to face him, she noticed that his eyes were twinkling and he looked almost friendly. Perhaps this was the time to disarm him. "There wouldn't be a problem if we joined forces, Mr. Morrison. Since you know about ranching and I don't, I'll let you decide on the asking price. All you have to do is agree to sell."

Dane raised his eyebrows and then he chuckled. "Nope."

"But why? Ranching's got to be hard work, even when the . . . uh . . . *guests* aren't here. Don't you want to retire while you're still young enough to have fun?"

"Can't say as I do."

The man was infuriating! Caitlyn drew a deep breath and forced the smile to stay on her face. "I don't understand. I'm sure you have other interests you'd like to pursue."

"Yup."

Caitlyn's smile grew wider. Now she was getting somewhere. "What are your other interests, Mr. Morrison?"

"Don't answer that, Dane!" Jerry stepped in before Dane could open his mouth; and when he turned back to Caitlyn, he was grinning. "You don't want to know his other interests. Trust me on that."

Caitlyn felt the heat rising to her cheeks. Dane Morrison was what Bitsy Beauchamp would call sinfully handsome. Whatever had possessed her to ask about his other interests?

"You're wasting your time, Ms. Bradford." Jerry wiped the grin off his face. "We already went over this ground while we were waiting for you, and there's nothing you can say to change his mind. Dane refuses to sell."

"And just where does that leave me?"

Jerry shrugged. "If Dane won't sell, you *can't* sell . . . unless he buys you out."

"Perfect!" Caitlyn breathed a sigh of relief. "I knew there was *something* I could do. How about it, Mr. Morrison?"

"Nope."

His answer surprised Caitlyn so much, she just stared at him for a moment. "But why not? I'm willing to negotiate."

"Nope."

Caitlyn's lips tightened. He was beginning to infuriate her. "Is that a *nope* you can't? Or a *nope* you won't?"

"Both. Looks like we're both stuck."

"There's got to be a way around it." Caitlyn turned to Jerry. "You're the lawyer. It's up to you to find a legal loophole in Aunt Bella's will."

That seemed to strike Jerry as funny because he chuckled. "There aren't any legal loopholes. Dad drew up this will and he knew what he was doing. You're welcome to hire another law firm to look it over, but you'll just be wasting your money. I read it over again while we were waiting for you. It's airtight."

"I could always contest it." Caitlyn glared at Dane again. "For all I know, this . . . this *cowboy* coerced Aunt Bella into leaving half of her property to him."

Dane straightened up in the chair, his blue eyes snapping. Though it was ridiculous, Caitlyn felt threatened, even though the width of the table separated them.

"Hold on, Dane." Jerry reached out to put his hand on Dane's arm. "Ms. Bradford didn't mean it. She doesn't know you, and she's pretty upset right now. Isn't that right, Ms. Bradford?"

Caitlyn hestitated, but then she nodded. If she were forced to accept this man as her partner, it wouldn't be smart to get off on the wrong foot. "You're right. I apologize, Mr. Morrison. I spoke out of pure frustration, and that wasn't fair. It's just that I came out here to settle Aunt Bella's affairs and then I planned to leave and get on with my life."

Dane nodded, settling back down to a slouch again, but Caitlyn thought she saw a glimmer of understanding in his eyes. "No offense taken. It's like Jerry said. You don't know me or you wouldn't have said that. But as far as getting on with your life goes, I don't see why you can't do it right here at the Double B."

"Here?" Caitlyn's eyes widened. "It certainly isn't what I had in mind!"

"Maybe not, but it makes a lot of sense." Jerry turned to her. "It's like this, Ms. Bradford. Like it or not, you're stuck with owning half of a dude ranch that you can't sell. Your aunt didn't leave you with any other option."

Caitlyn thought about it for a long moment and then she sighed. "I guess you're right. I hate it when people don't leave me with any options!"

"But you *do* have an option." There was something close to sympathy in Dane's face as he leaned over the table to meet her eyes. "You're free to leave anytime you want to. I can run the ranch and send you a check for half the profits every month. I won't cheat you, if that's what you're thinking. Ask anyone in Little Fork and they'll tell you that."

Caitlyn nodded. Though it might be foolish of her, all her instincts told her that she could trust this man. "Trusting you isn't the problem, Mr. Morrison. Aunt Bella left me half of this ranch. It wouldn't be fair for me to bail out and still collect half of the profits."

"Then why don't you stay, at least for a while? It'll be a nice change from life in the big city and it's clear your aunt wanted you to get familiar with her operation. Give it a month's trial period. If you don't like life on the Double B at the end of that time, you can pull up stakes and leave."

What he said made sense and Caitlyn sighed. She was hooked and she knew it. "All right. But I insist on doing my share of the work while I'm here. What did Aunt Bella do?"

"She was the ranch hostess." Dane's blue eyes warmed perceptively and Caitlyn knew he was thinking of her aunt. "Your aunt took her meals with the guests, went out on most of the day trips with them, and just generally made them feel welcome. Do you think you could handle that?"

"Of course. There's no reason why I can't do that."

"Good." Dane reached across the table and held out his hand. "Then we're working partners?"

"Yes. We're working partners, at least for now." Caitlyn extended her hand so that he could shake it.

It happened the instant her fingers touched his, a wave of electricity that seemed to sizzle through her mind like fireworks. He had such a warm hand and the way his fingers gripped hers was surprisingly gentle. She shivered slightly, her body tingling with pleasure at his touch. For the first time since she'd arrived in Little Fork, she felt safe and comforted and protected. And she couldn't help wondering how it would feel to be in his arms, her body pressed up against his rugged strength.

"Guess I'd better be getting a move on." Jerry stood up, shattering the moment.

"Yes. Thank you for your help." Caitlyn jerked back her hand, hoping that Dane Morrison didn't have a talent for mind reading. Whatever had gotten into her? She rose to her feet on legs that trembled slightly and led the way to the door.

The simple act of doing something physical restored some of Caitlyn's composure. By the time she'd led Jerry down the hall and exchanged a few final words with him on the front steps of the ranch house, she was back in control. As she watched Jerry drive off in his truck, she almost managed to convince herself that her puzzling reaction to Dane Morrison's handshake had been a temporary aberration brought on by the emotional stress of her divorce. All the same, Caitlyn wasn't about to allow him to touch her again. There was no way that she wanted to put her theory to the test.

Caitlyn whirled around as she heard footsteps behind her. Dane had followed her. And now he was leaning against the door frame of the ranch house, studying her intently. As Caitlyn's green eyes met his, she thought she felt her heart skip a beat. Of course that was impossible. It happened only in the lyrics of country-western songs. But she was breathless and she found that it was an effort for her to speak. "Mr. Campbell seems very nice."

"Yup."

Caitlyn fought the impulse to step closer to him. Right before she'd left the ad agency, she'd been working on a campaign for a new line of perfume called "Allure." She could have borrowed from the highly successful campaign and featured Dane Morrison, dressed in his tight faded blue jeans and leaning against a bedroom doorway with the words *Got Allure?* flashing on the screen. With an effort, she lowered her eyes and tried to remember what subject they'd been discussing. Jerry Campbell. That was it. "Have you known Mr. Campbell long?"

"Yup."

He was back to the one-word replies that had made Gary Cooper famous, and Caitlyn felt the urge to giggle. He was obviously in his tough-cowboy, head-wrangler mode. She was very relieved that he hadn't seemed to notice her strange and puzzling attraction to him, but she couldn't stand here for the rest of the day avoiding his eyes. She'd ask him a question that couldn't be answered by a "yup" or a "nope."

"I meant it when I said that I wanted to be a working partner." Caitlyn took a deep breath and forced herself to look up at him. Spencer had always said that she was tall for a woman. Five feet, eight inches without shoes. But Dane Morrison towered over her, even when he was slouching, and that made her feel small and vulnerable. "What are my duties for tonight?"

"Take the night off. You're probably tired. If you want, you can poke around before the guests get back and learn the layout of the ranch house. I'll make sure that nobody comes in to bother you."

Caitlyn nodded. "Thank you. I don't think I'm up to meeting the whole staff today."

"All in due time. That's what your aunt used to say."

"I don't want you to think I'm a"—Caitlyn hesitated, trying to think of exactly the right word—"a lightweight."

"Nope."

"Good." Again, Caitlyn felt the urge to giggle. Now they were *both* doing Gary Cooper imitations. "Do you think you could give me more than a one-word reply? I don't do Gary Cooper as well as you do."

"Yup."

This time, Caitlyn's sense of humor got the best of her and she laughed. Was that an answering smile lurking in the depths of his eyes? "I'm serious about wanting to work, Dane. And I promise that I'll do my share."

"I'm glad you're calling me, Dane." His face crinkled in a smile. "Mr. Morrison makes me feel like Hank."

"Who's Hank?"

"My dad. But hardly anybody called him Mr. Morrison, either. Only the guy from the bank."

Caitlyn caught a hint of sadness in his reply and she decided that she wouldn't ask him about his father. It surprised her that she was so concerned about his emotions, but she was. "Learning the layout of the ranch house won't take me very long. What else do you want me to do?"

"Get a good night's sleep and be in the kitchen at eight to-morrow morning to eat breakfast with the guests." He pushed himself off from the door frame and sauntered down the wooden steps, turning at the bottom to grin up at her. "I'll tell Gibby to send you up a good dinner. He's our head cook."

Caitlyn smiled. He was being very nice. "Thank you, but I don't want any more to eat. Mr. Campbell and I had sandwiches on the way here."

"You ate one of Jerry's sandwiches?"

"Yes. They were huge, so I only had half, but . . ." Caitlyn's voice trailed off as she noticed the expression of alarm on his face. "Did I do something wrong?"

"If you ate one of Jerry's sandwiches, you did. What was in it?"

Caitlyn was still puzzled by his reaction. "It was ham. He told me that Millie made a mean smoked ham."

"Thank God!" He reached into his pocket, drew out a red bandanna, and wiped his forehead. "I thought we'd have to roll out the stomach pump there for a minute. Just promise me that you won't ever eat anything that crawls out of Jerry's kitchen."

Caitlyn shuddered at his choice of words. "Crawls? As in . . . in bugs?"

"It amounts to the same thing. Jerry wouldn't have seen fit to say anything, you being a stranger and all, but his dad suffered a cerebrovascular infarct last month."

"What's that?"

"It's a stroke."

"I . . . I'm sorry to hear that." Caitlyn was puzzled. She'd spoken to Jerry's father on the phone this morning and he'd sounded perfectly normal to her.

"It didn't leave much residual damage and only minor brain function was affected. Folks around here all know it, and they make allowances. And most of the time he's fine."

Caitlyn nodded. "But at other times, he's not?"

"Nope."

"What happens when he's *not* fine?" Caitlyn frowned slightly.

"Little things. Jerry came home a couple of times and found that his dad had shut off the refrigerator. Said it made too much noise and it was disturbing his peace."

"And that's why you told me not to eat anything that came out of Jerry's kitchen?"

He nodded. "We talked about it while we were waiting for you. Jerry's going to try gluing the control to the 'on' position. Of course, that won't keep his dad from unplugging it . . . if he gets the notion."

"That's . . . that's so sad." Caitlyn turned away slightly to hide the moisture that was welling up in her eyes.

"Not really. Jerry's dad sees the humor in his situation. He even laughs about how he got up last week and went out to mow the lawn at midnight."

Caitlyn was shocked. "Jerry's dad can *laugh* about losing part of his faculties?"

"He hasn't had another incident and he's on preventative medication. And he's lightened his stress load by turning the practice over to Jerry. If things go well, he may very well live out his life without having a recurrence."

"I hope so." Caitlyn nodded. "I think it's amazing that he's dealing with his condition so well."

"People around here take setbacks in stride. And he knows that he's lucky he lives out here and not in the city."

Caitlyn didn't understand his last comment at all. "Why is that?"

"It's different out here. Folks make allowances, and they believe in taking care of their own. The people in Little Fork don't mind if Jerry's dad gets up to mow his lawn in the middle of the night. If it happens again, some of 'em'll probably grab their flashlights and go out to help him do it."

Caitlyn smiled. If what he said were true, there was a big difference between Little Fork and Boston. Half the people in Boston didn't even know their neighbors, and the only time they noticed them at all was when there was a cause for complaint. "I'm glad you told me about Jerry's dad."

"Sure. You should know, now that you're living here. You'll probably run into him when you go to town, especially if you stop in at Millie's. He goes in every day for apple pie and coffee. Millie makes a mean apple pie."

"It sounds like Millie makes a mean everything." Caitlyn nodded. "Her sandwiches were excellent."

He began to frown. "But you only ate half?"

"Yes. I told you, they were huge. I don't usually eat lunch unless it's business, and then I . . ." Caitlyn hesitated, trying to remember what Jerry had told her about what they called their meals. ". . . I skip my evening meal."

He frowned and it was obvious that her answer had displeased him. "Did you have breakfast this morning?"

"No, but . . ." Caitlyn's voice trailed off. He was positively glowering at her.

"So, the only thing you've eaten all day is half of a sandwich?"

"Yes." Caitlyn nodded quickly. "But I'm really not hungry."

"That's not enough food to keep a prairie dog alive. There's no way I'm going to stand by and let you skip dinner tonight."

Caitlyn's mouth dropped open. How dare he tell her what and when to eat! "What do you plan to do? Force-feed me?"

"I will if I have to." He glared at her. "Gibby'll send you up a plateful of barbecue, and I want you to eat every bite of your dinner. We've got to fatten you up a little. You're way too skinny for comfort."

"And just whose comfort would that be?" Caitlyn bristled with outrage. Her figure was perfect, and she'd worked very hard to keep it that way.

"The guests' comfort. They'll start to think there's something wrong with our chow if their hostess has hipbones that could double as a hat rack."

He grinned and Caitlyn began to fume. Maybe the other ranch women in Little Fork, Wyoming, let themselves go, but she wasn't about to fall into that trap. She bit back a sharp reply and settled for an icy nod. "Is there any other part of my appearance that you'd like me to change?"

"Yup. Don't ever wear a business suit again. Our guests come here to relax and get away from all that. Put on some jeans and a shirt. That's standard wear around here. And do something about your hair."

"My hair?" Caitlyn was beginning to seethe. No one had ever dared to criticize her appearance before. "What's wrong with my hair?"

"It's too fancy. The way I see it, you've got two choices. Either chop it off or put it in pigtails. It's just going to put people off if you run around here looking like a fashion model."

The man was insufferable. Caitlyn turned on her heel and marched back inside. She had almost finished hanging her clothing in Aunt Bella's closet before she realized that his latest criticism had really been a compliment: He thought she looked as beautiful as a fashion model.

She sat down on the edge of Aunt Bella's bed and replayed their conversation in her mind. He had ordered her to eat all of her dinner. Dinner, not supper. People out here called their evening meal supper. Jerry had told her that. And now that she thought about it, Mr. Dane Morrison had been surprisingly well-informed on a variety of subjects. He'd understood the legalities of her aunt's will; he'd known all about land ownership and checkerboarding, and he'd spoken knowledgeably about Jerry's father's medical condition. There was the hint of mystery about him, of secrets that he wasn't telling. Caitlyn was beginning to suspect that her new partner was much more than the simple, sexy, and highly irritating cowboy that he pretended to be.

The ranch hands were waiting at the bunkhouse when Dane came in. He told them that Bella's niece wasn't up to meeting them until tomorrow and sent them back to their duties. Of course Gibby wasn't so easily dismissed. He wanted to know all about Caitlyn Bradford.

Dane filled Gibby in—not the whole story, but part of it. He told Gibby about his half-ownership of the ranch and how it couldn't be sold out from under them. At the same time, he warned Gibby that Caitlyn Bradford could still make trouble for them. As an equal partner, she had the power to veto any decision involving the Double B. Dane didn't think she'd argue much about the day-to-day running of the ranch; but if she did, they'd be deadlocked and everything would come to a screeching halt.

Gibby promised to explain everything to the staff and warn them to walk on eggshells around Ms. Bradford. Their jobs were secure, but they should all be careful to treat Caitlyn Bradford with the same respect that they'd shown to Bella. If they minded their p's and q's, everything should turn out just fine.

That was only part of the story and Dane knew it. As he walked to the corral, he thought about Caitlyn Bradford and frowned. He hoped she didn't turn out to be some kind of animal activist. There would be trouble if she believed that it was cruel to break a horse to saddle. And there'd be hell to pay if she thought that the mountain lions and the occasional bear who sometimes came down to terrorize their livestock shouldn't be deprived of the right to feast on their herds. He could probably bring her around to his way of thinking if he showed her the bloody carcass of one of their lambs or colts, but that was just one more thing he'd have to deal with, one in a long line of things.

But those were small problems in the giant scheme of things. The real problem lay with Caitlyn herself, and the way she'd affected him. He'd dated some during the time he'd spent at the Double B Ranch. He'd even had a couple of uncomplicated, highly enjoyable affairs. But not one of those women had ever socked him in the gut the way Caitlyn Bradford had.

He knew the reason she'd changed to her business suit. She'd felt threatened by him and she'd wanted to set him in his place. She'd done her damnedest to be smart and tough, to take control over a situation that had frightened her. Her hard-line approach might have worked with Jerry, if Dane hadn't been in the room. But Dane hadn't been fooled for an instant. There had been a curious vulnerability in her lovely green eyes that had positively tugged at his heartstrings.

Dane hadn't lied when he'd said that he couldn't buy her out. There was no way he could afford to pay her what half of the Double B Ranch was worth. And he didn't want to buy her out, even if he were able to raise the money. Bella had wanted her to come out here and spend some time on the property she'd loved. It had been Bella's dying wish and Dane wasn't about to deny it.

He wished that Bella were still here so she could see that her niece was a carbon copy of her. Caitlyn Bradford was a prickly little thing on the outside. She had courage and gumption, just like Bella, and she had refused to back down until she'd exhausted every argument. When she'd finally accepted the inevitable and realized that there was no way she could find a way around the terms of Bella's will, she'd declared that if she had to remain partners with him, she'd be a working partner. And then she'd swallowed her pride and asked him what to do.

Bella had thrown them together for a reason. Sick as she'd been, she'd insisted he turn off the morphine drip so there couldn't be any question that she was in her right mind when she met with Jerry's dad to change her will. He knew exactly why she had checkerboarded the ranch and left half to him and half to her niece. Right before she drew her last breath, she'd squeezed his hand and made him promise to forget his unhappy past. And even though he hadn't known the details of her will before Jerry had told him today, it was pretty obvious what Bella had intended. She'd linked them through the terms of her will, hoping that he might make Caitlyn forget her past and that she might do the same for him.

Dane chuckled, picturing Bella looking down at him and grinning as her final matchmaking scheme got off to a start. In a way, he really hated to disappoint her. Bella had been the mother he'd never known, and he'd loved her every bit as much as a son could love his mother. But Bella had been deluding herself if she'd thought her little plan would be successful. Caitlyn Bradford was his polar opposite, and it just wasn't going to work.

FIVE

Caitlyn groaned as bells clanged loudly in her ear. She sat up with a jolt, reached out to turn on the light by the side of the bed, and stared at the source of the noise in shock. It was an old-fashioned alarm clock. Why wasn't she using her electronic alarm clock, the one that woke her with soothing music? Had the power gone off, causing her to resort to this antiquated windup clock?

It took her a moment to notice the time and when she did, she gasped. How could it possibly be six o'clock in morning? She'd just closed her eyes.

Had she set this old clock wrong? Caitlyn pressed the button that silenced the clanging set of bells that sat like little ear muffs on either side of the clock's face and stared at the hands with bleary eyes. One straight up, one straight down. It was six o'clock, all right. And she knew that the clock wasn't broken, because it was still ticking.

Why had she set the alarm for this ungodly hour of the morning? She didn't have to be at her desk in the corner office at the Sinclair Agency until ten. She never scheduled a meeting before eleven and it took her only fifteen minutes to drive to the office. The only other time she'd ever gotten up at six in the morning had been the time her secretary had booked her on an early overseas flight. She had been furious about the departure time, especially since it had been too late to reschedule, and her secretary had never made that particular mistake again.

Caitlyn was about to burrow back under the blankets when she noticed that the lamp beside her bed wasn't the smart chrome-

and-glass fixture that the interior designer had chosen for her bedroom. And the bed she'd been sleeping in didn't have her feather-soft mattress. She blinked, staring around her in growing confusion. Walls paneled in knotty pine. Red chenille curtains at the windows. A framed painting of a herd of wild horses on the wall. Where was she?

Then the confusion cleared and she groaned again, remembering why she'd planned to get up at the crack of dawn. She owned half of Aunt Bella's Double B Dude Ranch and she'd agreed to join the guests for breakfast.

With an expletive that Spencer and his mother would have found shocking in the extreme, Caitlyn threw off the covers and jumped out of bed. This was the first day of her new life and she'd made a promise to her partner, Dane Morrison. She'd be in the breakfast room at seven-thirty, smiling and ready to start the day, even if it killed her.

Her morning shower didn't take long, just a brief dash under the water to dispel the last vestiges of sleep from her eyes. She toweled off on one of Aunt Bella's red bath towels that were embroidered with the Double B logo, and walked briskly to her closet to decide what to wear. Dane's insistence on jeans and a shirt left her little choice. She'd worn her blue jeans yesterday and they were hopelessly rumpled. The crease was gone and they'd lost their shape. They had to be cleaned and pressed. Thank goodness she'd thought to buy a second pair.

Once she'd dressed in the snow-white jeans and the checkered blouse of blue-and-white gingham that the salesgirl at The Gap had said was perfect Western wear, Caitlyn sat down in front of Aunt Bella's old-fashioned dressing table and surveyed her reflection in the mirror. Dane had told her to do something with her hair. Chop it off, he'd said, or put it in pigtails. Caitlyn wasn't about to risk cutting her own hair, but she supposed that she could braid it. She brushed it, parted it in the middle, and set to work.

Five minutes later, Caitlyn gave up the effort. She knew how to braid—that wasn't it—but she wasn't skilled enough to divide each side into three separate parts and then braid it neatly. There must be another, simpler hairstyle that would satisfy her partner's requirements.

A ponytail. The moment Caitlyn thought of it, she brushed her hair back and secured it with one of the rubber bands from Aunt Bella's desk. Now all she needed was a pair of shoes.

She had forgotten to buy boots. Caitlyn frowned as she stared at her shoes, all neatly arranged in rows at the bottom of the closet. Sandals would be ridiculous and high heels were definitely out. The only pair of shoes she owned that wouldn't be totally inappropriate were the white sneakers that she'd worn for her aerobic classes. Caitlyn put them on, tied a blue silk scarf around her neck like a bandanna, and marched to the door. She was as ready as she was ever going to be.

As she walked along the hallway, Caitlyn told herself she couldn't possibly be nervous. She had held conferences with tough and irascible clients, managed her household staff with ease, and arranged parties for hundreds of guests. Dane had told her that there were only twelve couples who'd booked reservations at the Double B, and surely she could handle that. All she had to do was sit at the table and make conversation with them as they ate their breakfast. There was no reason to be nervous. None at all.

The kitchen and dining hall were connected to the ranch house by a covered breezeway. Caitlyn walked down the sidewalk and smiled as she breathed in the fresh air. Rows of pink and yellow daisies were planted on either side of the sidewalk, and it was really quite pretty.

At first, she'd thought it was odd to separate the two buildings, but the red-whiskered cowboy who'd brought her dinner had told her that breakfast preparations at the Double B began at five in the morning. Since the kitchen was housed in a separate building and the guests slept in the sprawling ranch house, none of them would be roused from their slumber by the sounds of clanging pots and clattering silverware. Now that the system made sense to her, Caitlyn thought that it was very clever of Aunt Bella to have arranged it this way.

She could hear cheerful voices inside the kitchen and Caitlyn took a deep breath as she pushed open the door. She hoped she

wouldn't have to do more than smile and nod at the ranch employees before she'd had her first cup of coffee. She wasn't a
people person in the morning. She needed time to enjoy a solitary
cup of coffee and gather her thoughts for the day. Ten minutes
was enough. After that, she could handle anything that came her
way.

"I see you made it."

Caitlyn winced as she saw Dane. He was here already, sitting
at the long oak table in the dining hall, a mug of coffee in his
hand. She turned to glance at the clock on the wall and realized
that it was precisely seven-thirty. It had taken her more time to
fix her hair than she'd thought it would.

"I should have guessed you'd be a walking zombie in the
morning." Dane patted the chair next to him. "Got the same
problem, myself. Sit down. I'll get you a cup of coffee and I
promise I won't say a word while you drink it."

Caitlyn managed a smile as she sat down in the chair he'd
pulled out for her. He was really very understanding, and that
came as a surprise. Spencer had been her polar opposite and he'd
never understood her craving for solitude in the mornings.

Dane came back to the table with a mug of coffee for her, and
true to his promise, he didn't say a word as he passed her the
ceramic sugar bowl and creamer. She waved them away, indicat-
ing that she took her coffee black, and picked up the heavy white
mug with the Double B logo to inhale the scent. Was anything
more marvelous than the scent of freshly brewed coffee in the
morning?

Her first sip was pure heaven. The coffee was strong and
steaming, just the way she liked it. Caitlyn closed her eyes, took
several bracing swallows, and opened her eyes to nod her thanks.
She'd never expected to find anyone who would truly respect her
need for privacy in the morning, and the fact that Dane had immediately understood her needs amazed her.

He grinned, sat back down in his chair, and picked up the
clipboard that sat on the table. He scrawled a note with the pen
that was attached to the clipboard by a chain and studied the
typed lines with a frown.

"Is something wrong?" Caitlyn surprised herself by speaking. She never spoke until she'd finished her first cup of coffee.

"Nope. Just checking the schedule."

He glanced back down at the clipboard and Caitlyn felt curiously rebuffed. She told herself that it didn't matter, that she hated conversation in the morning, but she found herself asking another question. "Is that the schedule for the day?"

"Yup." He turned to smile at her. "I thought you wouldn't want to talk until you finished your coffee."

"I don't, not usually, but this morning's different. What's on the agenda for today?"

"The guests are going on a day trip right after breakfast. They'll come back around four. After dinner, we're teaching them how to square dance. Have you ever done it?"

Caitlyn nodded, wincing slightly at the memory. "Only once and that was under protest. Our fifth-grade teacher decided that we should learn. We drew names for partners and I got Tommy Henderson. He wasn't very good at it."

"He stepped on your toes?"

He was grinning and Caitlyn grinned back. "Four times. And he was the biggest kid in our class. I brought an excuse from home the next day and sat on the sidelines until we switched to softball."

"You were good at that?"

"The best." Caitlyn nodded. "My dad taught me to play. We used to practice in the vacant lot across from our house."

"I bet you were a cute little kid."

Caitlyn felt the heat rise to her cheeks and she wondered why she was blushing. "No, not really. I had freckles and my hair was much redder than it is now. I used to pray every night that my hair would change color and my freckles would disappear."

"Your prayers must have worked." He laughed, a sound that Caitlyn found pleasant. "You didn't have freckles when you were twelve. And your hair was much darker by then."

Caitlyn stared at him in shock. "That's right. But how did you know?"

"There's a picture of you on the mantel in the living room. Bella said it was a snapshot that she took at your sixth-grade graduation. She had it enlarged and put it in a frame so she could show it to the guests. It's still there."

"If I'd only known, I would have sent her a more recent photo." Caitlyn blinked, fighting back tears. "I can't believe she kept it all these years."

"She loved you. She wouldn't have left you half of her ranch if she hadn't. If you want more coffee before the guests come in, you'd better get it now. They'll start trickling in any time in the next ten minutes."

Caitlyn picked up her mug and rose to her feet. She walked to the big urn on the serving table at the side of the room and took her time about filling her mug. By the time she turned to walk back to her chair, she was in control again. Had he deliberately given her something to do so she'd have the time she needed to compose herself?

"Whatever made you decide to wear *white* jeans?"

An amused smile hovered at the corners of his lips and Caitlyn sighed. It was clear their temporary truce was over. He was criticizing her appearance again. "They're my only other pair. I wore my blue jeans yesterday and they need to go to the cleaners."

"The cleaners?"

His lips twitched and Caitlyn stared at him curiously. He looked as if he were about to laugh. "The dry cleaners. Just tell me where to go and I'll take them in today."

"Let's see now." His lips were still twitching. "I guess that'd be Laramie."

Caitlyn's mouth dropped open. "Laramie? But that's almost two hours away!"

"There's not much call for dry cleaning around here."

"But how about your jeans? And the shirts you're wearing? How do you get them clean?"

"We wash 'em. The housekeeping crew comes in at ten—six women, all locals. Ida and Marilyn do the wash; Ellie and Joyce clean, and Gladys and Darlene change the linens and tidy up the guest rooms."

"I see." Caitlyn nodded.

"There's a laundry hamper in your room. Just toss your dirty clothes inside and they'll bring them back the next day, all folded and clean." He reached out to pat her hand. "Trust me, jeans don't need to be dry cleaned. They wash just fine."

Caitlyn nodded again. "Okay, if you say so. But do they press them, too?"

"Press jeans?" He stared at her for a moment and then he laughed. "Nobody but a city girl would worry about having her jeans pressed, but they could probably run them through the mangle if you ask."

"No." Caitlyn imagined the reaction she'd get if she asked two local women to press her jeans. "That's quite all right. But what do you do with things that can't be washed, like silk and satin?"

"We don't wear things like that on the ranch."

Caitlyn raised her eyebrows. "Not even the guests?"

"If a guest wants to wear a satin cowboy shirt for a party, he takes it with him and has it cleaned when he gets home. We don't provide any laundry service for the guests, unless it's some kind of emergency. Bella decided, early on, that it was one headache she could do without. She added a line to her brochure telling them to bring enough clothing for their stay."

Caitlyn nodded, imagining the complaints that could arise if an article of clothing was improperly pressed or cleaned. Aunt Bella had been wise in not providing laundry service.

"Come on, Caitlyn. It's time to play hostess." Dane got up and motioned toward the door. The first of the guests was starting to trickle in.

Caitlyn nodded and rose to her feet. "I'm ready. What shall I do?"

"Just smile and tell 'em good morning. And try to learn their names. I'll help you out with that."

Caitlyn nodded, putting on her most charming smile. She knew it was crazy, but her knees were trembling as she followed Dane to the doorway. What if Aunt Bella's guests didn't like her? Would they refuse to come back next year?

" 'Mornin', Miz Rothstein." Dane grinned at the heavyset blonde who'd just come in. Then he turned to her husband and pumped his hand. " 'Mornin', Ralph. You folks sleep all right?"

"Yup. Gotta be all that fresh air."

Caitlyn bit back a giggle. Mr. Rothstein had a New York accent and his reply sounded curiously out of place.

"Meet Caitlyn, Bella's niece. She came out here from Boston to help run the place." Dane turned back to her. "These good folks are Marsha and Ralph Rothstein. This is their fifth year with us."

"Good morning, Mrs. Rothstein, Mr. Rothstein." Caitlyn smiled. "I hope you're enjoying your stay at the Double B."

Marsha Rothstein nodded. "We always do. We were so sorry to hear about Bella. You must miss her very much."

"I do." Caitlyn's smile wavered a bit. "I hope you'll share some of your memories of Aunt Bella with me. I never had the chance to visit her out here and I'd really like to know more about her friends and her life."

"Of course we will." Marsha Rothstein gave her a friendly smile.

"You bet." Ralph nodded, his broad face creasing in a smile. "Bella was the salt of the earth."

After the Rothsteins, Caitlyn met nine other couples. They all seemed nice and they appeared to be enjoying themselves at the Double B. As the second to the last couple approached on the walkway, Dane nudged her and leaned close to whisper in her ear.

"Just smile and nod. Don't say anything else. I want your opinion of them later."

Caitlyn raised her eyebrows in surprise, but the couple was approaching too rapidly to ask any questions. The woman was a petite brunette and she wore jeans and a long-sleeved blouse made of pink denim. As she walked, one sleeve of her blouse pulled up slightly and Caitlyn noticed a series of dark bruises on her wrist, as if someone had reached out to grab her so tightly that it had caused injury.

The woman's husband was tall and distinguished, and Caitlyn got the impression that he would be more comfortable in a three-piece business suit than the tan jeans and embroidered cowboy shirt that he wore. For some strange reason, she formed an instant dislike for him. Perhaps it was the arrogant way he carried himself, forcing his wife to hurry to keep up with his long strides.

Coupled with the scowl that he was wearing, he looked stern and forbidding, not a nice man at all.

"Good morning, Mrs. Benning." Dane greeted the brunette politely, but he didn't reach out to shake her hand. When he turned to her husband, Caitlyn noticed that his smile was strained. "I hope your evening was satisfactory, Mr. Benning."

Mr. Benning gave a slight nod. "Yes. Did you fire the careless maid who broke my wife's perfume bottle?"

"The situation has been handled, Mr. Benning. From now on the head of our housekeeping staff will personally service your room."

Mr. Benning's brows furrowed in a very unattractive frown. "I suppose that'll have to do. Can you personally vouch for her honesty and reliability?"

"I can." Dane's words were clipped. "She's been with us for five years and we've never received a complaint."

"That means nothing. You know as well as I do that some people are too timid to complain, even when they have cause."

Dane nodded. "I'm sure you're right. But she's also the wife of a local minister. I doubt that Reverend Jenkins would have married anyone who was less than honest."

"Perhaps." Mr. Benning didn't look convinced, but he turned to his wife. "Come along, Cynthia. If we don't hurry, the toast will be cold again this morning."

The moment they were out of earshot, Caitlyn turned to Dane. "Who were *they?*"

"Cynthia and James Benning. They're new this year. And if I have anything to say about it, they won't be back."

Caitlyn nodded. "I agree completely. He looks mean and I noticed that she had bruises on her wrist."

"She probably has more bruises that you can't see. He's a heavy drinker; and when he gets smashed, I suspect that other things get smashed, too. And that includes his wife."

"I knew there was a reason I didn't like him." Caitlyn frowned. "I don't usually take such an instant dislike to anyone."

Dane nodded. "I felt the same way the first time I laid eyes on him. Hold down the fort, Caitlyn. I'll be right back. Marsha's got her hands full juggling her plate and her cup of coffee. Something's going to go soon if I don't help her."

Caitlyn smiled as Dane crossed the room to help Marsha. He really took good care of their guests. But her mind returned to Cynthia Benning's problem, searching for a way to help.

"Okay. Situation's handled."

Dane smiled and so did Caitlyn. She'd thought of a way to help Mrs. Benning. "I've been thinking about Mrs. Benning. Perhaps I can do something to make certain that her husband doesn't abuse her while they're here at the ranch."

"How?" Dane stared at her curiously. "You won't be able to prove that there's anything wrong. I already asked her about the bruises on her wrist and she gave me some cock-and-bull story about how he caught her when she tripped. She'd never agree to lodge a complaint against him, if that's what you're thinking."

Caitlyn shook her head. "That wasn't what I was thinking. I know that most abused wives are afraid to come forward. Who has the room next to the Bennings?"

"The Rothsteins. They've heard her crying in the middle of the night. Ralph mentioned it to me. At first they assumed that she was having a nightmare, but they began to suspect that something was up when it happened three nights in a row."

"Do you think that Ralph might be willing to do a little acting job for us?"

Dane stared at her curiously. "Maybe. What did you have in mind?"

"I thought I might strike up a conversation with Mr. Benning and mention that he shouldn't be concerned if he hears Ralph's beeper going off in the middle of the night. I'll say that he prefers to be treated like a civilian while he's on vacation, but the precinct back home still needs to contact him on a regular basis."

"That might just work." Dane began to grin. "I'll talk to Ralph and clue him in. They were pretty concerned about Mrs. Benning, and I'm sure he won't mind playing a cop on vacation."

"Good. By the way, did the maid really break Mrs. Benning's perfume bottle?"

"I asked her about it, and she said that it was already broken when she went in to clean the room."

"You didn't fire her, did you?"

"Nope." Dane shook his head. "I've known Darlene for over four years and she's not the type to lie. If she'd broken it, she would have come to tell me right away."

Caitlyn nodded. "That's what I thought." But she didn't have time to say any more because the last couple was coming in, a young husband and wife who were jogging down the walkway, holding hands.

"Sorry we're late." The woman grinned at Dane, blushing slightly.

Her husband nodded, his face reddening slightly. "I couldn't find my . . . uh . . . the string tie I wanted to wear."

Caitlyn glanced at the young man's neck. He wasn't wearing a string tie.

"That's okay. We don't stand on ceremony here and you've still got plenty of time for breakfast. I want you to meet Caitlyn Bradford. She's part owner of the Double B." He grinned as he turned to Caitlyn. "These folks are Mr. and Mrs. Palmer."

Caitlyn smiled at the young couple. They looked very much in love. "I'm glad to meet you."

"Me, too." Mrs. Palmer shook Caitlyn's hand. "It's Susie and Danny. We're on our honeymoon."

Caitlyn nodded. Now she understood why they'd been late. "Congratulations. I hope you like the ranch."

"We do." Danny Palmer grinned at her. "It's really romantic out here in the West."

Caitlyn smiled, suppressing the urge to laugh. The Palmers would have probably found anyplace they'd chosen for their honeymoon romantic.

When the Palmers had gone off to fill their plates at the long buffet table, Dane turned to Caitlyn. "Come on, partner. Let's go join our guests."

"Good idea." Caitlyn gasped slightly as Dane took her arm to walk her to the buffet table. She could feel the heat of his fingers through the material of her blouse and her heart pounded so loudly, she was afraid he might hear it. Why did her new partner have this strange effect on her? Other men had held her arm before. It was simply common courtesy. But it had never affected her like this. When Dane held her arm, she found herself wishing that she'd worn a short-sleeved blouse so that she could feel his warm fingers on her bare skin.

"Here we are. Let's dig in."

Caitlyn nodded, almost afraid to speak for fear her voice would betray her. But then she noticed that the honeymooners were in line just ahead of them and she raised up on tiptoe to whisper in Dane's ear. "I notice that Danny Palmer didn't find his string tie. Do you think that he made a thorough search?"

"Yup." Dane's eye closed in a conspiratorial wink. "But it'd be pretty unusual to find a string tie where Danny was probably looking."

SIX

Caitlyn was proud of herself. She'd managed to speak to Mr. Benning before their breakfast was over and he'd seemed quite subdued after she'd planted the idea that Ralph Rothstein was with the New York police. Caitlyn had no illusions that she'd solved the problem, but the action they'd taken might give Mrs. Benning a rest from her abusive husband, at least while they were vacationing at the Double B.

Dane had done his part. Caitlyn had watched as he'd spoken to Ralph and she'd noticed the grin that had spread across Ralph's broad face. It was clear that he was all set to enjoy his role in their scheme. Perhaps, if Mrs. Benning had time to think about her situation, she might take some sort of action to improve her life.

The last of the couples had just left the dining hall and Caitlyn leaned back with a satisfied smile. To use a phrase of Bitsy's, she'd "worked the room," managing to speak to each one of their guests, even if it had been only a friendly sentence or two. She had memorized their names, linking them to the proper faces, and she could now greet them personally when she saw them again.

"You'd better eat something." Dane came back from his post at the doorway and plunked down in a chair. "All you did during breakfast was nibble like a rabbit on a piece of dry toast."

Caitlyn frowned. He was criticizing her again. "I told you yesterday, I never eat breakfast. I'll eat something for lunch, or dinner, or whatever it's called."

"That's not good enough, but your appetite will probably pick up when you've been here for a while. At least you finished the plate that Gibby brought you last night. He said there was nothing left when he came to collect it."

"He's right. There was nothing left." Caitlyn couldn't quite meet Dane's blue eyes. The portions on her plate had been so huge that only a sumo wrestler could have eaten it all. After she'd finished what she'd wanted, she'd opened the back door of Aunt Bella's quarters and given the rest to one of the ranch house dogs.

"I saw you talking to Mr. Benning. Did everything go okay?"

"Yup." Caitlyn grinned as she deliberately used what seemed to be one of his favorite words. "I don't think we'll have any more problems with them while they're here. What did Aunt Bella usually do after breakfast?"

"She went with the guests on their day trips. Would you like to ride along?"

Caitlyn nodded, pushing back her chair and standing up. "That sounds like fun."

"Then follow me. The guests are all out at the corral saddling up. You ride, don't you?"

"Of course." Caitlyn crossed her fingers, a gesture left over from her childhood that was meant to negate any lie that was told. She'd never been on a horse in her life, but she wasn't about to admit it. Dane might not let her go along and she really wanted to see the ranch.

As they walked down the path to the horse barns, Caitlyn convinced herself that she hadn't actually lied. He'd asked her if she rode and she had ridden on the back of an elephant once at a fund-raiser at a zoo. He hadn't specified the animal, and she hadn't asked. And how difficult could it be to sit on the back of a horse and let it carry her down a trail? Even children rode. She'd seen them riding the ponies in the park.

Good heavens, they were big! Caitlyn's eyes widened as she eyed the horses in the corral. The ponies she'd seen in the park had been a lot smaller. She took a deep breath for courage, joined the line of guests to wait her turn, and watched as Marsha Rothstein was helped into the saddle. The sight gave her courage. Marsha was forty pounds overweight and middle-aged, while she was much lighter and younger. If Marsha could ride, she could ride, too.

"You're sure you've ridden before?"

Dane was staring down at her and Caitlyn almost told him the truth. But she didn't. She just smiled and nodded and hedged a little. "It's been a while, but it's like riding a bicycle, isn't it?"

"Pardon me?"

Caitlyn winced as she looked up to meet his eyes. Could he tell that she was lying? "You know. They say that once you learn to ride a bicycle, you never forget."

"If you're talking about muscle memory, you're right to a certain extent." Dane looked amused. "If you're sure you're all right here, I'll just go on up and speak to the boys."

Caitlyn nodded and watched him walk up to the employees who were helping the guests mount. She swallowed past the lump of fear in her throat and hoped her hands wouldn't shake when she got into the saddle. Another glance at Marsha Rothstein reassured her. Marsha and Ralph were perched on the backs of their horses, smiling and talking as if riding were the easiest thing in the world. She hadn't really lied to Dane. She'd be just fine.

Dane gestured to Jake, calling him over for a private talk. "I want you to put Ms. Bradford on Nanny."

"Nanny?" Jake's eyebrows shot up in surprise. "But we never use Nanny for the day trips. She's slow as molasses and we're always having to wait for her to catch up with the rest of the line."

Dane nodded. "I know. Just do it, Jake. That's an order."

"You're the boss. Just so long as you know that Nanny's gonna hold us up somethin' awful."

As Jake went off to get Nanny, Dane glanced at Caitlyn. Her eyes were huge, her face was pale, and she looked about as nervous as a person could look. He could see that her legs were shaking in her silly white jeans, and he was willing to bet his share of the Double B that she'd never been on horseback before. All the same, there was a stubborn expression on her pretty face

and he couldn't help but admire her gumption. She was determined to ride along with the guests, despite the fact that she was
scared to death.

He hadn't been planning to go out on the day trip; but as he
watched Caitlyn, he changed his mind. Somebody had to see that
she didn't hurt herself, and she'd never tell the boys that this was
her first time on horseback. He motioned to Floyd, who was
leaning against the fence looking bored, and told him to saddle
Warrior for him.

"You're goin' on the day trip?"

"Yup."

Dane could understand why Floyd looked surprised. He
wasn't in the habit of accompanying the guests, preferring to use
the time to accomplish other, more pressing ranch business.
"Trevor's in charge while I'm gone. If something comes up that
you boys can't handle, let me know right away."

Floyd walked off to saddle Warrior and Dane bit back a grin.
The boys probably thought he was sweet on Caitlyn Bradford, and
they'd have a high old time imagining the worst while they were
gone. But Bella used to say that gossip was like fire and Dane knew
that it was true. It wouldn't take the bunkhouse gang long to discover
that there wasn't any fuel for their speculations and the whole thing
would die down as quickly as it had flared up.

Dane turned back to the line and saw that there were only
three couples in front of Caitlyn. Her eyes met his and she
dropped her gaze quickly, but not before he'd seen the panic that
was beginning to emerge in those startling green depths. He gave
her a grin and walked quickly toward her, enjoying the relief that
washed over her face.

"Are you going along on the day trip, Dane?"

"Yup." Her voice was trembling slightly and he gave her a
grin as he draped a casual arm around her shoulders. "I figured
I'd better, or Bella would come back to haunt me for not keeping
an eye on her greenhorn niece."

Dane helped her into the saddle himself, and Caitlyn was sur-

prised at how easily it went. Before she knew quite what was
happening, she was sitting on the back of her first horse.

"Comfy?"

He grinned at her and Caitlyn nodded, picking up the reins
and holding them loosely, the way she'd seen the guests do.
"What's my horse's name?"

"Nanny. She's a mare with a nice, easy gait. Just give Nanny
her head and I think you'll get along just fine."

"I'm sure we will." Caitlyn frowned slightly. Had he guessed
that she'd never ridden before and requested a gentle horse for
her? But she didn't have time to ask him because he was busy
adjusting the stirrups and, the moment that he'd finished, the long
line of horses started to move forward.

Caitlyn's heart went into panic mode as Nanny stepped forward to follow the other horses. Would she make a fool of herself
and fall off right here in the paddock, or the corral, or whatever
it was called? But she soon caught her balance and she breathed
a small sigh of relief. This wasn't so bad. All she had to do was
hang onto the reins, keep her feet in the stirrups, and not look
down.

The moment Caitlyn thought of it, she looked down. She
couldn't help herself. She grabbed the saddle horn, feeling light-
headed, and then she looked back up again, swallowing past the
lump of fear in her throat. She'd never been comfortable with
heights and she was a long way up from the ground. It was a
little like sitting on the top step of a bumpy, moving ladder, and
she didn't like it at all.

"Are you doing okay?"

Caitlyn glanced to the side and saw that Dane was riding beside her. She prayed her voice wouldn't betray her as she choked
out a reply. "Fine. I'm doing just fine."

"Good. It takes a while to get accustomed to riding again.
Just let me know if you have a problem."

Caitlyn nodded, her knuckles white on the reins. "I will."

At that precise moment, the lead horses started to go faster.
Caitlyn felt her teeth rattle as Nanny broke into a lumbering gait.
She didn't know whether it was a trot, a canter, a walk, or some-
thing else. She'd heard the terms, but she had no idea what they

meant. Whatever Nanny was doing, it took Caitlyn long moments to adjust to the new speed. But Dane was watching her and she managed to smile through her gritted teeth.

She'd heard that it was impossible to be terrified for long. The body simply made adjustments and the terror receded to an uncomfortable, but acceptable level. That seemed to be true because, after the first few minutes of riding, Caitlyn seemed to feel much less frightened. She hadn't made a fool of herself; she was still in the saddle, and she was actually beginning to enjoy the feeling of the sun and the breeze on her face.

"Hold on, Caitlyn. I'll be right back."

Dane smiled at her and then he wheeled his horse to the side and moved up the line. Caitlyn watched in pure amazement as he maneuvered his horse next to Marsha Rothstein, leaned sideways in his saddle, and grabbed the rein she'd dropped. Marsha smiled as she reached out to retrieve the long strip of leather.

"Sorry, Dane." Caitlyn could hear Marsha's voice clearly over the clopping of the horses' hooves on the hard-packed trail. "You'd think I'd know better, wouldn't you?"

Dane laughed, a cheerful sound that made Caitlyn smile. "You've got to stop talking with your hands when you're riding, Marsha."

"I know. I just forgot, that's all." Marsha laughed, too. "Habits of a lifetime are hard to break. New Yorkers always gesture when they talk."

"Pretend you're from Cleveland." Ralph spoke up and several of the other guests turned to laugh. Caitlyn smiled, but she didn't dare risk laughing for fear the sound might startle Nanny.

And now Dane was riding back to her. Caitlyn held on to her reins tightly, not about to drop them the way Marsha had. No one had to tell her that Dane was an excellent rider. She could see that for herself. The horse and rider were moving as one, each respecting the other's wishes and knowing the other's limitations. Caitlyn wondered how long it would take her to feel as comfortable on horseback as Dane seemed to be.

There was something very erotic about the sight of a strong, handsome man on a powerful horse. Caitlyn felt her breath catch in her throat as she watched Dane thread his way past the other guests in line. Color stained her cheeks as she wondered what it would be like if he swept her up into his arms and held her in front of him on the saddle. Just watching him made her want to be part of that powerful bond between man and beast.

Caitlyn's cheeks grew even more flushed as she imagined Dane's arms around her and his body pressed close to hers. What had happened to her detachment? She'd thought that her divorce had left her numb, indifferent to men and sex. But she certainly didn't feel numb right now. Her whole body tingled as Dane rode up to her and her eyes met his.

"Hold the reins a little looser, Caitlyn. Here, I'll show you." Dane reached out to take the leather strips she held and his fingers brushed hers. "Hold them in one hand, like this, between your fingers. Use your other hand to hold the loose ends."

"Okay. I've got it." Caitlyn found she was trembling as he handed them back. Just the touch of his fingers had made her blush. She could feel the heat in her cheeks.

"The sun up here's deceiving, Caitlyn. The air's a lot thinner at this altitude and more of the ultraviolet rays get through. You'd better put on some sunscreen when we stop to rest the horses. Looks like you're starting to burn."

Caitlyn dropped her eyes and nodded. She was burning, but not from the sun. It was Dane and the feelings he'd awakened in her, the feelings she'd thought were safely buried. Just looking at the man made her knees feel weak.

"Are you all right?"

"I'm fine." Caitlyn didn't look at him for fear she'd start thinking about how attractive he was. She'd keep everything business-like around him. It was safer that way.

"I'm going up to check on the schedule with Jake. Don't try anything fancy. Just concentrate on moving in synch with Nanny and you'll be okay."

Caitlyn watched him ride off and then she did exactly what he'd said. She kept her eyes straight ahead and tried to concentrate on moving with her horse the way that Dane seemed to do so effortlessly. It took her a while to get the hang of it, but after a few minutes, she managed to adjust her body to Nanny's even gait. Riding Nanny was a lot like standing on the deck of

Spencer's schooner. She had turned into a decent sailor when she'd learned to roll with the motion instead of bracing herself against it.

It was much more comfortable to ride like this. Caitlyn smiled as she grew more confident. Now that she was more accustomed to riding, she didn't have to concentrate so hard. She could gaze at the scenery around her, enjoy the fresh air and the incredible blue sky. Her thoughts could roam free, just as long as she didn't think about Dane Morrison.

The moment she told herself not to think of him, she did. She could see him up ahead, talking to one of the other ranch hands. His face was in profile and he looked just like a cowboy in a Western movie, grinning at his companion and holding the reins casually in one strong, tanned hand.

What would it be like to be loved by a man like Dane? A shiver of pure heat turned Caitlyn's face pink and she trembled slightly. She'd seen him gentle his horse before he mounted, running his hand along Warrior's sleek flank and stroking the side of his neck. Just the thought of those same hands stroking her skin made Caitlyn's breath catch in her throat. She'd never had this reaction to any man before, not even Spencer.

Caitlyn tore her eyes away and tried to concentrate on the trail. But a startling memory popped into her head and her eyes widened with surprise. Her former college roommate had flown in on the day before Caitlyn's wedding and they'd spent the evening together. Amy had splurged on a bottle of Dom Perignon, and they'd popped the cork after dinner in Caitlyn's small apartment.

To love. Amy had offered a toast and they'd smiled as the tiny bubbles rose in their glasses. And then Amy had asked a strange question. *Do you really love Spencer?*

She had laughed and said that she did, assuring Amy that she wouldn't want to marry Spencer if she didn't love him. Amy had seemed satisfied for a moment and then she'd asked what Caitlyn loved the most about Spencer.

Caitlyn remembered her answer, word for word. She'd said, *Spencer is handsome, intelligent, and kind. He's also very loyal and completely devoted to me. That's love, isn't it?*

Maybe. Amy had frowned slightly. *But you could say every one of those things about a pet dog! Tell me how you really feel about Spencer.*

Caitlyn had nodded, telling Amy how safe Spencer made her feel and how he never tried to hold her back, even though he was technically her boss. She'd mentioned that Spencer supported her personal decisions and always took the time to listen to her.

No, that's not what I mean. Amy had taken another sip of champagne. *I asked you how you really felt about him, Caitlyn. And you're giving me a laundry list of his good qualities. Maybe we'd better try it from a different angle. When Spencer's not with you, do you feel like a part of yourself is missing? Do you long to be together night and day? When he kisses you, do your knees turn weak?*

Caitlyn had nodded because that was what Amy had seemed to want. But she'd known in her heart that it hadn't been quite true. She supposed she missed Spencer when they weren't together, but she'd never really thought about it. And while it might be nice to be with him night and day, they had their own lives to lead. Spencer's kisses were wonderful, that part was true, but her knees had never actually turned weak.

Amy had refilled their glasses and then she'd winked at Caitlyn. *Just as long as you see the heavens open up when he makes love to you, you're doing the right thing.*

Caitlyn had laughed, amused by Amy's description of how she should feel. Amy had just completed her master's thesis on Byron's love poems and it was obvious that the study of his verses had affected her former roommate's outlook. Once Amy got into the real world, she'd learn that not everyone turned into a blithering idiot when they were in love.

All the same, Caitlyn had thought about Amy's words several times during the night and she'd reminded herself that not all loving relationships revolved around sex. Spencer possessed all the qualities she admired and their sex life was good—even though she'd never seen stars or blinding colors or the heavens opening up before her eyes. Those were just silly phrases from romantic prose and nothing like that actually happened in real life.

Or did it? Caitlyn frowned, unconsciously tightening her grip on the reins. Had Amy been right in suspecting that she hadn't loved Spencer enough? She hadn't missed him when they'd been apart; she'd never longed to spend every waking moment with him, and her knees hadn't turned weak when Spencer had kissed her. And the heavens had never opened up, not once in the three-and-a-half years she'd spent as Spencer's wife.

Dane had turned around now, and he was coming back to her. Caitlyn felt a warm glow spread through her body and she started to tremble again. Would her knees turn weak if Dane kissed her? All the man had to do was look at her and she felt flushed and eager, like a woman on the brink of . . . of . . .

Love? Caitlyn's face turned pale at the thought. Was she starting to fall in love with Dane Morrison?

Bitsy had warned her about this. Caitlyn forced herself to be calm. It was called rebounding, and it happened to many women who had been recently divorced. Bitsy had told her to go through a "cooling-off" period before she even thought about starting a new relationship. It was too easy for someone who had been disappointed in love to go from one bad experience straight into the arms of the next man who came along.

Caitlyn sighed. She felt curiously vulnerable and her emotions were in turmoil. She must be rebounding, and that meant she'd have to be very careful around Dane. He was handsome, intelligent, and very masculine, exactly the type that a new divorcée might find irresistible.

Without really realizing what she was doing, Caitlyn gathered up the slack in the reins. She'd nip her attraction to Dane in the bud before it had time to cause a problem. If her new partner thought that she was just another vulnerable divorcée who would tumble into his bed, he was completely mistaken.

Nanny's head jerked back and Caitlyn gasped. What was going on? And then Nanny reared up and Caitlyn was flying out of the saddle, tumbling to the ground like a stone.

SEVEN

Caitlyn groaned. She was sure that every bone in her body was broken. She blinked, looking up at the branches of a towering pine, and moved her arm slightly. She couldn't do that if it was broken, could she?

"Just stay right there. Don't move a muscle."

It was Dane's voice and it held a note of command that Caitlyn had never heard before. "What . . . what happened?"

"Nanny threw you. It's lucky you landed in that nice soft bed of mud."

"It's *not* soft!" His face appeared above her and Caitlyn stared up at him accusingly. "I thought you told me that Nanny was gentle."

"She is. You pulled up tight on the reins. That signal means stop to a horse."

"Oh." Caitlyn winced, realizing that she hadn't been giving him her full attention when he'd explained what to do with the reins. "I think I'm all right. Will you help me up?"

"Nope. I need to check you for broken bones. Just stay still and tell me if anything hurts."

Caitlyn stared up at the pine boughs high above her as he ran his fingers over her arms, probing gently. Then he felt her ribs on each side, and she started to blush. "What do you think you are? A doctor?"

"Close enough. You can't grow up on a ranch without recognizing a broken bone when you meet one. Hold on, Caitlyn. I'll be through in a minute."

Now his hands were moving down her legs, first the left and

then the right. He fingered both her ankles and then he leaned over her. "Nothing's broken, but you'll probably have some good-sized bruises. Tell me what day it is."

"A lucky day for you, an unlucky day for me."

The words tumbled out of her mouth before she could stop them, but he just laughed. "I guess your funny bone's not broken. Come on, Caitlyn. What day of the week is it?"

"Wednesday."

"And the month?"

"June." Caitlyn gave an exasperated sigh. "Do you want to know who's president?"

"Nope. I'd rather not think about that. Do you think you lost consciousness?"

Caitlyn shook her head. "If I did, it was only for a second or two. Can I please get up now?"

"Grab my hand and I'll help you."

His hand was warm and she steeled herself not to react as he helped her to her feet. The man's touch was electric, sending a jolt of pleasure through her. She straightened, pushing herself away from him, and took a few tentative steps, relieved that her feet seemed to work normally.

"Okay. Let me check out the back of your head."

She stood, rock still, as his fingers moved over her head. She knew enough about first aid to know that he was checking for bumps and possible skull fractures.

"Any nausea?" He waited until she shook her head. "Double vision?"

Caitlyn fidgeted. "No. I told you, I'm fine. The only thing that's hurt is my pride. I don't even have a headache."

"Okay. Lean up against this tree and wait for me. They're stopped right around the bend. I'll ride up and tell them you're okay."

Caitlyn nodded and watched him mount with one fluid motion. When he had disappeared around the bend in the trail, she glanced down at her clothing and groaned. She'd torn one sleeve of her blouse, and her white jeans were filthy. She brushed off as best she could and then she turned to Nanny, who was munching on grass by the side of the trail. "I'm sorry, Nanny. You didn't do anything wrong. I'm the one who messed up."

It didn't take Dane long to come back. He dismounted, dropped the reins, and strode over to her.

"Your color's better." He smiled, reaching out to brush a smudge of dirt from her cheek. "I'll call for the Jeep. One of the boys'll come out to pick you up." He reached into his pocket and pulled out a cell phone.

"That's really not necessary, Dane. I don't want to go back to the ranch. Just help me back on Nanny and let's catch up with the guests."

He stared at her in shock for a moment, as if he couldn't believe what she'd just said. "Are you sure you want to ride again?"

"I'm positive. If you're thrown, you're supposed to get right back on. Isn't that right?"

"Well . . . that's what they say, but . . ."

"Then that's what I'll do." Caitlyn interrupted him. "We wouldn't want me to develop a fear of horses, would we?"

That made him grin. "I don't think *we* are apt to develop a fear of anything."

"Let's do it, then. Come on, Dane. They're getting further ahead with every minute we waste."

Dane rode behind her on the narrow trail. Caitlyn Bradford had courage and a sense of humor to boot. There weren't many other greenhorns who would climb right back on a horse after they'd been thrown, but she hadn't batted an eyelash as he'd helped her back into the saddle. And then she'd asked him to explain about the reins again, to make sure that she wouldn't make the same mistake twice. She was every bit as tough as Bella, and then some.

Caitlyn Bradford was as pretty as a picture, as stubborn as a mule, and as sharp as a tack. Dane chuckled as every one of the hackneyed phrases occurred to him. All together, it was a pleasing package. And she was riding rather well now, better than a beginner usually did. She'd held herself stiffly at first, but now he could see that she was much more relaxed in the saddle. Perhaps she figured that once she'd been thrown, the worst had happened and she didn't have to worry about it anymore. He guessed that was true, in a way, but he wasn't about to let her get in any more trouble, at least not today.

Caitlyn looked good on a horse. Her hair turned the color of bronze in the sun and her cute little ponytail swung back and forth, sweeping against her back. It was soft, like silk, and when he'd examined her for any sign of skull fractures, he'd had the impulse to loosen her ponytail and run his fingers through her shining hair. Of course he hadn't, but he'd thought about it all the same.

She was strong for a woman. He'd felt the muscles in her arms and legs and figured that regular workouts had been a daily part of her schedule back in Boston. Even though he still thought that she was too thin, it was apparent that she took care of her body. Once she got more comfortable with riding, he'd try her on a more spirited horse. Caitlyn could turn out to be a fine rider, if she wanted to work at it. She had good balance and a natural grace. If she wanted, he'd help her choose a perfect mount and encourage her to bond with her horse. Once a horse and a rider developed an understanding of each other's movements and needs, they usually became a team.

As Dane watched, she stiffened slightly and reached up to rub her arm. She had to be getting tired, and the aches and pains from her fall would start to bother her before long. Dane really hadn't wanted to let her go on riding, but she'd had a point about getting right back on Nanny. She wasn't a quitter and she was stubborn. She'd probably want to ride all the way back to the ranch at the end of the day trip just to prove to him that she was tough enough to do it.

He wouldn't let her ride on the return trip. He'd think of some reason to send her back in the Jeep. It would have to be a good reason, an excuse that would let her save face. Maybe he'd say that Nanny was favoring a leg and she shouldn't be ridden back.

Caitlyn made a small sound and he urged Warrior forward, coming up beside her on the trail. "You all right?"

"Of course." She was smiling and he smiled back. "It's so beautiful here. I've never been in the mountains before."

He gestured toward the vista that was spread out before them. "Those peaks are the Medicine Bow Mountains, and they're part of the Rockies. I always think of *America, The Beautiful,* when I come up here."

"Do you mean the *purple mountain majesty* part?"

She had caught his meaning immediately and he grinned. "Yup."

"They really *are* purple." She felt as if they were sharing a secret. "I'm beginning to understand why Aunt Bella never came to visit me in Boston. If I owned a place as beautiful as this, I'd never want to leave it."

He laughed, reaching out to pat her shoulder. "Maybe it just hasn't sunk in yet, Caitlyn, but we *do* own a place like this."

Caitlyn's legs were trembling with fatigue when he helped her to dismount, but she wasn't about to admit it. She reached out to rub her aching back and then she looked around her in awe. They had stopped at a beautiful lake in the pines, and the sun glistened on the clear blue water. It was so lovely, it reminded her of something straight out of a fairy tale and she wouldn't have been at all surprised if Dane had told her that it was enchanted.

"What happens now?" Caitlyn turned to Dane, her eyes shining.

"They'll unpack all the gear and set up over there on the bank." Dane pointed to a sandy stretch of beach. "We'll fish for an hour or so, and then we'll have a shore lunch."

"Fish?"

"Yup. It's just one of the activities we offer. Fish and Game comes out every year to stock the lake, but you shouldn't mention that to the guests. Most of them like to think they're fishing in a lake that's entirely natural."

"Oh. Of course." Caitlyn nodded quickly. "But the lake *is* natural, isn't it?"

"It's not man-made, if that's what you mean. It's been here

since the first maps were drawn of the area, and there's an old Indian legend about it. They called it Star Lake."

Caitlyn smiled, taking a wild guess. "Because they could see the reflections of the stars in its depths?"

"That's part of it, but it's a little more involved than that. Legend has it that two bright stars fell in love and wished to become mortal. They fell to earth and when they landed, they created this lake."

"And they died here?" Caitlyn stared at the lake in fascination.

"Not according to the legend. They still live in the depths of Star Lake, and if you listen carefully, you can hear them singing for joy on quiet nights."

"That's lovely." Caitlyn sighed. "Have you ever heard the singing?"

"Nope. But the legend does turn out to have some basis in fact. Star Lake was created by a meteor. It has a sheer dropoff, about three feet from the shore, and the lake bed is a crater."

Caitlyn nodded. "Did it ever have fish?"

"Plenty, but the locals overfished it. You can't really blame them. It's a perfect spot. Now that Star Lake is part of the Double B, we're careful about maintaining a natural balance. Whenever Fish and Game comes out here to seed it, they do it with indigenous fingerlings."

"So the fish are small?"

"Not all of them. Bella started seeding Star Lake when she bought the ranch and the guests don't catch them all. We've got a few lunkers lurking in the depths."

Caitlyn nodded again. She assumed a lunker was an old, very large fish, but she didn't want to ask and take the chance that she was wrong. "What kinds of fish are there?"

"Brown trout, walleyes, and bluegills, mostly. One of the guests pulled up a largemouth bass last year, but we don't see many of those. You've fished before, haven't you?"

"Yes." Caitlyn nodded, grateful that there was no need to cross her fingers this time. He'd asked her if she'd fished, not if she'd ever caught a fish. And she had fished, once. She had been six-years old, and they'd rented a lake cabin for a week. Her father had baited her hook and helped her drop her line into the water.

She'd sat on the dock with him for an hour. Neither of them had gotten so much as a nibble, but she *had* fished before.

He was staring at her and Caitlyn blushed. Perhaps she should amend her answer. "I've fished, but I've never caught anything. That still counts, doesn't it?"

"Sure, it does." He grinned at her. "And I can practically guarantee that you won't get skunked today. I was up here last week, and the lake is packed so full, they're practically begging to be caught."

"Are you saying that the fish in this lake are suicidal?"

He threw back his head to laugh and Caitlyn laughed with him. "Nice line, Caitlyn. I'll use it with the guests. Come on. Let's pick out some gear and join the party."

"I'm ready." Even though her legs were sore, Caitlyn did her best to match her strides with his as they walked toward the array of fishing poles that the ranch hands had set out on a tarp. But his legs were much longer than hers, and it didn't quite work. She settled for walking as quickly as she could, taking three steps to his two. But he wasn't like Mr. Benning. The moment that he noticed that she had to hurry to keep up with him, he shortened his stride.

"This one looks about right for you." He picked up a fishing rod and handed it to her. "Careful of the hook."

Caitlyn nodded and stared down at the barbed hook that was attached to the end of her line. She'd never really examined a fishing hook before, and it looked extremely dangerous. She didn't remember her father using hooks like this, but perhaps that was because he had baited it with a round ball of cheese before he had given it to her. "What kind of bait are we using?"

"Grubs. There's no restriction on live bait when you fish on private land."

"You mean . . . live grubs?" Caitlyn managed to hide her shudder of revulsion at the thought.

"Yup. The fish won't bite on 'em if they're dead. When they're alive, they wiggle and the motion attracts the fish."

Caitlyn just nodded. She couldn't speak. She found the notion of piercing a live grub with a hook positively repulsive.

"The next step is to bait your hook. Come on, Caitlyn." He

motioned her toward the shoreline. "There's a big pail of grubs over there."

Caitlyn did her best to maintain a pleasant expression as she followed him over to the pail of grubs. She looked down at the pile of writhing, slimy-looking creatures and felt her stomach churn.

"Some of the female guests don't like to bait their own hooks." He looked down at her with a knowing grin. "I guess it bothers them. Do you want me to bait your hook for you?"

Of course she did. But Caitlyn's pride reared up again and she shook her head. There was no way she'd admit that the sight of all those white, wiggling grubs made her sick. "No, thanks. I know how to do it. You can go help somebody else."

"Are you sure?"

He was still wearing that smug grin, and Caitlyn had the urge to slap him. It was obvious he thought that she didn't have the stomach to bait her own hook. That made her determined to prove him wrong, and she looked up at him defiantly. "I said I could do it! Just bait your own hook and go fish!"

"Anything you say." He reached into the bucket and pulled out a fat white grub. "Just remember to hook it securely so it can't wiggle off . . . see?"

Caitlyn averted her eyes as he attached his grub to the hook. She wasn't about to watch. When he was finished, she nodded as if she'd been watching. "If you stand here staring at me, you'll make me nervous. Go on ahead. I'll bait my hook and join you in a minute."

The moment he'd left, Caitlyn glanced around for a way out of her difficulty. She found a stick a few feet away from the bucket and used it to flip out a grub that looked as dead as a doornail. It didn't wiggle at all as she picked it up with her folded handkerchief, and after a few very careful attempts, she managed to attach it to her hook.

"All ready?" Dane grinned at her as she marched over to join him.

"You bet." Caitlyn threw her line into the water before he could notice that her grub wasn't wiggling. "Has anybody caught anything yet?"

"Not yet, but we just started. Give it a couple of minutes and they'll be pulling them out left and right."

"I got one!"

Caitlyn whirled as they heard an excited voice. It was Marsha Rothstein and she was pulling in a flopping fish. Marsha grabbed the fish, removed the hook, and held it up by its mouth for everyone to see.

"Attagirl, Marsha!" Dane gave her the high sign and several other guests called out to congratulate her. Caitlyn managed to add her voice to the rest, but she was worried as she turned back to tend to her own line. She hoped that the fish were smart enough to tell a live grub from a dead one, because she certainly didn't want to catch anything. There was no way she wanted to reach out and grab a fish with her bare hands.

As time ticked by, Caitlyn began to relax. She hadn't even had a nibble and that was fine with her. It was beautiful out here by the lake and she could stay here happily for hours. There were long benches made from fallen logs along the shoreline, and it felt good to sit in the sun with the mountain breeze cooling her face. Most of the guests were catching fish, and Caitlyn called out her congratulations to each of them. It was a bit like a party, and she even forgot to feel guilty about the way she'd fooled Dane with the dead grub.

"Hand me your pole, Caitlyn." Dane turned to her. "I want to check your line."

Caitlyn experienced a moment of panic. If he checked her line, he'd discover that her grub was dead. But she couldn't tell him that, so she handed him her rod and held her breath while he reeled in her line.

"Looks fine to me." He cast her line back into the water. "You did a good job of baiting your hook, Caitlyn."

Caitlyn's eyes widened. "My grub's still alive?"

"Yup. You're bound to catch something before long."

Caitlyn swallowed hard as she took back her pole.

"What's the matter?"

"Nothing. I'm fine." With a silent apology to the disgusting creature that she'd impaled, Caitlyn kept on fishing. What else could she do? And then Mrs. Benning called out in excitement.

"I'd better go help her. She's got one." Dane patted Caitlyn on the shoulder. "Reel in your line and cast out again. I'll be right back."

Caitlyn did, shuddering slightly as she caught sight of her wiggling grub. She had managed to cast quite well, she thought, and she turned to watch as Dane helped Mrs. Benning pull in her fish. She looked proud and happy, and Caitlyn was glad. She was just wondering whether Mrs. Benning's success at fishing would give a boost to her self-confidence when she realized that her own line was snagged on something.

What should she do? Dane was still helping Mrs. Benning and she didn't want to interrupt. She'd seen Dane jerk up on his line to free his hook and she tried to do the same. But nothing happened and Caitlyn didn't want to jerk so hard that she'd break her line. She had just decided to put her pole down and wait for Dane to come back to help her when she felt an enormous tug on her line.

Instinctively, Caitlyn tugged back. Had she actually caught a fish? She stood up and walked to the edge of the shore, peering out to see if she could spot anything lurking in the depths. She was just taking another step closer when her line jerked again, with so much force that it toppled her headfirst right into the lake.

EIGHT

Dane felt his heart thump hard as he raced to the spot where Caitlyn had tumbled into the lake. He didn't even know if she could swim. Why hadn't he asked her? But she was up, sputtering and coughing, but still holding her fishing rod in both hands. And as he threw off his boots and waded in to grab her, she turned to him, laughing.

"I must've hooked one of those lunkers you told me about. He pulled so hard, he tumbled me right into the lake."

"Are you sure your line's not hung up on something?" Dane stared at her in surprise. She didn't seem all that upset about her unceremonious dunking.

"Pretty sure. Whoops! There he goes again!"

"You're right. You've got a big one on the line." Dane chuckled. She was soaked through and through, and her cute little blouse clung to her in ways he really didn't want to think about right now. "Here. Let me take your pole."

She shook her head so hard, her wet ponytail sprayed him with water. "No way, cowboy! I hooked him; I'll bring him in. Just tell me what to do."

"Reel him in very slowly. Keep it nice and even and don't jerk. Did you set the hook?"

She giggled. "Of course I did, but it was a total accident. I thought my line was caught on a branch so I jerked it back a couple of times. That's setting the hook, isn't it?"

"It should amount to the same thing." He watched as the tip of her pole bowed sharply. "Not so fast. You don't want him to snap your line. Play him a little. Give him a little more line."

"How do I do that?"

Dane stepped up behind her, reaching around to cover her hands with his. She was standing pretty close to the drop-off and she'd hooked a fighter. If he didn't anchor her, it could pull her right over the edge. "Just let me loosen the drag."

He continued to hold her, straddling her feet with his. He could feel the tension in the fiberglass pole right through her hands. She had hooked a lunker. There was no doubt about that.

"Now I reel him in again, slowly?"

"Yup. You do it. I'll just steady you. If you think he's pulling too hard, just let him take a little more line." To Dane's surprise, she was doing a good job of working the fish. He concentrated on guiding her hands and steadying the rod and did his best not to think about the way her body was molded to his. "By the way, can you swim?"

"Isn't it a little late to ask that question?"

There was laughter in her voice and he grinned. "Yup. Can you?"

"Yes. My trainer said it was great exercise, and I used to do laps on the weekends."

"You had your own pool?"

She nodded. "Two. One was a black-bottomed grotto, but it wasn't really big enough for laps. It was more decorative than anything else. The other was a lap pool. You must know the type. Long, narrow, and flat on the bottom?"

"Yup." Dane grinned. Bella had said that her niece had married well. Caitlyn's ex-husband must have been rich. "Do you miss it?"

She shook her head. "No. At least, not as much as I thought I would. How much line is out there, anyway?"

"A lot." Dane glanced at her reel and did a quick calculation. It was clear she wanted to change the subject, and he didn't blame her. He didn't like to talk about his former life, either. Bella was the only one he'd told about Beth. "I'd say he's got about twenty-five feet to play with. Try to bring him in a little. Maybe we can spot him."

She began to reel in the fish, cranking him closer and then giving him a little more line when he resisted. Unlike some of the other novices he'd coached, Caitlyn seemed to sense when the fish was about to rebel and gave him just enough leeway to make him think that he was winning. She took her time. It was a slow process. But gradually the line on her spool grew larger. "We ought to be able to see him pretty soon. You're doing fine, Caitlyn."

"I watched a couple of fishing shows."

Dane was surprised. "You were interested in fishing?"

"Not really." She didn't loosen her grip on the rod. "I only did it when I couldn't sleep, and there wasn't much choice at five o'clock on Sunday mornings. I watched a lot of infomercials, too."

Dane nodded. He'd done that himself during the long, lonely nights once Beth was gone. "Did you ever have the urge to pick up the phone and order anything?"

"No, but I almost called a psychic hotline once."

"You did?" Dane was surprised. She didn't seem to be the type of woman who'd call a stranger for advice about her life. But she was grinning and he realized that she must be teasing him. "What stopped you?"

"I decided that the one thing they were bound to be right about was that my phone bill would be a lot more expensive. And I guess I . . . I really didn't want to know my future. Can you see my fish yet?"

"Nope." Dane peered into the water, accepting the abrupt way she'd changed the subject. "He's still too deep, but it shouldn't be . . . there he is, Caitlyn! He's jumping!"

"I see him! He's beautiful!"

She shivered and Dane felt her excitement. And then she settled back down to working her fish again. Long moments passed without a word and then she sighed.

"I think he's getting tired. He's still pulling, but he hasn't really tugged hard for a while."

"That's good, but be careful when you bring him up toward the surface. He's bound to fight then. Remember that you're his enemy and he doesn't want to be caught."

"Right." She nodded. "I can't say I blame him. I wouldn't want to be caught, either."

She continued to reel in the fish as Dane steadied her. And then he spotted her fish. He was huge, more than fifteen pounds, an old granddaddy of a walleye. "There he is, Caitlyn! He's about ten feet out, just to the right of us. Can you see him?"

"Yes! He's even bigger than I thought he was!"

Dane turned and saw that the guests had gathered in a group on the shore to watch Caitlyn's struggle with the fish she'd almost landed. "Bring me the net, Jake. I think we're gonna need it for this beauty."

"Got it right here, boss."

Jake waded out into the water to hand him the net. He'd already taken off his boots and rolled up his jeans, and Dane nodded his approval. Jake moved forward. "Nice job, Miz Bradford. We're all watchin', and you're doin' just fine."

"Thanks."

When Caitlyn smiled at Jake, Dane felt a totally unreasonable surge of anger. He didn't want Jake anywhere near his new partner. "Go on back to the shore, Jake. Ms. Bradford doesn't need any distractions right now."

"Whatever you say, boss."

Dane did a slow burn as Jake flashed him a knowing grin and then turned to wade back to the shore. Jake probably thought that he was trying to pick up on Caitlyn himself, and all he was doing was steadying her a little, helping her to land her fish. Making a move on his new partner was the furthest thing from his mind.

She was starting to tremble now, and Dane steadied her with one arm. "You've almost got him, Caitlyn. Just bring him in, nice and easy, and I'll net him for you."

"He's . . . he's a monster!"

Dane laughed as Caitlyn caught full sight of her trophy fish. Her eyes were as wide as a kid who'd just seen Santa for the first time. "Just a little further, Caitlyn. Keep up an even pressure and angle him over to me."

She followed his instructions perfectly and Dane was impressed. If she'd learned all this from a fishing show, perhaps he should record a couple and show them to the guests before they came out here the next time. He watched for another few seconds and then decided it was time to ready the net. "I have to let go now, Caitlyn. Spread out your feet and brace yourself for a struggle."

"Okay." She moved her feet apart and planted them firmly on the bottom. "I'm ready. Just don't miss him with the net, Dane!"

Dane dipped the net in the water so it wouldn't splash when he moved it. Then he stepped out forward, reached out with both hands, and scooped up the thrashing fish.

There were cheers from the guests on the shore and Caitlyn laughed as she reached out to touch her fish. "Show me how to take out the hook, Dane. I want to do it myself."

"Let's get him up on the shore first." Dane grabbed her with one hand and carried the net with the other. "You don't want to chance losing him now."

"How much do you think he weighs?"

"Over fifteen pounds, I'd say." Her face was flushed with success as Dane hefted the net. "You caught a trophy fish, Caitlyn. If you want to have him mounted, I can call Roy Watson in Laramie. He's the best taxidermist around."

She thought about it for a moment and then shook her head. "I don't want him stuffed, Dane. I'd just feel bad every time I looked at him."

"Do you want to eat him for dinner tonight? Gibby's got a way with fish."

"I don't think I want to do that, either." Her brow puckered. "He fought so hard. He never gave up, not even at the very end. Maybe I'm just being sentimental, but I'd really rather take out the hook and . . . and let him go back to what he was doing before I caught him."

Her answer pleased him because he felt the same way. An old lunker like this deserved to live out the rest of his days in the lake. "It's your decision to make, Caitlyn. He's your fish."

"Do you think I'm crazy?"

"Nope. Would you like to take a picture before we release him?"

She nodded and gave him a huge smile. "That would be perfect! Does anybody have a camera?"

"We always carry along a couple of cameras. It was Bella's idea. After our guests leave, we get the film developed. And then we mail out copies to each one. Come on, Caitlyn. If we're gonna keep this big guy alive, we've got to hurry."

The next few minutes were busy. They brought Caitlyn's lunker into the shallows, and Dade showed her how to remove the hook. She did it perfectly and then he held her fish up by the mouth while Jake and Sam took pictures of her with the fish. Some of the guests had cameras, too, and they all promised to send Caitlyn copies when they got their film developed. Then it was time to release Caitlyn's fish.

"I can do it if you don't want to get wet again." Dade grinned at her.

"Again?" She grinned right back.

Dane glanced at her. "Guess you're right. You're so soaked, a little more water won't make any difference. We'll take him back out to the drop-off. Just follow me, but stay a step behind. I don't want you to fall over the edge."

"That wouldn't make any difference, either!"

Caitlyn was a truly amazing woman. He'd half expected her to primp a little before the pictures were taken, maybe ask one of the guests if they had a mirror and use it to smooth her hair or put on some lipstick. But she'd been much more interested in how the fish would look and she hadn't seemed to care about her own appearance at all. And even though she was soggy from the top of her head to the toes of her sneakers, he had to admit that she still looked good. Come to think of it, she'd probably look good buck naked, coming out of the shower.

Those kinds of thoughts could get him in big trouble. Dane pushed that delightful image out of his mind and turned his attention back to the fish. They were nearing the drop-off and he motioned for her to stop. "We'll do it here. We don't want to touch his scales if we can avoid it. That's bad for a fish. He's still pretty lively, so I don't think we'll have to help him much."

"I'll do it." Caitlyn reached out and hooked her finger in the walleye's mouth. She was straining a bit as she lifted him, but she managed and Dane was impressed by her strength. "What now?"

"Just lower him into the water and head him in the right direction. He'll get the idea."

Dane watched as she lowered the lunker into the water. She

was smiling, and he drew out the camera he'd taken from Jake and snapped a picture. "Okay. Pull him forward a little and then let him go."

She followed his directions and gave a little shout as the fish sprang into action. "He's fine. Look at him go!"

"Yup." He snapped another picture of her excited face and then he stuck the camera into his pocket. He was just in time because she threw her arms around his neck and gave him a hug.

"Thank you, Dane! That was more fun than anything I've ever done in my life!"

Dane's arms tightened around her instinctively. Her body was pressed up against his so sweetly, his breath caught in his throat. He had the sudden urge to kiss her, right then and there, and he barely managed to control himself. And then she pulled back, turning toward the crowd on the shore.

"He's gone! He swam off right away!"

Several of the guests applauded, but Dane heard Jake muttering to Sam. "Still don't see why she let him go. That could've been a record."

"Women!" Sam rolled his eyes. "There's no telling what they'll do next."

Caitlyn turned to him, and it was clear from her amused expression that she'd heard Jake and Sam's muttered comments. "What do *you* think I should do next?"

"Go back to the ranch house, get into some dry clothes, and take the rest of the day off." Dane looked down at her. "The breezes up here have teeth. Once the excitement wears off, you're gonna feel 'em."

Caitlyn opened her mouth and he knew she was about to object, but she nodded instead. "You're right. I am a little chilled. But you don't have to leave on my account. Just help me up on Nanny. I can follow the trail back to the ranch house."

"Nope. I've got some paperwork I should do, anyway. I'll call for the jeep."

"But can't we ride?"

He stared down at her with utter amazement. She'd already been thrown once and she'd been dunked in the lake. And she wanted to get back on the horse that'd thrown her and *ride* back to the ranch house?

"Why are you looking at me that way?"

She blinked and Dane bit back a grin. Sam had been right. You never knew what a woman was going to do next, especially if that woman was Caitlyn.

"I don't want you to ride. It's . . . uh . . . ." Dane thought fast. He'd have to latch onto an excuse that she'd swallow. "Nanny doesn't cotton to carrying wet riders on her back."

"But I wouldn't be on her back. I'd be sitting on the saddle and Nanny wouldn't even know that I was wet."

"Your legs would still touch her." Dane hoped she wouldn't know that he was lying through his teeth. "And Nanny's always been peculiar about that. Some horses just hate the water, and Nanny's one of 'em."

She stared at him for a moment, and then she capitulated. "Okay, then. I won't ride Nanny. Is your horse afraid of water, too?"

"Nope." Dane grinned, thinking about all the streams he'd ridden through on Warrior.

"Then there's still no reason to call for the jeep. Since you're going back to the ranch house, you can take me along on Warrior."

"You mean you want to ride double?"

"Yes." She was clearly pleased with her solution to their problem. "I don't weigh very much, and your horse is big. He wouldn't mind, would he?"

Dade knew when he was defeated. "No, Warrior wouldn't mind."

"Good. The minute we get back, I'll jump into a hot shower and then I'll join you in the office. If there's paperwork to do, I can help."

Dade gave in to the inevitable. She was one stubborn woman. And while Warrior wouldn't mind if they rode double, he certainly would. If the way she'd hugged him after her fish swam off was any indication, he was in big trouble. The long ride back to the ranch, with Caitlyn sitting in back of him on the saddle and pressing her sweet body against him, would be pure torture.

NINE

Caitlyn groaned as she stepped out of the shower. Dane had warned her that she'd be sore from her fall, but she hadn't expected the stiffness to set in quite so soon. As she raised her arms to towel off her hair, she actually winced in pain. What was wrong with her arms? She hadn't hurt either one of them when she'd tumbled off Nanny's back.

The lunker. She must have strained her arm muscles when she'd reeled in her lunker. Or perhaps it had happened when she'd lifted the trophy fish to let him go. It didn't really matter, because the whole experience had been worth every ache and pain.

Caitlyn remembered the way her fish had darted off when she'd released it. Jake and Sam had been shocked when she'd decided to let it go. It was clear they thought that she was crazy not to keep it. But Dane had approved. She'd seen it in his eyes. And he had been impressed with her for hanging onto her pole when the lunker had pulled her into Star Lake. He'd even told her as much on their ride back to the ranch house. And that had made her even more determined not to let any aches and pains she might feel get the best of her.

She opened Aunt Bella's medicine cabinet and gave a big sigh of relief as she spotted a bottle of aspirin. Extra-strength aspirin ought to fix her up just fine. She shook out two tablets, popped them into her mouth, and swallowed them with tap water from the faucet.

She tried not to wince as she finished toweling off and walked into her bedroom. The aspirin she'd taken wouldn't start working for at least twenty minutes. What she really wanted to do was to climb back in bed and pull the covers over her head, but she couldn't. She'd promised to help Dane with the paperwork, and that was exactly what she was going to do.

Caitlyn squared her shoulders and marched to the closet to find something to wear. She chose the least dressy of her outfits, a pair of light grey slacks and a pale-yellow, short-sleeved sweater. The materials weren't appropriate for ranch wear, but the style was simple and perhaps Dane wouldn't notice that her slacks were made of silk and her sweater was cashmere.

She shouldn't have suggested riding double. Caitlyn's cheeks burned with embarrassment as she started to dress. She'd recognized the hungry look in Dane's eyes when she'd spontaneously hugged him in the lake. He was attracted to her. She was sure of it. She'd been playing with fire when she'd insisted that Dane let her ride with him on Warrior, and only the fact that he was a gentleman had kept her from being burned.

Caitlyn sighed as she sat down in the chair in front of Aunt Bella's dresser and began to dry her hair. Her head told her that she didn't want any sort of romantic relationship with Dane. It was too soon. She wasn't ready. So why had she given in to the impulse to snuggle close to him in the saddle and lean up against his hard body?

By the time she'd finished drying and brushing her hair, Caitlyn still didn't have any answers. Her good sense told her to steer clear of her new partner, but her body was in total disagreement. There was only one thing to do. She simply had to figure out some way to regain control of her emotions before she made a real mess of things.

Caitlyn stared at her reflection in the mirror and tried to imagine what Amy would say if she were here right now. But Amy was the very last person she should ask for advice in a situation like this. Amy was an incurable romantic. If Caitlyn admitted that she trembled every time Dane looked at her and her knees turned to jelly when he did nothing more than slip a friendly arm around her shoulders, Amy would decide that she was in love.

No, she didn't want Amy's advice. Amy believed that life was chock full of hearts and valentines and that everyone had a perfect mate. She'd declare that Caitlyn had found hers in Dane, and that was nonsense. Bitsy's advice would be better. Bitsy was older and she was about as far from a starry-eyed romantic as a woman could get.

Bitsy would say that Caitlyn's attraction to Dane wasn't love at all, that it was simply desire. She'd say that Caitlyn would be fine as long as she was very careful not to get emotionally involved. And then Bitsy would encourage her to go for it, to have a little fling and get her sexy partner out of her system.

Bitsy's advice wouldn't work, either. Caitlyn tried to think of someone else to ask. If Aunt Bella were here, she'd ask her what to do and she'd follow her advice. But Aunt Bella wasn't here. She was dead and Caitlyn was on her own. And she shouldn't forget that Aunt Bella was the one who'd thrown her into this whole situation in the first place.

Sitting here thinking wasn't going to solve her problems. Caitlyn stood up and walked to the door. One of her co-workers at the ad agency had cured herself of binging on chocolates by eating a three-pound box at one sitting. Perhaps she should try that with Dane. She'd continue to work with him closely, be with him whenever possible, and hope that she'd eventually burn out on him. And once her crazy desire for him had died a merciful death, they might even wind up as friends.

Dane glanced at the clock as he heard footsteps approaching in the hall outside. It couldn't be Caitlyn, not this soon. He'd never known any woman who could shower, dress, and fix her hair in less than an hour. Even Beth had taken that long, and Beth had been near perfect as far as he was concerned. Dane gave a wry smile. And now she was growing more perfect with each year that passed. He knew that he was falling into the trap of forgetting Beth's imperfections and concentrating only on her good qualities, creating her as a feminine ideal in his mind.

The footsteps stopped and Dane glanced up from the pile of paperwork on his desk. It *was* Caitlyn! She was standing in the doorway, looking gorgeous in a pale-yellow sweater that clung to her curves.

"Am I late?"

"No." Dane shook his head. "I just got here a couple of minutes ago myself."

She walked to the chair in front of the desk, but she didn't sit down. He stared at her wondering how anyone could look that good after having been thrown from a horse and dunked in a lake. Then he realized that she was waiting for him to tell her what to do.

"There's coffee if you want it." Dane gestured toward the cart against the far wall. "It's fresh. I made it when I came in."

She poured herself a cup, carrying it back to the desk. "What do you want me to do?"

I *want you to throw your arms around my neck and kiss me. And then I want you to* . . . He pushed the errant thoughts out of his mind and sighed. "Sit down and make yourself comfortable. How are you feeling?"

"I'm just fine."

"No headache, dizziness, or nausea?"

She shook her head. "None of that. I feel exactly the same way I felt when I got up this morning. I'm just a little bit stiffer, that's all."

"Did you notice any bad bruises from your fall?" Dane studied her face intently. If she dropped her eyes, he'd know that she was lying. He'd noticed that about her the first time they'd met.

"Not yet." She shook her head. "I suppose I'll have some by tomorrow."

Dane nodded. He was glad that she was being truthful with him. "I've got aspirin in the desk."

"Aunt Bella had some in her medicine cabinet." She picked up her cup and took a sip of coffee. "I took two when I got out of the shower."

"Aspirin'll do fine for now, but you might need something stronger by tonight. Do you know if you have any drug allergies?"

She shook her head. "I don't think I do."

"Has a doctor ever prescribed Vicadin for you?"

"Vicadin?"

She looked puzzled and Dane explained. "It's an analgesic, a combination of synthetic codeine and Tylenol."

"I don't think I've ever taken it. But I did take something with codeine in it when I sprained my wrist playing tennis."

Dane nodded. "Okay. I'll give you a couple before you turn in for the night. If you wake up in pain, take one."

"But isn't that a prescription drug?" she questioned.

"Yes, it is." Dane nodded. "The Double B has an emergency medical kit, and Doc Henley keeps us supplied with the drugs he thinks we might need."

"And *you* dispense them?"

"I'm the only one who has the key." Dane patted her hand. She was right to be cautious, but it was clear that she didn't understand life on the ranch. "The Double B's a working ranch and we have our share of accidents. If we can't get to Doc Henley or he can't come out to us, we've got to be prepared to give emergency treatment."

She considered his explanation. "I see. And this Doc Henley trusts you to do that?"

"Yup. I'm the only one who's had the proper training." Dane changed the subject before she could ask any more questions. "I was just going over Gibby's supply list when you came in."

"And Gibby's the head chef?"

"Cook." Dane corrected her. "If you call Gibby a chef, he's likely to throw one of his spiders at you."

"The kitchen has *spiders?*"

"Not the kind you're thinking about." Dane laughed at the shocked expression on her face. "A spider is a cast-iron frying pan."

"I'm really glad to hear that," she admitted wryly. "Why doesn't Gibby want to be called *chef?*"

"He says they all talk funny and wear silly hats. And he doesn't think they should be so snooty about their cooking since they have other people to do all the preparations before they start and they don't even have to do the dishes when they're through."

"He's right," she agreed. "Thanks for warning me. I'll be very careful not to call him a chef."

Dane handed her copies of Gibby's weekly supply order and the menus he'd planned. "These are for next week. I made copies for you."

"Thanks." She glanced down at the papers and a tiny crease appeared on her forehead as she studied them carefully. "How many guests will we have?"

"We've got another twelve couples coming in on Sunday afternoon and they'll stay for one week."

"How many meals is that?" Dane noticed that she looked a bit shocked at the amount of food on the list.

"Seven breakfasts, six lunches, and seven dinners."

She nodded, glancing down at Gibby's supply list again. "A hundred and twenty-five *dozen* eggs? That would be over five cartons for each guest!"

"Yup. A guest eats an average of three eggs every morning for breakfast. He's here for six breakfasts, and that's a dozen-and-a-half eggs right there. Gibby makes egg salad twice a week, and that's another six eggs for each guest."

She nodded. "I see. But that would account for only two dozen per guest. What about the rest?"

"You're forgetting the staff. They eat, too. And Gibby makes a lot of cookies, pies, and cakes. There aren't many desserts that don't use eggs. He also bakes his own bread. And then there are things like pancakes, casseroles, scalloped potatoes, and corn pudding."

She stared at him for a moment and then she laughed. "The Council for Raising Cholesterol Levels would applaud you!"

"Probably, but most people ignore their diets while they're on vacation, and the food at the Double B is wholesome and well balanced. Our guests get plenty of exercise, much more than they would on a cruise ship or at a fancy beach resort. All in all, it's pretty much of a trade-off."

"You convinced me." She glanced down at the list again. "I see chicken, pork, and turkey, with what probably amounts to a whole cow on here. And there seem to be plenty of fresh vegetables on the list."

"Yup." Dane wondered if she'd catch the one thing that was missing from Gibby's list. "So you'd sign off on this order?"

"I think so. Everything on the menu seems to be here, including the staples. Except . . . where's the coffee?"

"Good for you!" Dane beamed at her. He hadn't expected her

to catch it, but she had. "We don't buy our coffee locally. The beans are shipped directly to us from a mail-order company, and we have a standing order."

"The coffee's really good," she commented. "I noticed that this morning."

"It should be. It's not cheap, and we grind it fresh for every pot. Your aunt loved good coffee and she did a lot of shopping around before she found a supplier she liked."

"I'm glad Aunt Bella was particular about the coffee." She took another sip from her cup. "It's some of the best I've ever tasted."

"That's what our guests say. They used to ask for the name so they could buy it when they got home."

"They *used* to?"

He nodded, pleased that she'd caught his deliberate use of the past tense. "Yup. When the distributor realized that he was getting so many phone orders from our guests, he decided to supply us with brochures and order blanks that they could take home with them."

"Do you get a discount?" Her eyes began to sparkle as he shook his head. "You should. The Double B is advertising their product by passing out brochures and order blanks."

Dane could see her excitement mounting. "You're right. How would we go about applying for a discount?"

"I'll take care of it. Just give me one of their brochures and I'll call. I'm sure they'll agree when they realize the number of new customers they've made. They might even spring for some sample packets that we could give to the guests. A brochure is easy to misplace. It's just a piece of paper. A sample packet has much more value, especially if you already know you like what's inside."

Dane pulled out the drawer where he kept the brochures and handed her one. "When do you want to call?"

"Just let me check to see where they're located." She scanned the brochure and glanced at the clock. "It's two-thirty in San Francisco, and the head of their marketing department should be back from lunch. I'll call right now. There's no time like the present, right?"

"Right." Dane pushed back his chair and stood up. "Let's switch places. It'll be easier if you sit behind the desk. Do you want me to leave while you make the call?"

"Why would I want you to leave?"

Dane shrugged. "I just thought you might find it easier. Some people don't like an audience when they talk on the phone."

"I don't have that problem." She grinned. "I've made calls from conference tables with twenty people listening in on a speaker phone. Stay or go, whichever you prefer. It really doesn't bother me."

"I'll stay then." Dane sat down in her chair.

"Good." She pointed to the pad of paper on his desk. "Is it okay if I use this to make notes?"

He nodded, watching as she flipped to a blank page and took a pen from the holder on the desk. She was a study in contrasts. She acted like a high-powered executive, used to making decisions and business deals. But she looked like a teenager with her pretty red hair pulled back in that cute little ponytail.

"Mr. Sherman, please. This is Ms. Bradford's office calling." Dane stared at her in shock. She was speaking with an English accent and she'd completely changed her voice. "No, I'll hold. Ms. Bradford said that it was important that she speak to Mr. Sherman immediately."

She must have noticed his shocked expression because she winked at him. And then she scribbled a note on the pad and turned it around so that he could read it. It said, *Important executives never make their own business calls.*

"Mr. Sherman?" She spoke in that different voice again. "It's Leonna Smythe-Holmsby from Ms. Bradford's office. Just a moment, please."

Dane grinned. She was good! She winked at him again, wiggled her eyebrows, and waited for a minute before she spoke.

"Mr. Sherman." Her voice was her own now, but her tone was businesslike and efficient. "Caitlyn Bradford here, from the Double B Ranch. I have some sad news regarding my aunt, Bella Bradford, the former owner of the Double B. She passed away six weeks ago."

In the ensuing silence, Dade assumed that Mr. Sherman was expressing his sympathies. And then Caitlyn spoke again.

"Thank you, Mr. Sherman. As I'm sure you know, Aunt Bella chose your coffee, personally, for use at the Double B. I tasted it this morning and I'm happy to report that it's an excellent product. Now that my partner and I have inherited the operation, we'd prefer to continue our business association with you."

She had jotted him another quick note, and Dane leaned forward to read it. It said, *I've got him hooked.*

"That's true, Mr. Sherman. It's an association that's been of benefit to both of us. But there's one aspect of our relationship with your company that puzzles me. You do have an advertising department, don't you?"

Dane leaned back and listened as she made her pitch to Mr. Sherman. Even though he could only hear one side of the conversation, he realized that she was playing him like the lunker that she'd hooked, letting him think that he was in control of their conversation, but reeling him in, bit by bit, until she'd landed the discount she wanted.

But Caitlyn didn't stop there. Dane grinned as she arranged for hundreds of sample packs for their guests. She even managed to negotiate bonus points for the Double B, redeemable for free bags of coffee beans and awarded for any large orders that their guests placed.

"Thank you, Mr. Sherman." She gave Dane a triumphant smile. "It's been a pleasure doing business with you."

When she'd replaced the phone in the receiver, Dane stood up and applauded. "You're really good at that, Caitlyn."

"Thank you." Her cheeks turned pink with his compliment and she looked even prettier. "It's really not that difficult."

"Maybe not, but I couldn't do it."

"Of course you could," she assured him. "All it takes is self-confidence and the ability to make them think that you're doing *them* a favor."

Dane shook his head. She was too modest. "I think it's a bit more than that. You made Mr. Sherman want to please you."

"That's right." She nodded quickly. "But you could do that, too. Most people want to please *you,* don't they?"

Dane shrugged. "I don't know. I've never spent any time thinking about it."

"If you had, you'd know that they do. Sam and Jake would do anything for you, and I suspect it's the same for any other member of the Double B staff. They all want your approval."

"I'm their boss," Dane reminded her. "That's the reason they want to please me."

"Not necessarily. You're not my boss and I still want to please you. How do you explain that?"

Dane watched as her cheeks turned red. She looked terribly embarrassed, and it was clear that she hadn't intended to tell him that. He wanted to see how she'd try to wiggle out of the trap she'd unwittingly set for herself, but that would be cruel. He had to give her some way to save face. "That's not so hard to explain."

"It's not?"

"Nope." She couldn't quite meet his eyes. "I know how to run the Double B and you don't. You want to learn how from me, and that causes you to think of me as your boss, even though we're really partners."

She seized the excuse he'd offered like a lifeline. "Of course. You're right."

"And there's another factor, too."

"Oh?" Her eyebrows shot up and she stared at him. It was clear she was anxious about what he was going to say next.

"You're hungry. I wouldn't be surprised if you were plum light-headed from lack of food. Let's go raid the kitchen and see what we can rustle up for ourselves."

A relieved smile flashed across her face. "That's a great idea. I *am* really hungry, now that you mention it."

Dane got to his feet and motioned toward the door. He'd saved her pride and that made him feel good. But as she walked down the hall with him, he couldn't help grinning. Caitlyn Bradford wanted to please him, and he could think of several dozen ways that she could do that. But most of them involved slipping into his bedroom in the middle of the night, and he wasn't about to mention them, at least not yet.

TEN

It was Sunday and the guests had left. Caitlyn had waved them off and then she'd gone to her room, feeling vaguely depressed, to shower and dress for the new batch of couples who'd be arriving before nightfall. She was surprised that it had been so difficult to say goodbye. She'd actually felt as if she were losing friends.

Caitlyn pulled on her blue jeans and surveyed the contents of her closet. Her blue-and-white cotton blouse was in the wash, and it was too warm to wear a sweater. She had brought her whole wardrobe, but she still had nothing to wear. Life on the Double B didn't require evening gowns, designer cocktail dresses, or smart little business suits.

She'd simply have to make do with what she had until she could drive into Laramie and replenish her wardrobe. Caitlyn pulled a silk turquoise blouse off the hanger and slipped it over her head. It was too dressy, but she didn't have anything else.

As Caitlyn reached out to flip off the closet light, one of her favorite evening gowns caught her eye. It was made of soft green chiffon with a silk underskirt and a beaded silk bodice that was held in place with spaghetti straps. She'd worn it only once, on her honeymoon, and it had cost a small fortune. If she stayed on at the Double B, she'd never have the occasion to wear it again.

Caitlyn took the dress off the hanger and carried it over to the mirror. She held it up in front of her and thought about the night she'd worn it. It had been a command appearance at the French Embassy. They'd gone to represent the Sinclair family, and she'd spent the evening chatting with the wives of powerful men. To tell the truth, the affair had been tedious and boring, and she remembered feeling relieved when it was time to leave.

She'd cause quite a sensation if she wore this dress to one of the Double B's Saturday night dances. Caitlyn giggled as she thought of Dane's reaction if she waltzed through the door of the barn-like building wearing this particular dress. He'd tell her she'd gone plumb crazy and spirit her back to her room before anyone could laugh at her. Of course she wouldn't wear it; it was totally inappropriate for a square dance, but it would almost be worth it to see the shocked expression on his face.

Caitlyn thought about her new partner. Dane was a puzzle that she couldn't quite figure out. There were times when he was the quintessential cowboy with his "yups" and his "nopes" and his colorful western phrases. But at other times, he had an air of sophistication about him that was surprising for a head wrangler on a ranch. He'd been educated. She knew that. And she was willing to bet that he'd attended a top-notch college. At the same time, she didn't doubt that he'd been raised on a ranch. He had the kind of knowledge about ranching that you couldn't get from books or even from talking to ranchers. It had to have come from years of experience. But Dane also knew a lot about the stock market. And just yesterday, he'd mentioned an exhibit that he'd seen at the Metropolitan Museum of Art. There were a lot of puzzling things about Dane Morrison, including the fact that he'd immediately run for the bottle of club soda when she'd spilled barbecue sauce on one of her silk blouses. It had been the right thing to do, but how had he known that?

There was a knock on her door, and Caitlyn crossed the room to answer it, dropping her designer cocktail dress on the bed as she passed by. The guests had left an hour ago and their new batch of couples wasn't due to arrive for at least three hours.

"Miz Bradford?"

It was Lisa Thornton, one of the high school girls they'd hired to help out in the summer, and Caitlyn smiled at her. She liked the friendly brunette. "Hi, Lisa. What can I do for you?"

"I need to leave early, Miz Bradford, but Tricia promised to cover for me."

Caitlyn nodded. Lisa's eyes were shining and she looked very excited. "That's fine, Lisa. What is it? A special date?"

"No, Miz Bradford." Lisa blushed. "Mom just called and she said I won the state essay contest. And I have to go to Cheyenne on Friday night to accept my award at a big banquet. It's going to be real fancy and I have to go home and run up something to wear."

"Run up something?" Caitlyn was confused. Was this another colorful Western expression?

"I mean, I have to sew it." Lisa explained. "I don't want to ask Mom for the money to buy a new dress. We barely make it, now that Dad's gone. My summer job here has helped out a lot, but I haven't been able to put that much money away."

Caitlyn stared at Lisa for a moment and then she nodded. She knew precisely what she was going to do. "What type of dress would you like, Lisa?"

"I'm not sure. Something really elegant, I think. The governor's going to be there to present the award and I'll have to get up in front of all those people."

Caitlyn nodded. Lisa was close to her size. "Take a look at the dress on my bed and tell me if you like it."

"This one?" Lisa walked closer and reached down to touch the material. "It's beautiful! Would you let me copy the pattern? I wouldn't have to take it apart or anything. I could just sketch it right here, if you wouldn't mind, and . . ."

Caitlyn interrupted her. "Try it on, Lisa. See if it fits you."

"Are you sure?"

"I'm sure. I'd really like to see how it looks on you."

Lisa didn't wait for a second invitation. Her pretty brown eyes were wide as she shed the jeans and shirt that she wore and slipped the dress over her head. Caitlyn zipped it up for her and led her over to the mirror. "I think it's gorgeous on you."

"I think so, too." Lisa laughed, turning around slowly to admire the cut of the dress. "I wouldn't copy the beadwork on the top. Beads are too expensive and it would take too long. But this style is just perfect. And the color is beautiful! I wonder if I could find some material like this in Laramie."

The material was expensive imported silk, and Caitlyn

doubted that a Laramie fabric shop would carry anything close to it. "I don't think you can, Lisa, but you don't have to look. The dress is yours."

"Mine? But . . ." Lisa stopped, staring at her in shock. "You mean that I can borrow it for the banquet?"

"No, you can have it. I'll unzip you and then I'll find a bag for it. I know I've got several in my closet."

"But . . . why would you give *me* something like this?" Lisa still looked shocked.

"Why not? You have an occasion to wear it, and I don't. And if I stay out here on the Double B, I won't be attending any fancy banquets or cocktail parties."

"Nobody's ever been *this* nice to me before." Lisa's lower lip trembled and she looked ready to burst into tears. "I . . . I just don't know what to say."

"You don't have to say anything. Just have a good time at the banquet and make us proud of you."

Once Lisa had left, wearing a huge smile and holding the dress bag reverently, Caitlyn sat down and thought about her first week at the Double B. Giving Lisa the dress had lifted her spirits. She'd felt wonderful when she'd seen the expression of awe on Lisa's face. But as nice as that had been, it hadn't completely erased the depression she felt.

The week hadn't been all bad. Caitlyn tried positive thinking. She'd done some things right. Getting the discount from Mr. Sherman had been one of them. She'd also caught a trophy fish and she was riding a little better, although she still wasn't entirely comfortable on Nanny's back. She'd learned to braid her hair, and that was an accomplishment. And Mrs. Benning hadn't appeared with any new bruises, thanks to her plan. But there were countless other things that hadn't gone well at all.

Caitlyn attached a ribbon to the bottom of the thick plait of hair that hung down her back. She had been stung by a bee and nearly bitten by a rattlesnake when she'd poked her hand into a bush to investigate the strange sound she'd heard. And when she'd tried to weed the flower bed that ran along the sides of the breezeway, she'd ended up killing several of the flowers. She'd fallen off the fence at the corral, right in front of a group of guests, and she'd made the mistake of smiling at Jake once too often. He'd taken it as the wrong kind of encouragement, and at the square dance last night, she'd been forced to use her authority as part owner of the ranch to order him to leave her alone.

She walked over to the bed and sat down to put on her shoes. They really hadn't been designed for wear on a ranch. The toes had curled up when she'd soaked them in the lake, and there was a cut on the side of the left one from an encounter she'd had with a sharp rock. The white had turned to a dusty gray, and she didn't dare wash them because she had nothing else to wear while they dried. They were wearing out quickly, and Caitlyn knew that they weren't long for this world. She needed boots and she'd have to get some soon. Life on the ranch required boots.

Caitlyn thought about all the things she'd need if she stayed on at the Double B. She needed more jeans, shirts, and socks. And she also needed some washable dresses that she could wear to the Saturday-night dances. As Dane had pointed out, there was no dry cleaning available out here, and almost every item in her wardrobe needed to be dry cleaned. Her wardrobe was all wrong for life on the Double B.

It was time to face facts. Caitlyn sighed and dropped her head in her hands. She could handle a conference room full of finicky clients with ease, but she simply wasn't cut out for life on the ranch. She liked it—that wasn't the problem; but it seemed that every time she tried to do something, she did it wrong. To make matters even worse, Dane was incredibly good-natured about it. He didn't even grumble when he had to step in to fix something she'd botched. He was always cheerful and he'd been the soul of patience with her. And that was another thing that was wrong with life on the ranch. Dane Morrison.

Caitlyn had stuck to her plan to work closely with Dane, but her desire for him hadn't diminished. If anything, it had grown stronger, and now she was even dreaming about him. Her dream last night had been much too real for comfort. She'd actually dreamed that Dane was taking off her clothes and running his strong hands over her body! She knew she couldn't control her dreams, but sometimes she found herself musing about him in the middle of the day, imagining what it would be like to kiss him, and wishing that he'd take her off to a private spot in the purple mountains and make love to her.

It had to stop. Her thoughts about Dane were driving her crazy. Every night, alone in her bed, she found herself fighting down the impulse to put on something incredibly sexy and slip through the deserted halls to knock on his door. She had to do something. If she didn't stop thinking about Dane like this, she'd make a total fool of herself.

Caitlyn gave a wry laugh. At least one thing was good about life on the ranch. She hadn't thought about Spencer once. Any regrets she'd had about their divorce had vanished into thin air. She no longer cared that Ardis was having Spencer's baby. It simply didn't matter to her at all. Caitlyn didn't miss her former life and she was very glad she'd left it when she had.

Life on the Double B was interesting. Caitlyn had to admit that. When her old wind-up alarm clock began to clang at six in the morning, she'd found herself actually jumping out of bed. Each new day was an adventure filled with exciting discoveries. It could also be frustrating and sometimes embarrassing, but no one could call her life on the Double B boring.

Dane strode down the hall in a clean pair of jeans and a freshly laundered Double B shirt. The new guests would be here in less than an hour, and he had to be sure that everything was ready for them.

"Hi, Mr. Morrison."

"Hi, Lisa." Dane grinned at one of his favorite summer employees. Lisa Thornton was always pleasant and friendly, and she was a hard worker, too. He glanced at the dress bag that was hanging over her arm and his grin grew wider. "Big date tonight?"

Lisa giggled slightly and her cheeks turned pink. "No, Mr. Morrison. This dress is for the award banquet in Cheyenne. When I told Miz Bradford that I won the state essay contest, she gave it to me."

"That was nice of her." Dane wasn't all that surprised. He'd seen enough of Caitlyn to guess that she was a generous person.

"I . . . I think it's really expensive." Lisa lowered her voice to just slightly above a whisper. "Do you think I was wrong to accept it?"

"Nope. Caitlyn wouldn't have offered it if she hadn't wanted you to have it. What kind of dress is it?"

"It's real silk with a chiffon overskirt." Lisa unzipped the garment bag to show him. "And look at all the beadwork. Beadwork like this is expensive. I can tell it's hand sewn."

Dane caught sight of the designer label. "You're right, Lisa. It's expensive."

"I wish I could do something for her in return," Lisa confided. "Except I can't think of anything to do. All I really know how to do is sew, and she's got a whole closetful of expensive dresses."

"I think you just hit on a perfect thing to give her, Lisa," Dane whispered conspiratorially. "You say Caitlyn's got a whole closetful of expensive clothes, right?"

"Yes." Lisa waited for him to continue.

"Did you see anything that she could wear for our Saturday-night square dances?"

"No." Lisa understood at once. "But I could make her something like that. Do you think that I should?"

"That's up to you, Lisa, but I think she'd like it a lot."

"Then I'll do it!" Lisa paused, considering. "What color do you think it should be?"

Dane didn't have to think. "Green," he said. "It should have some green in it to match her eyes."

"You're right," Lisa concurred. "I've got a bolt of green-and-white calico that would be perfect on her. Do you think I should make it a surprise?"

Dane raised his eyebrows. "Can you? I mean, don't you have to have fittings and things like that?"

"No." Lisa shook her head. "Ms. Bradford and I are the exact same size, so I won't even have to ask her to try it on before it's finished. Thanks, Mr. Morrison. I'm going home right now to get started on it!"

Dane watched Lisa hurry off, a satisfied expression on her face. The dress that she'd sew for Caitlyn wouldn't have a designer label, but he was sure that Caitlyn would like it much more than any of the expensive outfits in her closet. She was self-conscious about her designer clothing. He'd seen the way she'd tried to tie bandannas around the necks of her silk blouses so no one would notice that they were too dressy to wear on the ranch. It hadn't fooled anybody, but she'd tried. She didn't have any ranch clothing at all. Even her blue jeans had a designer label. He'd thought about it last night, and he'd come up with one way to help her out. There was a box of Double B shirts in the office. They were men's shirts and they'd be too big on Caitlyn, but he'd take her one and see if she could figure out some way to make it work. It was red and it wouldn't go with her hair, but he had a feeling that Caitlyn would wear it anyway. She'd been a real fashion plate when she'd first set foot on the Double B, but Dane suspected she'd re-ordered her priorities when she'd decided to stay and help him run the ranch. He guessed that the shirt was a test, of sorts. He'd just give it to her and see what happened. He admired Caitlyn Bradford already. She was one tough lady, just like Bella. If she wore the red shirt to greet their new batch of guests, he'd know that she was really adjusting to life on the Double B.

Caitlyn groaned as she pulled the shirt from the box. It was red and she'd never been able to wear red. But it was made of cotton and it could be washed. And it was an official Double B shirt. Dane wore them all the time, and so did the rest of the ranch employees. She was tired of being different, of being a city slicker and a greenhorn and an outsider. If all it took to be accepted on the Double B was to wear this official shirt, she'd do it.

She slipped it over her head and laughed. It was way too large. Dane had warned her about that. The sleeves were at least four inches too long and it hung on her like a bulky sack, but that didn't really matter. Caitlyn rolled up the sleeves, left the bottom three buttons open, tucked up the tail as best she could, and tied the ends in a knot around her waist. Then she walked to the mirror and winced at her reflection. The color was truly dreadful on her. It clashed with her hair and made her look like a cherry tomato with a darker red stem. Her friends back in Boston would be horrified if they saw her in this outfit. They'd probably suggest that she go in for counseling, and gather together to whisper that poor Caitlyn's divorce had unhinged her mind. But none of that mattered out here on the Double B. There simply wasn't time to worry about fashion. Other things were much more important, like working together and being accepted and letting everyone know that you were willing to do your share. Dane wouldn't have given her this shirt if he hadn't wanted her to wear it. She had two choices. She could refuse to wear anything that wasn't her size and color. Or she could wear it and make Dane happy.

Caitlyn glanced at her reflection once more and made up her mind. She whirled on her heel and marched out the door to join the man who meant much more to her than fashion ever had or ever could.

ELEVEN

Caitlyn managed to keep the polite smile on her face even though one of the guests, Mr. Allen Kennedy, was beginning to try her patience. He'd monopolized her from the moment he'd arrived, and now he wanted even more of her attention. "I'm afraid I don't know much about fly fishing, Mr. Kennedy. You'll have to ask my partner about that. He's right over there at the chuck wagon."

"No problem." Mr. Kennedy got up from the table, and Caitlyn breathed a sigh of relief. He'd told her that he was a Los Angeles producer and he was always on the lookout for locations for his movies. But instead of leaving to talk to Dane, Mr. Kennedy grabbed her arm. "Come on. I want you to show me the corral."

Caitlyn shook her head. "Sorry, Mr. Kennedy. I can't leave right now. But if you ask Dane, I'm sure he'll be happy to—"

"You don't seem to understand," he interrupted her. "There's a reason why I want *you* to show me. I need to see how you'd look in that milieu."

"Me?"

"Yes, Caitlyn. By the way, Caitlyn's a good name. I like it. I don't even think we'd have to change it."

"Change it?" Caitlyn forced herself to smile at him pleasantly. "I have no intention of changing my name, Mr. Kennedy."

"Call me Allen. Everyone's on a first name basis in Hollywood. I think I could work with you, Caitlyn. How would you like to try out for the part of the ingenue in my next film?"

He was grinning at her, and Caitlyn had all she could do not to tell him to get lost. He was a middle-aged man, handsome in a slick, oily sort of way, with an *I won't take no for an answer* attitude. She doubted that he was a producer at all, even though his driver's license had sported a Los Angeles address. He reminded her of a high-pressure salesman who'd go to any lengths to close a sale.

"I'm much too old to be an ingenue, Mr. Kennedy." Caitlyn knew that if she'd met him under any other circumstances, she would have ended their conversation several minutes ago. But Mr. Kennedy and his wife were guests at the Double B and it was her job to be polite to him.

"You could be right." He stared at her critically. "But we could age you down a little. You can't be in the biz for thirty years without learning a few tricks."

This had gone far enough. Caitlyn smiled politely and shook her head. "Thank you, Mr. Kennedy, but I'm not interested in an acting career. And if you came out to the Double B to scout locations, I'm afraid I'll have to disappoint you. We don't allow film crews on our land."

"That's what they all say . . . at first." He chuckled and patted her arm. "Money talks, Caitlyn. That's a fact of life in the fast lane."

Caitlyn sighed, wondering just how long she could keep a smile on her face. "I'm sure it is, Mr. Kennedy, but we're simply not interested in becoming a film location. If you're looking for a Western setting, you could discuss your project with the mayor of Little Fork. I understand they shot a film there a couple of years ago."

"Maybe I'll do that." Mr. Kennedy nodded. "But I still want to see that corral. You're not being very friendly to a paying guest, you know."

Caitlyn bit back a sharp retort and got to her feet. "Of course, Mr. Kennedy. Please follow me."

"I still think you could play an ingenue."

He was following her so closely, Caitlyn was uncomfortable. There was no way she was taking him to the corral by herself. She led him straight to the chuck wagon and gestured to Sam. "Hi, Sam. This is Mr. Kennedy and he wants to see the corral.

Would you please give him a tour and answer any questions he has?"

"Sure, Miz Bradford." Sam gave her a knowing grin. "Come on, Mr. Kennedy. Let's go pick out a horse for you to ride tomorrow."

Mr. Kennedy turned to give her a dirty look as Sam led him away. That made Caitlyn smile, her first genuine smile since the pseudo-producer had decided to monopolize her evening.

"Everything okay?" Dane walked up to her, a quizzical look on his face.

"Right as rain." Caitlyn repeated one of Gibby's favorite phrases. "Mr. Kennedy said he wanted to see the corral and I asked Sam to give him a quick tour."

"He wanted to see the corral at night?"

"That's right." Caitlyn started to grin. "He wanted me to take him, but I didn't think that was such a good idea."

"Why not?"

Caitlyn shrugged, trying to look perfectly innocent. She wasn't about to tell Dane that Mr. Kennedy had tried to pick up on her. "I don't know that much about horses and Mr. Kennedy asks a lot of questions. I just thought it would be better for both of us if Sam gave him the tour."

Dane took Caitlyn's arm and led her to a deserted table. He'd seen Kennedy trying to move in on her, and he'd been about to rescue her when she'd palmed that aging womanizer off on Sam. From the grin Sam had given him right before he'd led Kennedy away, he'd known exactly what was going on.

"Stay put, Caitlyn. I'll get us some coffee."

Dane walked toward the chuck wagon. It was pretty clear that Kennedy had set his sights on Caitlyn, and he wasn't the type to give up that easily. He intended to warn the boys to keep an eye out for Caitlyn, but before he could open his mouth, Gibby grabbed him by the arm.

"Keep an eye on that guy from California, Dane. He got a little too friendly with Miz Bradford. She was smart enough to bring him over to Sam, but he's bound to try it again."

Dane nodded. "I'll do that, Gibby. How did you find out about Kennedy?"

"Sam passed the word. Can't let anything happen to Miz Bradford. She's a real nice lady."

"Yes, she is." Dade filled two cups and carried them back to the table. Maybe Caitlyn didn't know how much it had meant to the boys, but the minute she'd appeared in that Double B shirt, they'd felt that she had thrown in her chips with them. He'd heard Jake say that it was a shame it wasn't a different color, one that showed off her pretty hair, and Dane intended to do something about that. First thing tomorrow morning, he'd call the company that made up their shirts and order a couple in a different color and a size that would fit her.

He was grinning as he walked back to the table, and Caitlyn looked up at him. "You look happy tonight."

"I am. I think we've got a good bunch of guests, with the exception of Mr. Kennedy. Steer clear of him, Caitlyn. He's trouble."

"I will." She dropped her eyes and blushed, her cheeks almost as red as the shirt. "Have you met Mrs. Kennedy?"

Dane nodded, remembering the blonde who had signed the guest register. "I saw her when they checked in. She's a Barbie."

"Her name is Barbara?"

"No." Dane chuckled. "Her first name is Bambi and she used to be a *Playboy* centerfold. She told everyone that the moment she arrived."

She cocked her head to the side, regarding him curiously. "Then why did you call her Barbie?"

"I didn't call her Barbie. I called her *a Barbie*," Dane corrected. "It's pretty clear she spent a fortune to look just like the doll."

"She's a blonde?"

Caitlyn leaned forward and Dane swallowed hard. Her ranch shirt was buttoned all the way up, but she was still incredibly sexy. She looked like a teenager wearing her boyfriend's shirt, and he almost wished that he'd given her one of his.

She was waiting for an answer and Dane nodded. "She's a California bleached blonde. And she must have gotten a deal on cosmetic surgery because she's had everything done. Tucks, face lifts, enhancements, you name it. She's fighting hard to turn back the clock."

"How old is she?"

"Her driver's license says she's forty-two, but she looks ten years younger. You know the type. She's not about to age gracefully."

"You noticed a lot about her," she teased. "Anything else?"

"She's got a sunlamp tan, and certain parts of her anatomy don't wiggle when she walks."

Caitlyn giggled, a sound that pleased him a lot. She had a good sense of humor. "I understand. But where is she? I thought I talked to everyone here at the barbecue."

"Mr. Kennedy came alone. Right after they checked in, Bambi went to her room with a bad case of jet lag. I assume she's still there."

"Jet lag?" Caitlyn stared at him, as if he were crazy. "But that doesn't make any sense! How can she possibly have jet lag? There's only an hour's time-difference between California and Wyoming."

"Yup."

It took her a minute, but then she nodded. "I get it. A Barbie always suffers from jet lag, even if it's only a two-hour flight. Am I right?"

"You got it." Dane chuckled and reached out to take her hand. "You're not going to turn into a Barbie when you grow up, are you, Caitlyn?"

She looked shocked as she shook her head. "Never. I intend to age gracefully, the way my mother did. I might touch up my hair a little, if the gray doesn't look good on me, but that's as far as I'll go."

"No tummy tucks or facelifts?"

"Absolutely not. Cosmetic surgery is like a roller coaster. Once you get on, there's no way to get off before they stop the ride. My former mother-in-law fell into that trap, and now she's stuck with a thirty-year-old face on a sixty-year-old neck. I can understand why a movie star or a model might have to do it. It's the price they have to pay for choosing a profession that's so appearance-oriented. And I guess I can understand why Mrs. Kennedy feels that she has to do it."

"Why's that?"

"If her husband's the person he says he is, he's surrounded by beautiful women every day. I'm sure she feels that she has to compete with them."

Dane raised his eyebrows. She had a good point. "Do you think her husband is really a producer?"

"He could be, but somehow I doubt it. He drops too many famous names and he's too quick to tell everybody what he does. If I were a big producer, I'd want to get away from it while I was on vacation."

Dane agreed with her. "Do you want to find out if he's telling the truth?"

"It really doesn't matter." She shrugged. "Let him have his little fantasy, if that's what he wants. It won't change my attitude toward him either way."

Dane grinned. "You don't like him, do you?"

"Not much. But he's a guest and I have to be polite to him. And I *am* looking forward to meeting his wife."

"Why is that?"

She giggled and Dane knew that she was setting up for a punch line. "I've never met a saint before. And she's got to be one to put up with Mr. Kennedy."

He was touching her face, and Caitlyn shivered in pleasure. His touch lit little fires under her skin and made her want more. He stroked her arms and she sighed, reaching up to clasp her arms around his neck. Now he was lifting her up into his strong arms and carrying her through the trees to a wooded glen filled with soft waving grass and brightly colored flowers. There was a red velvet blanket in the middle of the glen, and he gently placed her down on it. But red didn't go with her hair and she changed its color to a deep midnight blue. And it was midnight. She could see the stars twinkling like candles in a soft black sky, singing their song of love to fill her heart with gladness.

One by one, the stars began to swim, streaking across the sky and leaving light trails in their wake. They jumped and whirled, playing like puppies in a darting game that made the moon laugh with a deep rumbling sound. Louder and louder the rumbling grew until even the stars took flight. They streaked for cover at the edges of the sky and disappeared in flashing bolts.

Now the moon was weeping, alone in the sky. His playmates were gone and he was lonely. His great tears fell in bursts and patters, pounding down to a thirsty earth below.

And then his face blocked out the sky. Their lips met in a fiery kiss, igniting a blaze of passion that left her weak and trembling. He trailed kisses down her body, pinpoints of pleasure that made her gasp in wonder. She trembled and sighed as he caressed her and then covered her body with his own. She cried out in rapture, spiraling out of control, spinning and whirling and rising toward the light that suddenly appeared in her eyes. And then the moon spoke . . .

"Caitlyn? Wake up, Caitlyn. We've got a problem. I need you."

"Huh?" She sat up, blinking at the light. It was a candle inside a glass chimney. There was a face behind it, a ruggedly handsome face that she recognized immediately. It was Dane, and he looked very upset. "What . . . what is it? Dane? What are you doing in my room?"

"Lightning hit the horse barn and I've got to go out and help. I need you to reassure any of the guests who wake up."

Suddenly she was awake, and she gave a quick nod. "Of course. Just give me a second to throw on some clothes. Are the horses all right?"

"Yes. The boys got them all out. They're safe in the corral, but storms like this get them spooked. We're going to have our hands full until the lightning and thunder die down."

She nodded. "Go ahead. I'll take care of the guests."

"You'll need this." He struck a match and lit the hurricane lamp that sat on her dresser. "The electricity went out and there's something wrong with the backup generator. I don't have time to fix it now."

"How about the guests? Do they have candles in their rooms?" Caitlyn knew that this was an emergency and she didn't stand on ceremony. She just jumped out of bed and pulled on her jeans, glad that she'd worn her old flannel college nightshirt to bed.

"There are a box of matches and a hurricane lamp in every room, but some of the guests may not know how to light them. I stopped to fire up a couple of lamps in the hallway so no one would stumble down the stairs."

"Okay. No problem." Caitlyn turned her back, pulled off her nightshirt, and reached into her dresser to grab the sweater on the top of the stack. It happened to be sky-blue cashmere that was embroidered with a field of colorful flowers, but this wasn't the time to worry about the way she looked. "I'm ready."

"Shoes." He pointed to her bare feet.

She blushed, following his gaze down to her feet. As a gesture of defiance, on the day she'd gone in to sign her divorce papers, she'd painted her toenails bright pink. Spencer abhorred painted toenails and even though no one had seen them, it had given her great satisfaction to stand in the tastefully decorated law offices with bright pink polish on her toenails.

"Nice polish. Somehow, I didn't think you were the type to paint your toenails."

"I'm not." Caitlyn shot him a look that told him not to ask any questions. She'd intended to remove the polish the moment she'd returned home, but Bitsy had been there to take her to lunch and she'd forgotten all about it. And now it would have to wear off because she'd forgotten to bring any nail-polish remover.

The blush still staining her cheeks, Caitlyn slipped her feet into her tennis shoes and tied the laces. "I'm ready now. Are any of the guests awake?"

"Only one."

The concerned tone of his voice could mean only one thing. "Mr. Kennedy?"

"Yup."

He looked so anxious, she gave him her best self-confident grin. "Don't worry, Dane. I'll be fine. Just go on out and help the boys."

"If you're sure . . ."

"I am." Caitlyn picked up the lamp. "Use my back door. It's closer. I'll take care of everything in here."

He pushed open the back door, letting in a driving gust of rain, and hesitated. "Maybe you should wake the Randalls. This is their third year with us and I know they won't mind getting up to help you out. I don't want you to be alone with Kennedy."

"Okay." Caitlyn nodded quickly, just to reassure him. "But I told you, there's really no problem. I can handle Mr. Kennedy with one hand tied behind my back."

TWELVE

The long hallway leading from her quarters to the main part of the ranch house was dark, and Caitlyn was glad she had the lantern. Dane had given her a box of wooden kitchen matches, and she struck one to light the lantern that hung near the entrance to the large living room. She glanced in, wincing as she saw Mr. Kennedy sitting on the sofa, and then ducked back before he could see her. She'd check on the rest of their guests before she went in to talk to him.

Her legs were trembling as she climbed up the curving wooden staircase to the second floor. There were no sounds from any of the guest rooms. Caitlyn didn't see how it was possible, but all the guests were still asleep. Perhaps that was good. It might have been difficult for her to reassure them when she was so nervous herself.

She'd never liked storms. Caitlyn shivered as she walked along the long hallway. And this was the worst electrical storm she'd ever experienced. The rain pelted down on the wooden shingles of the roof and it reminded her of a steady snare drum roll. Lightning flashed in an irregular rhythm, illuminating the corridor brightly for a moment and then plunging it into darkness again. Each lightning bolt was accompanied by a deafening crack of thunder, and Caitlyn couldn't help thinking of every horror movie she'd seen. She knew it was just a storm and there was really no danger, but the noise and the fury made her want to run to a safe place and hide until it was over.

Should she wake the Randalls? Caitlyn hesitated at their door. If she had some company, she wouldn't be so frightened. The storm had totally unnerved her, but it seemed selfish to wake them. The guests had a full day planned for tomorrow and the Randalls would need their sleep. She'd just have to conquer her fear; that was all. Dane was depending on her.

Once Caitlyn had assured herself that no one needed her assistance, she retraced her footsteps. There was only one lamp at the head of the stairs, and she held her breath as she descended into the darkness. She really didn't want to go into the living room to reassure Mr. Kennedy, but she had no choice. She was the hostess and he was a guest. It wouldn't be hospitable to leave him there alone.

She hesitated at the door and took a deep, calming breath. There was no need to be nervous. She'd dealt with men like Allen Kennedy before. It was entirely possible that he'd gotten the message last night at the barbecue when she'd handed him over to Sam for the tour of the corral. Even if he hadn't, he wouldn't dare to try anything when the other guests might wake up at any moment.

He looked up as she entered the room, and Caitlyn gave him a smile that was polite, but distant. "Are you all right, Mr. Kennedy?"

"I am now." A grin flashed across his fleshy face. "I figured you'd come to check up on me."

Caitlyn nodded, setting her lamp down on the nearest table. "Of course. We want everyone to be comfortable. I'm sorry that the storm woke you."

"It didn't. I wasn't sleeping. I was thinking about you." He got up from the sofa and moved closer to her. "I was very disappointed that you didn't give me the tour of the corral. I thought it would give us time for a personal chat."

Caitlyn wanted to take a step back, but she stood her ground. "We've already had our personal chat, Mr. Kennedy. You offered me a part in your movie and I turned it down. I haven't changed my mind. I'm simply not interested in becoming an actress."

"Oh, that." He shrugged, moving even closer. "We can talk about that another time. Right now, I'd rather talk about us."

"Us?" Caitlyn managed to keep her voice neutral, but her heart began to thud in her chest. Was he going to be difficult?

"I know that you're attracted to me, Caitlyn. It's in your eyes when you look at me, and you can't hide it."

Caitlyn shivered. The man had an ego that wouldn't quit. "I'm sure you're a very nice person, Mr. Kennedy, but I'm a member of the staff and we make a point to never become personally involved with a guest. I'm here to make your stay at the Double B as pleasant as possible, but that's it."

"You're giving me the company line, but we both know that rules are made to be broken. You don't have to worry about my wife, if that's your problem. She never wakes up in the middle of the night. And now that your boyfriend's not around, I figured we could . . ."

"That's quite enough, Mr. Kennedy." Caitlyn interrupted him before he could dig himself in any deeper. "You're obviously not afraid of the storm, so I'll leave you to your own devices. I have to check on the other guests."

He grabbed her arm, pulling her close. "Not quite yet. I'm not through with you, Caitlyn. You said you wanted your guests to be comfortable, and I'm very *uncomfortable*. Don't you think it's your duty to do something about that?"

"No, Mr. Kennedy." Caitlyn fought down her urge to slap him and settled for giving him an icy glare. She wasn't about to ask him why he was uncomfortable when it was so readily apparent. "That's a problem you'll have to take up with your wife. And now, if you'll excuse me . . ."

"I expected you to say no." He wore a smug grin as he interrupted her. "Girls like you always do. You just want a man to overpower you so you don't feel guilty after it's over. I understand you, Caitlyn. You're just like Bambi was when I met her. You need a little persuading, and I'm just the guy to do it."

Caitlyn didn't say anything. It was useless to struggle. He was holding her too tightly, and it would only alert him that she intended to resist. He wasn't a large man, and she could get away if he let down his guard. Caitlyn forced her body to relax and managed to produce what she hoped he'd think was a smile.

"That's better, Caitlyn. I knew you'd love it when you got used to the idea. I'm never wrong about girls like you."

He relaxed his grip slightly, believing in his own fantasy, and

Caitlyn knew she'd never have a better opportunity. She shoved her hands against his chest with all her strength and kneed him in the groin when he staggered back. As he dropped to his knees, gasping for breath, she whirled and raced for the door.

It was dark in the hallway, and Caitlyn was grateful. She could hide in the shadows if he recovered enough to chase after her. She slipped down the dark corridor, her sneakers soundless on the carpet runner, glad that she knew the layout of the ranch house much better than he did. She wanted to run straight to her rooms and lock the door, but there were the other guests to consider.

Caitlyn ran up the back staircase to the second floor and headed straight for the Randalls' door. Dane had been right. She should have asked the Randalls to help her instead of going down to the living room by herself.

Would there be trouble about what had happened? Caitlyn's hand trembled as she knocked on the door. She really didn't think that Mr. Kennedy would mention that he'd tried to seduce her and she'd countered his advances by kneeing him in the groin.

"Who is it?"

Caitlyn gave a sigh of relief as she heard Mr. Randall's voice behind the door. "It's Caitlyn Bradford. I know it's an imposition, but I really need your help."

Once Caitlyn had explained that lightning had struck the horse barn, Sue and Ted Randall were eager to help. She waited while they dressed, and they came out to help her light the rest of the lamps in the hallway.

"What's wrong with the generator?" Ted sounded concerned.

"Dane didn't say. He just told me that he didn't have time to fix it. He had to go out and help with the horses."

"I'll take care of it." Ted nodded quickly. "I know that generator like the back of my hand. It conked out last year, and I helped Dane get it running again. I'll just find a couple of the other guys to help me."

"I'll go put on some coffee," Sue offered. "The boys are going to be soaked when they come in, and Gibby's probably out there with them. The stove in the kitchen is gas, isn't it, Caitlyn?"

"Yes." Caitlyn felt proud that she was able to answer. She

didn't know much about the kitchens, but she'd noticed the gas ranges. "Do you think we should wake the others?"

"Might as well," Ted responded. "They're a good bunch and they'll all want to help. You start knocking on doors at the other end of the hall, and we'll meet in the middle."

Ted was right. The moment the guests learned about the problem, they all wanted to help. They gathered at the head of the stairs.

"There's a row of slickers on the wall by the door that leads out to the breezeway," Caitlyn said, and everyone hurried to put one on.

"The only people missing are the Kennedys," Ted commented to his wife. "Did you wake them?"

"Yes," Sue assured him. "But they're not coming down. Allen Kennedy said Bambi took a sleeping pill. He's going to stay with her."

Caitlyn breathed a sigh of relief. Mr. Kennedy must have recovered enough to get back to his room, and she, for one, was glad that he had decided to stay there. "I don't think he'd be much help anyway," she said wryly. "Let's find out what everyone wants to do."

It didn't take long to divide the guests into groups. One older couple, the Bergstroms, had been spending their vacations at the Double B for the past four years. They volunteered to take one group of guests out to the horse barn to help with the horses. Ted took another, smaller group off to work on the generator. A third group, consisting of mostly women, followed Caitlyn and Sue to the kitchen.

The kitchen looked eerie in the darkness. Caitlyn found several hurricane lanterns hanging on the walls, and after she'd lit them, the huge room looked much friendlier. "The first thing to do is to make coffee. Does anyone know where Gibby keeps his supplies?"

"I do." Mr. Humphries spoke up. "He gave me a tour the last time we were here. Doris and I are retired now, but we used to run a truck stop. We'll take over in here, if you don't mind."

Caitlyn grinned at the older couple. "Thanks. I haven't been here long enough to learn how the kitchen works. You'll let us know if you need any help?"

"Sure. Come on, Doris. Let's get to work."

Hank and Doris Humphries seemed to know what they were doing, and Caitlyn breathed a sigh of relief as she watched them open cupboards and search for the coffee. They found a couple of old-fashioned hand-crank coffee grinders, and Doris brought them over to the kitchen table with several sacks of coffee beans and two large bowls.

"You can take turns grinding. Fill the top up with beans, grind them all down, and then pull out the drawer and dump them into these bowls. We're gonna need lots, so just pass it to the next person when your arm gets tired. Hank and I'll get the pots filled with water."

It didn't take long with all of them working together. They each took a turn grinding, and Caitlyn was amazed at how delicious the beans smelled. When they'd filled the bowls, she carried them over to Doris and asked what they could do next.

"Start going through the cupboards. There's got to be some disposable coffee cups around here somewhere. Look for thermoses, too. And sugar. We'll go without cream. The less we open the refrigerator, the better until the generator's fixed."

In very little time, the kitchen was fragrant with the smell of freshly brewed coffee.

"Here's a thermos." Sue plunked a giant metal thermos down on the counter next to the stove. "I'm going to fill it up and take it down to Ted and his crew."

Caitlyn nodded. "And I'll take some thermoses out to the horse barn."

When the coffee was ready, Sue left with a thermos, a stack of paper cups, and a handful of sugar packets. Caitlyn stood by the counter and waited as Hank filled her thermos. "I wish I knew how to make breakfast. Everyone'll be hungry when they come in."

"Don't you worry about that, honey," Doris reassured her. "We'll do it. Gibby's kitchen is even better than the one we used to have. You just tell the boys to start heading this way in a half hour or so, and we'll see that they get a hot meal."

"But this is your vacation!" Caitlyn frowned as she added a handful of sugar packets to her box. "You shouldn't have to work on your vacation."

Hank laughed. "This isn't work; it's fun. Doris and I were just talking about how we miss feeding a hungry crowd."

"Well . . . if you're sure you don't mind . . ."

"We don't." Doris grinned. "Go on, honey. We'll take care of things in here. You just get that hot coffee out to your man."

Caitlyn pulled on a slicker, tying the hood securely under her neck. Then she picked up the heavy box and stepped out into the driving rain. She was halfway down the path to the horse barn when she realized that she was no longer afraid of the storm. The lightning still flashed and the thunder still boomed, but it didn't bother her in the slightest. And then she remembered what Mrs. Humphries had called Dane and she felt warm all over, despite the gusts of icy rain that pelted against her face. *Her man.* The politically correct movement would take umbrage at the thought that one person could belong to another, but she wouldn't mind at all if Dane really were her man.

It was cold and Dane was soaked to the skin by the icy rain, but he warmed inside as he remembered how Caitlyn had blushed when he'd noticed her bright pink toenails. He wasn't quite sure what they signified, but that didn't matter. She'd tell him eventually. Caitlyn wasn't the type to keep secrets for long.

She'd looked so lovely, sound asleep in Bella's bed with the covers twisted around her beautiful legs. There had been a half smile on her lips, and for a brief moment, he'd wondered if she could be dreaming about him. Then he'd caught himself liking that idea a lot and he'd pushed it right out of his mind. The last thing he needed was for Caitlyn Bradford to fall in love with him.

Dane hadn't wanted to wake her, but he'd really needed her help. Every able-bodied hand had gone out to the horse barn, and there'd been no one else to see to the guests. Caitlyn had rallied like a trooper the moment he'd explained the situation. She'd even jumped out of bed without a trace of false modesty and pulled on her clothes while he'd waited for her. Even now, remembering the glimpse he'd caught of her naked breasts made the sweat pop out on Dane's forehead.

He shouldn't have left her to deal with Kennedy, but his place had been out here with the boys. Caitlyn hadn't seemed worried about it. She'd even assured him that she could handle Kennedy with one hand tied behind her back, but he was still concerned about her. He just hoped that she'd taken his advice and gone up to get the Randalls.

The horses were calming down a little now that the thunder and lightning were receding. It was still raining cats and dogs, but they'd moved the skittish mares under the lean-to, and that had helped. Warrior had stayed calm through it all, and Dane was proud of him. He glanced over to see Rob Bergstrom approaching, and he gave a welcoming grin. "Hey, Rob. Hell of a way to wake up, huh?"

"That's okay. Some of the guests wanted to help, so Mary Ellen and I brought them out."

"Thanks, Rob. We can use all the experienced hands that we can get. Is Caitlyn all right?"

Rob laughed. "She's more than all right. She's got all the greenhorns in the kitchen, helping to make coffee. She said that lightning hit the horse barn."

"That's right. The rain doused the fire before it could do much damage, but we pulled the horses out anyway. I figured we'd wait until daylight to make sure it's not smoldering somewhere."

"That makes sense. You should have some lights out here soon. Ted Randall and a couple of others went to work on the generator. He was pretty sure they could fix it."

"I don't have any doubts about that." Dane started to grin. "He's a technical consultant for a big power company back in Wisconsin. Do you really want to help, Rob?"

"That's why we came out here."

"Good. Let's move the colts into the feed shed. We'll have to be smart about where we tether them. If they get near the feed, they'll eat themselves sick."

"No problem. I'll organize the guys and we'll take care of it. You can go check on Caitlyn."

Dane's eyebrows shot up. "What makes you think I want to do that?"

"You've been glancing at the ranch house every other minute, and she was the first one you asked about. Kennedy's not bothering her, if that's what has you worried. He stayed in his room with his wife."

Rob hadn't missed a trick. "You're right," he admitted. "I would like to check on her. Do you think you can handle Warrior while I'm gone?"

"Sure." Rob nodded confidently and took the reins. "Warrior and I are old friends. I'll take him with me when we move the colts; it'll give him something to think about besides the storm. You go check on that pretty lady of yours."

Dane was amused as he walked off toward the ranch house. Rob had assumed that Caitlyn was his lady—and he guessed she was, in a way. He did feel an obligation to protect her until she'd adjusted to life on the Double B. He didn't want to think beyond that point. Looking too far into the future would only cause problems. He'd learned that with Beth. There was some truth in that old saying about the wisdom of taking life one day at a time. Each day he'd spent with Beth had been a precious gift, and he'd done his damnedest to hang on to that feeling right up to the end, when it had been so painful.

There was someone coming up the path from the ranch house and Dane started to grin as he recognized Caitlyn. She was carrying a huge box and struggling to keep her balance against the sheets of driving rain. He broke into a run, splashing through the puddles and arriving just in time to keep her from slipping.

"Caitlyn!" Dane reached out to steady her with one arm and grabbed the large box with the other. "Give me that. You're going to blow away out here."

She gave him a grateful smile and hung on to his arm as he helped her toward the corral. "I brought hot coffee for everyone. And Doris and Hank Humphries are making breakfast. They said to tell you to start sending the boys back in shifts so that they can warm up and have a hot meal."

"That's great." Dane was impressed. It seemed she'd organized the guests. "Did you have any trouble with Allen Kennedy?"

"Kennedy? He . . . uh . . . he went back to his room to stay with his wife. He said she took a sleeping pill and he wanted to be there in case the storm woke her."

Dane nodded, but he knew she hadn't given him the whole story. Kennedy wasn't the type to be so considerate of his wife. Kennedy was concerned with Kennedy. Period. And he'd noticed how Caitlyn had hesitated when he'd asked her if she'd had trouble. There wasn't time to go into it now, but he'd get the details later. Something must have happened to send Kennedy back to his room like a dog with his tail tucked between his legs.

When they reached the corral, Dane watched Caitlyn set up under the tarp they'd rigged, passing out cups of steaming coffee. The boys clustered around her like honeybees bunching up around a tasty flower and Dane knew it wasn't just the lure of hot coffee that made them grin. Caitlyn had managed to earn their loyalty, and it was clear they admired her for slogging all the way out here with coffee for them.

Dane stood back. His new partner was really something. There wasn't a ranch hand who didn't like her and even Jake was acting like a gentleman around her. She'd won their respect and their affection. She had courage—or maybe it was stubbornness, but it didn't really matter. She was a part of the Double B team.

There was something else, too, and Dane's grin grew wide as he thought of it. Caitlyn Bradford was the only woman he knew who could look gorgeous and sexy in an oversized yellow slicker with rain dripping off the end of her nose.

THIRTEEN

It seemed her head had just touched the pillow when there was a pounding at her door. Caitlyn sat up in bed and glanced at the clock. It was nine in the morning and she'd had less than three hours' sleep. They'd stayed up until the storm had run its course, drinking coffee and talking, and everyone had agreed to cancel the morning ride and get some much-needed rest.

"Just a minute. I'm coming." Caitlyn winced and crawled out of bed. Her room was filled with sunshine, and it hurt her eyes. At least she didn't need to dress to open the door. She'd been so exhausted, she'd fallen asleep in her clothes.

"Yes?" Caitlyn pulled open the door and stood face-to-face with a bleached blonde who was wearing the kind of Western outfit you might expect to see at a costume party. Her lilac denim skirt was short, micro-mini length, with a purple silk fringe around the bottom. Her bolero jacket matched the skirt, and she wore a pair of white patent leather cowboy boots. Caitlyn didn't have to ask who she was, but Dane's description hadn't quite done her justice. On the other hand, nothing could have prepared Caitlyn for Bambi Kennedy in the flesh.

"I'm Bambi Kennedy, *Mrs*. Allen Kennedy to you!"

Bambi's whole body was trembling with rage, and Caitlyn wished that she could reach out and shut the door again. But she couldn't. Bambi Kennedy was a guest, and she had to be polite. "It's nice to meet you, Mrs. Kennedy. Is there something I can do for you?"

"Yes! Leave my Allen alone you . . . you husband stealer. You ought to be ashamed of yourself."

Caitlyn blinked. It was not a good start to the morning. "Excuse me?"

"Don't play innocent with me. You tried to seduce my husband last night."

Caitlyn blinked again, wishing her mind would work a little faster. "What makes you think that I tried to seduce your husband, Mrs. Kennedy?"

"I don't think it; I know it." Bambi's startling violet eyes glittered with the fanaticism of a recent convert. Tinted contact lenses. Caitlyn was sure of it. No one had ever been born with eyes in that peculiar shade of purple. "The storm woke me up, and I came down to find Allen. And there you were—with your arms around him! I was so upset, I ran right back up the stairs to my room and took a sleeping pill so I wouldn't have to think about it."

Caitlyn sighed. "Look, Mrs. Kennedy. Appearances can be deceiving. I assure you that I have absolutely no interest in your husband. He's a guest, just like all the other guests."

"Then I should warn the other wives about you."

"That's not what I meant, Mrs. Kennedy." Bambi's unusually full lips turned down in a pout, and Caitlyn wondered how many collagen shots she'd endured to keep them so plump. "If you knew me better, you'd realize that I treat all the guests the same. Husbands, wives—it makes no difference to me. I'm your hostess at the Double B, nothing more."

Bambi drew herself up to her full height and placed both of her hands on her hips. "You're lying. And I know why."

Caitlyn sighed again. She wished she could say that Allen Kennedy had tried to seduce *her,* but Bambi would never believe it. "I'm not lying, Mrs. Kennedy."

"Yes, you are. You're just like all the others. You think that Allen's going to cast you in one of his films, don't you?"

"No, Mrs. Kennedy, I don't. I don't *want* to be in a movie. I told your husband that last night when he offered me a part."

"That's another lie. I star in all of my husband's films. He'd never offer *you* a part!"

This was getting them nowhere. Caitlyn took a deep breath and tried to think of a way to end the confrontation. "Look, Mrs.

Kennedy. I told you before. I'm really not interested in your husband."

"Then why did you hang all over him at dinner last night?"

"I didn't, Mrs. Kennedy. Perhaps I spent more time with him . . . he asked me a lot of questions, but I also spent time with the other guests."

Bambi frowned. It wasn't a deep frown. Her skin had been tightened so much it didn't allow for much movement. "He said you wanted to take him on a tour of the corral—and he doesn't even like horses."

"I didn't take him, Mrs. Kennedy. Sam, one of our ranch hands, gave your husband the tour. He said something about locations and that he wanted to see the corral."

"Oh. Well . . . Allen's always scouting locations. That could be true. But I know what I saw in the middle of the night. You were in my husband's arms."

"Not for long. And it certainly wasn't my choice." Caitlyn's temper got the best of her. "If you'd stuck around, Mrs. Kennedy, you would have seen—"

"Caitlyn, darling."

A deep voice interrupted her, and Caitlyn whirled to see Dane. But why had he called her *darling?*

"And here's the prettiest guest ever to grace the Double B Ranch. Good morning, Bambi." Dane turned to smile at Mrs. Kennedy. "Or should I say, Mrs. Kennedy?"

"Bambi's fine."

Caitlyn noticed that Bambi was no longer scowling and she bit back a grin. Dane was being incredibly charming, and it was working to defuse Bambi's anger.

"I'm sorry the storm scared you so much last night, honey." Dane moved forward and drew Caitlyn into his arms, pretending to kiss her ear but whispering for her to be quiet, that he'd take care of Bambi. "Go ahead and catch a little more sleep. I know you had a rough night. I'll take Bambi in to breakfast."

Caitlyn nodded, hoping that Dane knew what he was doing. "All right."

"Will you let me escort you to breakfast, Bambi?" Dane reached out to tuck Bambi's arm in his, and Caitlyn could hear them as they headed down the hall at a slow pace. "Your husband was such a big help to me last night. You got yourself a real nice guy there. Poor Caitlyn's terrified of storms and I didn't have time to sit with her, but your husband offered to take over for me. You're not afraid of storms, are you, Bambi?"

Caitlyn heard Bambi giggle. "I've never been afraid of storms. They don't bother me at all."

"I wish Caitlyn would take a lesson from you. She gets so scared, she acts plumb crazy. She shakes and she cries and she hangs all over me every time the lightning flashes. And the thunder's even worse. If I didn't hold her down, she'd jump a foot."

"Really?"

"And how." Caitlyn heard Dane's laugh. "I told your husband to just hold her and calm her down. You don't mind that I asked him to do that, do you, Bambi?"

"No, not as long as it was just the storm. I thought, well . . . I saw him holding her and . . ."

"I'm afraid that's my fault." Dane's voice interrupted her. "He was going to wake you up and tell you what I asked him to do, but I told him to let you sleep. I'm sorry, Bambi."

"That's okay."

"Do you want to find him so you two can talk it over? He'd probably be flattered if he found out you were jealous."

"No." Caitlyn heard a note of panic in Bambi's voice. "Allen hates it when I'm jealous. He says a marriage should be based on trust and it's no good if it's not. I don't want him to know that I doubted him, not even for a second."

"Then I won't say a word about it. And I'll tell Caitlyn not to mention it, either. It'll be our little secret, okay?"

"Okay." Bambi sounded relieved. "But there's still one thing I don't understand. Do you know if Allen offered your girlfriend a part in his movie?"

"I think so. He said something about a Western setting, and Caitlyn told him we don't allow film crews on the Double B. He probably thought that if he offered her a walk-on part, she'd change her mind."

"Of course." Caitlyn grinned as the last trace of doubt in

Bambi's voice disappeared. "I should have known it was some-thing like that. I star in all of his movies, you know."

"That figures. I'll bet you're a good actress, too."

"Oh, it doesn't take much acting." Bambi giggled. "Not with the kind of films that Allen makes. Did you ever see *Hot Nights In Houston?* They showed it on cable last year, and . . ."

Bambi's voice trailed off as they went around the corner, and Caitlyn laughed, closing her door. She should have guessed that if Allen Kennedy made movies at all, they'd be X-rated.

Dane sighed as he spotted Caitlyn at a table with four of the guests. The incident with Allen Kennedy wasn't her fault, but they still had to deal with it; and he was pretty sure that the same sort of thing would happen again if they didn't take action. He'd wracked his brain trying to think of some nice way to tell her, but he'd never been particularly tactful. There was nothing to do but confront her with the problem and see if they could come up with a solution.

"Hi, Dane."

She gave him a friendly smile and Dane felt a sense of dread. She'd probably hate him after they'd had their little talk, but it had to be done. The whole fiasco with the Kennedys had turned out all right, but it had taken some fancy fence-mending on his part. And he didn't even want to think about what would have happened if he'd failed to spot Bambi marching toward Caitlyn's quarters in those ridiculous white cowboy boots of hers.

"Caitlyn." Dane moved forward to take her arm, turning to the other guests. "If you folks will excuse us for a couple of minutes, I need to talk to Caitlyn in private."

Caitlyn followed him to the door. "What is it, Dane? Is there something wrong?"

"You could say that. Come with me and we'll straighten it out. I thought we'd go to the office, but Gibby's in there, using the phone. I guess it's a choice of your place or mine."

"Let's go to mine. I need to pick up a book for Mary Ellen anyway."

Dane felt like a heel as they walked down the hallway and

entered her quarters. He'd come through this same door last night to wake her up for an emergency. And now here he was again, about to criticize her for something that wasn't really her fault.

A wry grin crossed Dane's face as he sat down on the edge of her bed and waited for her to find the book for Mary Ellen. When he'd fantasized about joining her in her bedroom, he'd had an entirely different scenario in mind.

"I just don't see how I could have done anything differently." Caitlyn stared at him in shock. "You *know* that I didn't lead Mr. Kennedy on."

"I know that you didn't do anything deliberately, but . . . well . . . just being you is what gave the man ideas."

"You want me to stop being *me?*" Caitlyn glared at him, but she couldn't stay angry for long. This whole thing was just too ridiculous.

"No, of course I don't. I know you can't stop being you. I just want you to stop looking so darned attractive."

"Okay." Caitlyn sat down next to him on the bed, fighting down the urge to cuddle up close. "Just how am I supposed to do that?"

"I don't know. That's why we need to talk. You look so sexy, you give the guys ideas and it doesn't matter whether they're married or not. The men can't help it. It's a . . . well . . . it's just a gut reaction."

"A *gut* reaction, huh?"

"You know what I mean." His face turned red, and Caitlyn giggled. And then she sobered as she realized what he'd said. "Every guy? Even you, Dane?"

"Uh . . . well . . . I wasn't talking about me, not exactly. I just meant that you're a very attractive woman, and that's what we've got to change."

Caitlyn couldn't help smiling. He looked so uncomfortable. And at the same time, she just wanted to move closer and put what he'd said to the test. He'd practically admitted that he was attracted to her, and *she* was certainly attracted to *him*. "So are you saying that you want me to try to look ugly?"

"Yup. That's it, exactly. We're going to lose business if the wives start to think of you as their competition."

"But I'm *not* their competition!" Caitlyn gave a sigh of pure exasperation. "I think you're making a mountain out of a mole-hill, Dane. I'm sure the wives know that I'm not competing with them."

"Do they? How about Bambi Kennedy? If I hadn't made up that story about you being so terrified of storms, she would have demanded their money back and dragged her husband home on the next plane."

"Are you saying that Bambi Kennedy's misconception was *my* fault?" Caitlyn demanded.

"Nope. I'm just saying that we have to be careful that it doesn't happen again. We don't want some wife going home to tell all her friends that a gorgeous divorcee is running the show at the Double B."

Caitlyn snapped her mouth shut before she could make a fiery retort. At least he'd said that she was gorgeous. She took a deep, calming breath and asked a question. "What do you want me to do?"

"I don't know, but you've got to figure out some way to be less provocative. I've watched the men, and their eyes pop out every time you walk by. Maybe you could be more careful about what you wear?"

"How? I'm already wearing the dowdiest clothing I have!"

"Maybe you could walk more like a man." He cocked his head to the side, regarding her intently. "Concentrate on striding and not wiggling your hips."

Caitlyn knew her eyes were glittering dangerously. The man was actually giving her advice on how to walk! "Anything else?"

"I don't know. Can you think of any way to make yourself less attractive?"

Caitlyn nodded, giving in to her urge for sarcasm. "I can think of several. If I shave my head and wear granny glasses, do you think that'll do the trick?"

"Shave your head?" He stared at her for a moment and then he sighed. "You're joking. Don't do that, Caitlyn. This situation isn't funny. I didn't even want to bring this up, but I'm at wit's end trying to look out for you and do my job at the same time. There's going to be trouble, and I just don't know how I can avoid it."

He looked so unhappy, Caitlyn felt tears start to gather in her own eyes. She turned away, plucking at the tufted bedspread. "Do you hate me because I've turned into a problem for you?"

"Hate you?" He sounded genuinely shocked. "Whatever gave you a crazy idea like *that?*"

"Because you don't like the way I look and you just criticized everything about me—even the way I . . . I walk. I know I'm a greenhorn or a city slicker or whatever you call it and I don't really fit in here, but I . . . I'd hoped that—"

Caitlyn's voice trailed off, and hot tears rolled down her cheeks. She felt bereft, as if she'd just lost a friend, and it was more than she could bear. And then she felt him reach out for her; and before she quite knew what was happening, he'd pulled her close and she was sobbing against his chest.

"Come on, Caitlyn. I didn't mean to give you such a hard time. I guess I've been around the boys too long and I've plumb forgotten how to talk to a beautiful woman."

"Then you don't . . . don't hate me?" She raised her eyes to his and she saw such naked yearning in his face, she began to tremble.

"No. I don't hate you. I could never hate you."

There was a long moment that seemed to last forever, and then Caitlyn felt her heart start to sing. Her lips parted and his head was lowering toward hers, pulled there by some invisible force. And at last his lips claimed hers and such sweetness flowed through her, she thought she'd faint.

"Beautiful Caitlyn." He groaned as their kiss took on a life of its own, blazing and searing every nerve in her body in a fiery burst of passion. Her arms lifted to wrap around his neck and she held him there while they explored each other, mouths melding, tongues tasting, bodies crushed together until both of them were shaking with need. And then he broke their embrace, setting her firmly away from him, and sighed. "I'm sorry, Caitlyn. That should never have happened. It was my fault and it won't happen again."

Caitlyn drew a deep breath and let it out in a shuddering sigh. She wanted to tell him not to be such a fool, that she wanted him to kiss her again. She wanted him to do much more than kiss her, but his eyes were troubled as they met hers and she knew that she didn't dare say any of those things.

"Well . . ." Caitlyn resorted to something that had always worked in the past to defuse a tense situation. "I guess you were right."

"I was?"

He stared at her as if she'd just lost her mind, and Caitlyn giggled. "I *must* be provocative."

"Believe me, you are!" He raised his hands in a gesture of mock helplessness, and Caitlyn knew he was grateful that she'd turned their kiss into something less serious than it had been. "I really had no intention of kissing you."

"I'm sure you didn't. It just happened, and we're lucky it was you and not a guest. What are we going to do about me, Dane? I don't want to lose business for the Double B. And I certainly don't want a repeat of what happened with Allen Kennedy."

"You've got to look less kissable." He grinned at her. "Could you wear something baggy and shapeless?"

Caitlyn shook her head. "I don't have anything like that in my wardrobe. Baggy and shapeless wasn't exactly the style for a female advertising executive in Boston. Do you want to look in my closet and see for yourself?"

"Sure." He stood up and held out his hand. "Let's go through your clothes and see if you have anything that'll cover you up a little more so the guys'll have less to look at."

Five minutes later, Dane had to admit that their search of Caitlyn's closet had been fruitless. Every item in her wardrobe was both expensive and tasteful, but it was apparent that she'd chosen her clothing to complement her figure and not to hide it.

"I'm sorry, Dane. I just don't have anything that's loose."

She turned to him with a worried frown, and Dane had all he could do to keep from taking her into his arms and kissing her again. The bed beckoned him, clearly visible out of the corner of his eye, and he imagined pulling off her clothes and pressing her down on the soft silk and satin dresses that were spread out on the mattress and . . .

"What's the matter?" She interrupted the sexy scene he was playing out in his head.

"Nothing. I'm just trying to come up with a solution." Dane forced himself to meet her green eyes and hoped that she couldn't read the thoughts that had been racing through his mind. "I guess you could order some work clothes from a catalogue, but they'll take a couple of weeks to get here."

"Maybe I could borrow a pair of jeans from one of the boys?"

"Nope." Dane dismissed her suggestion without a second thought. "Ned Bascom's the smallest of the bunch, and his jeans would still slip right down around your ankles."

"I guess that would be defeating the purpose," she murmured devilishly.

"Right." Dane couldn't help but appreciate her sense of humor. She was being very nice about the whole thing and she hadn't mentioned the kiss they'd shared again. "It's just a pity you're not Bella's size. The sort of clothes she used to wear would be just right for you."

She stared at him for a minute and then looked thoughtful. "What happened to Aunt Bella's clothes?"

"They're still here. Do you want to see them?"

"I certainly do!" she exclaimed. "What size was Aunt Bella?"

"Well . . . she was about your height, maybe an inch shorter. But she weighed more than you do. About thirty pounds, I'd say."

"And what type of clothing did she wear?"

Dane tried to remember. During the last two months of Bella's life, she'd been bedridden and he'd only seen her in flannel nightgowns and robes. He didn't want to tell Caitlyn that. It would only make her feel bad. "She wore blue jeans and cotton blouses, lots of outfits like that. And she was partial to denim, so she had some denim dresses and jumpers. She wore a lot of sweaters and flannel things in the winter, and she didn't own anything that couldn't be washed. I remember that she was always after Ida and Marilyn to wash her things in cold water so they wouldn't shrink."

The publishers of Zebra Bouquet are making this special offer to lovers of contemporary romances to introduce this exciting new line of romance novels. Zebra's Bouquet Romances have been praised by critics and authors alike as being of the highest quality and best written romantic fiction available today.

Each full-length novel has been written by authors you know and love as well as by up-and-coming writers that you'll only find with Zebra Bouquet. We'll bring you the newest novels by world famous authors like Vanessa Grant, Judy Gill, Ann Josephson and award winning Suzanne Barrett and Leigh Greenwood to name just a few. Zebra Bouquet's editors have selected only the very best and highest quality for publication under the Bouquet banner.

You'll be treated to glamorous settings from Carnavale in Rio, the moneyed high-powered offices of New York's Wall Street, the rugged north coast of British Columbia, the mountains of North Carolina, all the way to the bull rings of Spain. Bouquet Romances use these settings to spin tales of star-crossed lovers caught in "nail biting" dilemmas that are sure to captivate you. These stories will keep you on the edge of your seat to the very happy end.

4 FREE NOVELS As a way to introduce you to these terrific romances, the publishers of Bouquet are offering Zebra Romance readers Four Free Bouquet novels. They are yours for the asking with no obligation to buy a single book. Read them at your leisure. We are sure that after you've read these introductory books you'll want more! (If you do not wish to receive any further Bouquet novels, simply write "cancel" on the invoice and return to us within 10 days.)

SAVE 20% WITH HOME DELIVERY
Each month you'll receive four just published Bouquet Romances. We'll ship them to you as soon as they are printed (you may even get them before the bookstores). You'll have 10 days to preview these exciting novels for Free. If you decide to keep them, you'll be billed the special preferred home subscription price of just $3.20 per book; a total of just $12.80 — that's a savings of 20% off the publishers price. If for any reason you are not satisfied simply return the novels for full credit, no questions asked. You'll never have to purchase a minimum number of books and you may cancel your subscription at any time.

GET STARTED TODAY –
NO RISK AND NO OBLIGATION

To get your introductory gift of 4 Free Bouquet Romances fill out and mail the enclosed Free Book Certificate today. We'll ship your free selections as soon as we receive this information. Remember that you are under no obligation. This is a risk free offer from the publishers of Zebra Bouquet Romances.

FREE BOOK CERTIFICATE

Yes! I would like to take you up on your offer. Please send me 4 Free Bouquet Romance Novels as my introductory gift. I understand that unless I tell you otherwise, I will then receive the 4 newest Bouquet novels to preview each month Free for 10 days. If I decide to keep them I'll pay the preferred home subscriber's price of just $3.20 each (a total of only $12.80) plus $1.50 for shipping and handling. That's a 20% savings off the publisher's price. I understand that I may return any shipment for full credit no questions asked and I may cancel this subscription at any time with no obligation. Regardless of what I decide to do, the 4 Free introductory novels are mine to keep as Bouquet's gift.

Name _____

Address _____ Apt. _____

City _____ State _____ Zip _____

Telephone (   ) _____

Signature _____
(If under 18, parent or guardian must sign.)   BN09B9

For your convenience you may charge your shipments automatically to a Visa or MasterCard so you'll never have to worry about late payments and missing shipments. If you return any shipment we'll credit your account.

Yes, charge my credit card for my "Bouquet Romance" shipments until I tell you otherwise.
☐ Visa   ☐ MasterCard
Account Number _____
Expiration Date _____
Signature

Orders subject to acceptance by Zebra Home Subscription Service. Terms and Prices subject to change.

If this response card is missing,
call us at 1-888-345-BOOK.

Be sure to visit our website at
www.kensingtonbooks.com

BOUQUET ROMANCE

120 Brighton Road

P.O. BOX 5214

Clifton, New Jersey 07015-5214

AFFIX
STAMP
HERE

"So they wouldn't *shrink?*" Caitlyn practically crowed. "What if I washed some of Aunt Bella's things in hot water? Do you think they might shrink to fit me?"

"We won't rightly know until we try," Dane said, matching her enthusiasm. "After Bella died, I packed up all of her clothes and put them in the attic."

"You did?" An expression of surprise crossed her face. "But why would you do something like that?"

"Because I didn't want you coming out here to find all her clothes hanging in her closet, as if she were gone but she'd be coming right back any minute. I thought that might make you sad."

"That was . . ." She blinked back a rush of sudden tears. "That was very thoughtful of you. Thanks, Dane."

Her gratitude pleased him. He guessed that even before he'd met her, he'd wanted to take care of her—just because she was Bella's niece. He still wanted to take care of her, but now it was for another reason, one he didn't want to think about just now. "I'll go grab one of the boys and we'll carry the boxes down for you."

"But I can go up to the attic with you and go through the things up there. It's easier than carrying everything down."

"Nope." Dane walked her to the bed and sat her down. "It's an unfinished attic and there's no floor, just ceiling joists with a couple of pieces of loose plywood. You might step through and put a hole in the ceiling. And we'll have to use flashlights. There's no electricity in the attic. You wait right here where you're safe, and we'll bring the boxes down to you."

She looked as if she might protest, but then she acquiesced. "Okay."

Dane gave a big sigh of relief as he walked out of her room. What he'd told her was true. The attic had no floor . . . and no lights, either. But he hadn't mentioned the real reason he hadn't wanted her to come along.

When he'd taken the job at the Double B, Bella had given him permission to put all his extra things in the attic. Almost everything he'd brought from New York was stored up there under the rafters. There were boxes of books from his office library, personal photo albums with pictures of Beth, and even the collection of stuffed animals that Beth had kept in their bedroom.

If Caitlyn had seen all those moving boxes, she would have asked questions that were too painful for him to answer. It was better for both of them if Caitlyn Bradford didn't find out anything about his former life and the woman he'd loved.

FOURTEEN

"You want me to wash these things in *hot* water?" Ida Billings, the older woman who took charge of the washing at the Double B, eyed Caitlyn with real surprise. "But your aunt always told me to be careful not to shrink 'em."

"I know." Caitlyn patted one of the simple cotton blouses. "Aunt Bella was a lot bigger than I am. I want to wear some of her things, but they won't fit me unless they shrink."

"Hot water, huh?" Marilyn, Ida's younger sister, began to laugh. "That's taking a risk, isn't it, Ida? Bella just might come back to haunt us. She was always so insistent about her clothes."

Caitlyn glanced at the two large, raw-boned women and saw the glint of humor in their eyes. "No, I can practically guarantee that she won't come back to haunt you. She'll pick on *me* because I'm the one who told you to do it."

"She's got a point." Ida exchanged a grin with Marilyn. "I guess we're safe."

Marilyn turned to Caitlyn. "Okay, honey. We'll do it. But why do you want to wear your aunt's clothes?"

"I don't have anything else." Caitlyn decided to be entirely truthful. "All I've got is what I brought with me from Boston, and I can't wear any of those outfits. They're too fancy, and . . . well . . . I don't want to look like that anymore. I don't have anything that's right for the life out here. Even my jeans are wrong. And I *like* the life out here. I want to fit in the way Aunt Bella did."

Ida reached out to pat Caitlyn's hand. "I saw that beautiful dress you gave to Lisa Thornton. That was real nice of you, and

I can see as how you couldn't wear it out here at the Double B. The rest of your clothes are like that?"

"Yes." Caitlyn nodded vigorously. "They're all the kinds of things you'd wear to fancy dinners and parties. I've got some business suits, the kind that women executives wear, but they're all wrong for the ranch. And everything I own has to be dry cleaned."

Marilyn's brow wrinkled in thought. "You've got some jeans. We've washed 'em."

"Designer jeans," Caitlyn pointed out. "They're tight and they're . . . well . . . they're just too . . ." Caitlyn stopped and took a deep breath. "You've seen me wear them. What do you think?"

"Too sexy," Ida supplied promptly.

"Exactly. And that just creates problems." Caitlyn blushed, embarrassed, realizing she really wanted Ida and Marilyn to approve of her. "I don't want to look sexy. I want to look as if I *work* here. I thought that if I wore some of Aunt Bella's things, I'd . . . well . . . I'd blend in a lot better."

"You're right, honey," Marilyn proclaimed. "And you're real smart for thinking of it. We'll shrink these clothes up for you and then you'll fit in just fine."

"Don't shrink them too much," Caitlyn warned. "I don't want to wear anything that . . . that . . ."

"We know," Ida interrupted quickly. "You don't want to wear anything that shows off your figure."

"Right," Caitlyn breathed in relief. "Thank you for being so understanding."

Ida looked down at the denim jumpers, cotton blouses, and jeans that Caitlyn had brought in to be washed. "Bella always had such nice things. She could look real spiffy when she got all dressed up. 'Course she didn't do it much, out here on the ranch. There was no reason."

"Only when Jeremy came out," Marilyn recalled. "She always got spiffed up then."

"Jeremy? Are you talking about Jerry Campbell's dad?" Caitlyn's eyes widened as she caught Marilyn's meaning.

"Yup." Ida nodded. "We could always tell when he was com-

ing, because Bella would wear that nice perfume he gave her for
Christmas. It was real expensive—French. She said it was called
Channel Five."

Caitlyn grinned. If Jeremy Campbell had given Aunt Bella a
bottle of *Chanel No. 5*, he must have been quite serious about
her. "So Aunt Bella had a boyfriend?"

"Yup," Marilyn concurred. "I wish you could have seen them
at the dances. They always had such a good time."

"We always hoped they'd get married, but it never happened,"
Ida said sadly. "Maybe they would have if Jeremy's wife had
died sooner."

"His wife?" Caitlyn blinked. She hadn't really known Aunt
Bella, but the thought of her as a home wrecker just didn't fit
with the other things she'd learned. "Jeremy Campbell went out
with Aunt Bella when he was married?"

Marilyn shook her head. "Nope. He certainly didn't do that.
You'd better explain, Ida, before Miz Bradford gets the wrong
idea."

"Jeremy's wife, Sarah, was your aunt's best friend. And when
Sarah got sick, Bella stepped in to take care of her. There was
no one else to do it. The other kids were grown and they'd all
moved away, and young Jerry was away at law school."

"How about Mr. Campbell? Couldn't he take care of his
wife?"

"Not by himself. Sarah needed someone to tend to her during
the day, and Jeremy had to work in his office. It was a real problem, but the three of them got together to work something out.
The upshot was that Bella just packed Sarah up and moved her
out here."

Caitlyn was surprised. "Sarah left her husband?"

" 'Course not. Jeremy moved out here, too." Marilyn took
over the story. "It was Dane's idea. He slept out in the bunkhouse
with the boys, and Jeremy and Sarah moved into his rooms. It
all worked out real well."

"You said it was Dane's idea?"

"Yup," Ida said. "He helped to take care of Sarah, gave her
all her medicine, and doctored her when old Doc Henley couldn't

get out here. Sarah would've been stuck in the hospital in Laramie if it hadn't been for Bella and Dane."

Caitlyn nodded. Dane had told her that the people in Little Fork took care of their own. "What was wrong with Sarah Campbell?"

"I don't rightly know." Marilyn shrugged. "It was some kind of muscle ailment. She just got weaker and weaker until she ended up in a wheelchair."

"Bella was as good as gold to her," Ida added. "She built that ramp on the side of the house so she could wheel her down to the barbecues and the dances on Saturday nights. Sarah was as sharp as a tack right up until the end, and she never stopped being grateful to Bella for taking care of her. She told me once that she hoped that Jeremy would marry Bella when she was gone, but it never happened."

"Do you think that Jeremy wanted to marry Aunt Bella?"

"He surely did," Marilyn replied instantly. "Jeremy was real grateful to Bella. She was his rock."

"His rock?"

"Bella held him together through the whole thing," Ida explained. "After Sarah died, she let him stay on until he was ready to go back to his own house in town. That's when we thought something might happen between them. You see, Jeremy still came out here a couple of times a week and it was as plain as the nose on your face that he loved Bella. But then young Jerry finished up law school and came back and moved in with his dad."

"And you think that Jerry's moving back home kept his dad from marrying Aunt Bella?"

"That was part of it, maybe." Marilyn looked thoughtful. "This is just my opinion, so take it for what it's worth, but I think it was Bella's friendship for Sarah that got in the way, even after Sarah was dead. Those kinds of feelings don't die, you know. When you really love somebody, it just keeps going on and on for the rest of your life."

"I guess that's true." Marilyn's words disturbed Caitlyn. She'd thought she'd loved Spencer, but she no longer felt that way about him. She didn't feel anything at all. Did that mean she hadn't really loved him?

"You got to run along, honey, if we're gonna get this washing done." Ida patted her on the back. "We chewed on your ear for long enough and we gotta get back to work."

Dane whirled on his heel and walked back the way he'd come, thinking about what Marilyn had said. She was right about feelings and how they never died. He still loved Beth, even after almost five years without her. He'd come to find Caitlyn; they'd planned to go over the books together, but he didn't want to see her now. Marilyn's comment had raised all the old questions that still haunted him about his life with Beth.

Instead of heading back to the office, Dane walked outside and took a deep breath of the fresh, clean air. If he'd stayed in the West instead of taking the job in New York, would things have turned out differently? If he'd opted for settling down in a small Western town, a town like Little Fork, would Beth still be at his side?

Their life in New York had been fast paced and hectic. Dane hadn't realized that his work would put so many demands on his time. There hadn't been time to relax with Beth, to talk to her at the end of the day. Most nights, when he'd come home to their well-appointed high-rise apartment, she'd already been asleep. And in the mornings, he'd had to rush off without exchanging more than a few words with her.

There was no denying that they'd grown apart, each caught up in their separate lives. He'd had his heavy work schedule, and since he was never around, Beth had formed new friendships that had kept her busy. Of course he'd loved Beth and he knew that she had loved him in return, but there'd been no time for the long, intimate talks they'd shared before they'd moved to New York. Perhaps Beth had been lonely; he really didn't know. Or perhaps she'd even been frightened. Beth had never been the type to confide in anyone.

Dane sighed, leaning against the fence outside the ranch house and thinking about the first time that Beth had confided in him.

They'd been in high school, and he'd found her sitting alone outside the school building, tears in her eyes. He'd practically had to force it out of her—she was so afraid to trust anyone—but finally she'd told him that she was worried about getting a scholarship to college.

Beth hadn't gotten her scholarship, but it hadn't mattered in the end. They'd married straight out of high school and gone off to college together. They'd done it the hard way, both of them working night shifts and attending classes during the day. But they'd made it in five years and they'd both felt that they'd accomplished something.

He remembered their first apartment, impossibly tiny and cramped. Their furniture had been minimal—a small table, two chairs, a couch, and a bed that pulled out of the wall. Every wall except the one that contained the bed had been covered with makeshift bookcases. Beth had worked at an ice cream parlor and she'd brought home the empty cartons. They'd washed them out, filled them with sand, and used them to space out the cracked boards he'd brought home from the trash pile of a construction site.

At least they'd eaten well. Dane grinned as he remembered the gourmet meals they'd enjoyed. He'd worked as a waiter at a restaurant, and the cook had given him all the leftovers. It had seemed crazy to dine on *boeuf bourguignon* and lobster bisque when they'd had to save all their pennies for the bus passes they'd needed, but it had been fun. And then he had won a full scholarship, Beth had landed a teaching job, and they'd started to move up in the world.

Had it been worth it? Dane didn't know. Things had changed when their hand-to-mouth existence had taken a turn for the better. Perhaps their struggle had brought them together and, once they'd made it, the glue that had held their relationship together had begun to dissolve. In the beginning, they'd shared all their secrets. Beth had been his best friend, and he had been hers. But Beth hadn't shared the one secret that might have kept them together . . . until it had been much too late to do anything about it.

Rehashing the whole thing was getting him nowhere. Dane

squared his shoulders and attempted to put the unhappy thoughts out of his mind. It was over. He had to move on. Even Bella had told him that. He was about to turn around and go back inside when his cell phone rang.

He pulled the phone out of his pocket and answered the call. It was Jake, and he sounded so upset, Dane could barely make out his words. "Hey, Jake. Take a deep breath and slow down. I can't understand you if you talk so fast. What's wrong?"

Dane listened for a moment and then he winced. "Okay. I understand. Where are the guests?"

Dane gave a sigh of relief at Jake's answer. "That's perfect. Ride back and turn 'em around. Tell Sam to bring them back to the ranch house, and don't let them know what happened. You'd better not tell Sam, either. He's likely to tell one of his stories and scare them all to death. Just say you talked to me and there's been a change of plans."

Dane frowned as Jake spoke again. He was really agitated and Dane didn't blame him. "There's no problem with that. Billy's a lousy shot, so I'll leave him here to help out with the guests. You got your rifle with you? If you have to shoot, make it count; but don't take any chances. I'll be up there just as soon as I can. You stay put and wait for us, you hear?"

Dane clicked off the phone and changed directions, setting off at a run to find Gibby. It didn't take long to round up the boys. Five sharp peals on the dinner gong, the signal they used for emergencies, brought them in at a run.

Less than five minutes later, Dane, Slim, and Trevor—the best shots they had—were riding out with rifles slung over their saddles. The ranch jeep, with extra rifles and ammunition, followed behind. A marauding cougar was serious business. Chances were high that it was a female, and now that she'd found easy pickings on Double B land, she'd be back for more. They had to protect their herd of wild mustangs and the colts they'd throw in the spring. There were also the lambs from the domestic sheep that wintered up here and the Big Horns and mountain goats that lived on their land.

Dane wouldn't have been as concerned if it had been only one kill, but Jake had said that he'd found four fresh carcasses.

That meant that their cougar was killing more than she needed to survive. She was an assassin, plain and simple. She killed more than she could eat. That wasn't nature's way, and Dane and the boys had to stop her before she wiped out their whole herd.

Gibby was softhearted, but he'd understood the situation. He wouldn't mention it to the guests, and Dane had specifically warned him not to tell Caitlyn where they'd gone. There was no sense in worrying Caitlyn or having her get up in arms because they were going out to hunt down the animal who'd killed their stock. He'd tell her when it was over, but the less she knew about it now, the better.

Caitlyn was delighted that the guests were back so early. She'd planned to spend the afternoon helping Dane go over the books, but he had disappeared right before Sam had arrived with the guests. Gibby had told her he'd left to fix a fence that was down and it had something to do with the herd of wild mustangs that grazed in their foothills. She hadn't had a chance to ask many questions because Gibby had asked her to help Billy organize a roping contest.

Caitlyn straddled the top rail of the fence, surveying the corral. The guests were having a wonderful time and they cheered Mr. Sanders on as he tried to do one of the fancy tricks that Billy had showed them. As she glanced at the guests, there was only one person who seemed to be distracted. It was Joan Henderson, and her face looked strained as she watched the contest.

There was definitely something wrong. Caitlyn hopped off the rail and moved over so that she was next to Mrs. Henderson. "Hi, Joan. Would you like to take a little walk with me?"

"Sure." The woman turned to her husband, but George Henderson's attention was on Billy. "I'm taking a walk, dear."

"Are you enjoying yourself, Joan?" Caitlyn led her over to the tables that had been set up beside the chuck wagon for the barbecue.

"Very much," Joan replied, but Caitlyn noticed that her smile didn't quite reach her eyes. "I think this is the best vacation that we've ever had."

"I know something's wrong," Caitlyn countered. "When you left this morning, you looked happy, but now you seem troubled. Would it help to tell me about it?"

Joan opened her mouth as if she were about to deny Caitlyn's observation, but then she just nodded. "You're right. George gave me a beautiful watch for our anniversary last night. I wore it this morning when we went out for the day trip, and . . . and I lost it."

"I'm sorry." Caitlyn reached out to put her arm around the older woman's shoulders. "Where did you last see it?"

"I noticed the clasp was loose when we stopped for lunch at that grassy place at the top of the cliff."

"Stoney Point?"

"Yes, that's the place. I must have dropped it there." Although they were alone, she lowered her voice to a whisper. "I didn't mention it to George. He'd be so disappointed. I thought maybe I could ride up to Stoney Point tomorrow and look for it."

"I'll go up right now," Caitlyn told her guest. "If the watch is there, I'll find it."

"You're going up there alone?" Joan Henderson's eyes widened.

"No, I'll take one of the boys with me," Caitlyn decided. "It's not far, and we've got at least two hours before it gets dark. If we find it, you won't even have to tell George that you lost it."

"Oh, thank you." Joan looked relieved. "I know George saved for months to buy me that watch. It's got little diamonds around the face and the band is gold. And . . . and there's a message engraved on the back. It says *Our love is forever.*"

Caitlyn gave her a hug. "Don't worry. Stoney Point is flat, and any jewelry should be easy to spot while it's still daylight. You just go on back to George and try to enjoy the roping contest. When I get back, I'll take the watch up to your room and put it on your dresser. I promise."

FIFTEEN

Caitlyn felt free and relaxed as she drove up the trail toward Stoney Point. She'd changed her mind about asking Sam to go with her. She knew he would have agreed to help, but the rest of the boys were out with Dane and she hadn't wanted to take him away from the guests. Billy and Gibby needed all the help they could get.

Dane had made her promise never to ride out on horseback alone, so she'd taken her Explorer. The salesman had promised that it would perform as well as a truck, and Caitlyn had to admit that it was living up to his sales pitch. She hadn't had a bit of trouble driving up the steep trail. Perhaps she might have thought twice if the trail had been narrower, but she knew that Gibby drove the ranch Jeep to Stoney Point every week to deliver food for the picnics. If the Jeep could make it, her Explorer could do equally well; and thus far, her plan was working out just fine.

Before she'd left, Caitlyn had followed Dane's instructions and left a note for him on the office door telling him exactly where she'd gone. She was perfectly safe and she hadn't wanted him to waste any time worrying about her. As she rounded the bend, she gave a grateful sigh and pulled her vehicle over to the side of the trail. She was here—and not a moment too soon. The sun was already beginning to dip down toward the peaks of the mountains, and there wasn't any time to lose.

Caitlyn got out of the Explorer and started her search. The sun cast long shadows over the patch of grass at the top of the ridge, but there was still plenty of light. And if it got dark before she was through, she'd simply flick on the headlights to light up the area.

It was breathtaking up here, but Caitlyn didn't take time to admire the view. She had work to do. She started at the far edge of the area and walked in a straight line, back and forth, as if she were mowing the grass in even strips. It took quite a while, but she had to be thorough. If Joan had lost her watch up here, she was determined to find it.

But she didn't find it, and Caitlyn sighed as she covered the last stretch of grass. It wasn't here, and Joan would be terribly disappointed. She walked to the lip of the ridge and frowned as she gazed at the darkening vista. Had Joan stood here to admire the view? And had she waved her arm in a gesture that had loosened the clasp on her watch?

It was a long way down. Caitlyn felt dizzy as she took in the sheer drop. The last rays of the sun made something glitter on a bush that was growing out of a fissure in the steep rock wall. Caitlyn took a step closer, holding her breath, and squinted into the gathering darkness. There it was! Joan's gold watch was caught on an outgrowth about ten feet down from the lip of the ridge.

Could she hook it with a stick? Caitlyn looked around for a branch, but quickly discarded the plan. If she dislodged the watch, it might tumble all the way down to the rocks below. Without a thought for her clothing, Caitlyn got down on her stomach and inched toward the precipice. There was an outcropping of rock about six feet down. If she could slide down to that, she might be able to stretch out and grab the watch.

Heights had always frightened Caitlyn. She didn't even like to climb a stepladder. But she was the only one here and she couldn't ask anyone else to do it. Of course she could drive back down and ask for help. Dane should be back by now and he'd come back with her to retrieve Joan's watch. But that would be admitting defeat, something that Caitlyn really didn't want to do.

So, she took a deep breath. She'd do it. She'd conquer her fear and make Dane proud of her. He'd told her she had courage, and now she had to prove it. Heart in her throat, Caitlyn turned around so that she was stretched out with her feet facing the abyss below. She wiggled back until her legs were dangling over the edge and attempted to push down the terror that clutched her. It would be all right. She could do it. She *had* to do it. Her hand reached out to grab a small bush near the lip of the ridge, and before she could think about the awful things that could happen, she pushed herself over the edge.

There was a moment of sheer panic as she dropped, and then her feet hit the rocks below. The rocks didn't jut out very far, and she knew she had to be very careful. It would be best if she got down on her stomach and then reached out.

It took a minute to get into position, and the light was fading fast. A thought flashed through her mind. Dane had told her that night fell fast up here in the mountains. There was practically no twilight. Once the sun dipped below the peaks, it was dark. Caitlyn reached out, her arm trembling, and her fingers closed around the watch. She had it!

With shaking fingers, Caitlyn tucked Joan's watch into the pocket of her ranch shirt and took a moment to button the pocket. Then she got to her feet and stared up at the bush. All she had to do was grab it again and pull herself up to safety.

Caitlyn felt a moment of apprehension as she reached up. The bush was out of her reach. She'd have to jump to grab it. There was no other way. But could she do it? Could she jump that far? Of course she could. If she didn't want to stay down here all night, she had no choice.

Her legs were shaking, and Caitlyn willed them to be still. If they shook too much, she'd lose her balance. And then she jumped up, grabbing onto the bush and scrambling up against the sheer rock face. She'd almost made it when she heard a sound that sent terror wrenching through her. It was a screech, loud and close, an eerie scream that made her blood turn to ice in her veins.

And then she was falling, backwards into space, flailing her arms and still clutching the bush that had pulled right out by its roots. The eerie scream came again as she hit hard, her ankle twisting beneath her. There was a blinding flash of pain, too much for her mind to process, and then the darkness came crash-

ing down, mercifully wiping out her fear and, with it, any remnant
of rational thought.

The stars were out by the time Dane rode up to the corral. He
handed Warrior over to Jessie, with orders to rub him down and
stable him for the night, and headed back toward the ranch house
at a run. They'd have to cancel tomorrow's day trip. There was
no sense taking any chances. They hadn't seen hide nor hair of
the big cat though they'd heard her screaming in the distance.
Jake, Slim, and Trevor had stayed behind, hoping she'd show
once the sun went down. They were all good shots and they'd
finish her off if they spotted her. The other boys had helped to
set up their tent and unload extra weapons and ammunition.
They'd made a clearing, gathered enough fallen wood to last for
the night, and lit a fire before they'd left. Dane would drive the
jeep back up at first light, bringing more food and supplies.
They'd all agreed that they'd have to camp out near Stoney Point
until they bagged the cougar. None of them was willing to risk
the safety of the guests.

The cougar's cry had spooked the horses, and they'd brought
them all back. Even Warrior had laid back his ears and rolled his
eyes in fright. As Dane strode toward the ranch house, the jeep
pulled in, followed by the riders with the extra horses.

"You'd better get some grub and turn in early." Dane sighed
as they gathered around him. "I'll take Lloyd and Dix with me
in the morning. We'll leave at dawn."

"We're not gonna *ride* out, are we?" Dix asked the question.
He'd been with Bella for over six years and he was a seasoned
hand.

"Nope. The horses get too spooked around cats. We'll take
the jeep."

Once the plans were made and Dane had cautioned them not
to talk out of turn to the guests, he headed around the back of
the ranch house to find Caitlyn. She and Gibby would have to
plan some activities close to home until they got rid of the cougar.

Dane breathed a sigh of relief as he rounded the corner and
entered the fenced-in area they used for the barbecues. Gibby

was behind the counter at the chuck wagon and the guests were laughing and talking at the long picnic tables that had been set up for their use. He waited until the last guest had filled his plate and then he walked up to talk to Gibby.

"Any luck?"

"Nope." Dane noticed that Gibby looked concerned when he shook his head. "I left Jake, Slim, and Trevor up there for the night. They'll take turns standing guard. I'm taking Lloyd and Dix up in the jeep tomorrow to switch off."

"It's a bad one?"

"Yup. We'll keep the guests right here until it's safe. Can you and Caitlyn plan out something for them to do?"

"Sure. No problem." Gibby nodded. "She must've gone into town for somethin'. When I pulled the chuck wagon down here, I noticed that the Explorer was gone."

"Great." Dane sighed and headed into the ranch house. He'd told her to leave him a note if she left the ranch. Normally, he wouldn't have minded if she'd taken a little respite, but this wasn't a good time to do it. Of course she hadn't known that.

There was a note tacked up on the office door and Dane nodded. Good for her! She'd followed his instructions. He tore it off to read it, and his mouth dropped open in shock. Caitlyn had driven up to Stoney Point by herself. Her note said she'd explain when she got back. It was important and Dane shouldn't worry. She'd be back at the ranch before dark.

But it was dark and Caitlyn wasn't back. And Stoney Point was only a mile-and-a-half from where they'd spotted the cougar. Dane didn't waste any time thinking about what could have happened to keep Caitlyn from returning. He just dropped the note and set off for the chuck wagon at a dead run.

It was cold, bone-chilling cold, but her ankle felt like it was on fire. How could she be so cold when she was home, in Aunt Bella's bed, curled up under the lovely, comforting patchwork quilt? She'd just go to sleep again. She'd warm up again if she went back to sleep. Then she wouldn't think about what was wrong and how scared she was and how she wished that Dane would come to take her in his arms and save her from . . . what? Save her from what?

Caitlyn blinked, opening her eyes, and fear and memory came back with a rush.

Something was staring at her from the top of the ridge. Caitlyn made out the shape of a sleek body in the moonlight. A cougar. A *big* cougar. And it was staring at . . . at her.

Her breath caught in her throat, and she had all she could do to keep from crying out in pure terror. Did it know that she was down here? If she could see it, it could see her. It didn't need to see her anyway. An animal didn't have to depend on eyesight. It could *smell* her.

But it was watching her. It was staring straight at her! Was it thinking about jumping down here? *Could* it jump down here? Caitlyn shivered. Perhaps it would help if she played dead, but she wasn't sure that she could do it convincingly enough to fool the cougar.

She tried to think, but panic clouded her mind. With a supreme effort of will, she forced herself to concentrate. She had only one advantage, and that was her ability to think. Wild animals reacted on instinct.

The cougar hadn't come after her yet, and she must have been here for a while. The moon was bright and it was riding high in the sky. She had to do something to protect herself before the cougar decided to attack her. But what should she do?

Caitlyn tried to remember what cats were afraid of. They didn't like water, but there was no water down here. And maybe it was different for wild cats. What else were they afraid of? Fire. That was it. Cats were afraid of fire. If you protected yourself by a ring of fire, the wild animals would stay away. She'd seen it in a movie. It must be true.

You shouldn't believe everything you see in the movies, Caitlyn. Her father had told her that right after she'd seen something scary, something about monster invaders from outer space. But sometimes the things you saw in movies had some actual basis in fact. It didn't really matter. She didn't have any fire. But she did have matches. She'd been carrying them around ever since Dane had given them to her on the night the horse barn had been hit by lightning and the power had gone out.

Lighting one match wouldn't do any good. She needed a big fire, one that would keep the big cat at bay. She had tinder. She could feel branches beneath her legs. She'd landed on a ledge, and it was littered with fallen branches and pieces of old, dead wood. Was there enough to build a fire? Caitlyn didn't want to think about what would happen if there weren't.

Should she stay right where she was, hoping that the cougar would think that she was dead? Or should she move around and attempt to start a fire? Caitlyn wasn't sure which way was better, but her pulse was racing in fear and she knew that she couldn't stay motionless for much longer. She had to do something. She couldn't just stay here and hope that the cougar wouldn't attack her. She would attempt to light a fire the moment that the awful creature stopped staring at her.

A movement at the top of the ridge drew her eye. The cougar had started to move. Now it was pacing back and forth; and then, after a long breathless moment, it disappeared from sight. Did she dare to hope that it had left for good? No, that would be foolish. It knew she was down here and it would come back.

When? When would it come back? When it got hungry, of course. Caitlyn shuddered and pushed that terrifying thought out of her mind. It was time for action. This might be her only chance. She had to light a fire while the cougar was gone.

Caitlyn slipped her hand into her pocket and pulled out the matches. Six. She had six. Quietly, steathily, she reached out to gather the wood that was within her reach. Two pinecones. That was good. The pinecones would burn. And there were some dried leaves. She'd use the leaves for kindling.

Her hands were shaking as she arranged everything in a pile and she blessed her parents for having made her join the Girl Scouts.

There was a horrible scream above her, and Caitlyn's hands started to shake. She couldn't see the cougar, but it was still there. With trembling fingers, she struck the match against the rock ledge. It lit on the first try, and she touched the flame to the dried leaves and prayed that she'd done everything exactly right.

The leaves caught fire as Caitlyn watched. And then the dry branches began to smolder. Little flames licked upward, igniting the smaller branches; and then the bigger ones began to burn. She'd done it!

But it was such a tiny fire. Would it be enough to keep the cougar away? Caitlyn huddled close to the blaze and prayed that it would. There was the sound of soft footfalls above her, and Caitlyn looked up with terror. The cougar had come back and was staring down at her, the fire reflected in the yellow glow in its eyes.

She had to get more wood. She had to get lots of wood. Caitlyn ignored her throbbing ankle and stretched out on the ledge to pick up all the bits and pieces of branches that she could find. She had to keep her fire going. It was the only thing that might save her. As she added more wood, piece by tiny piece, she watched her diminishing supply with a sense of dread. All she could do was pray that Dane found her note and came up here to save her before her wood ran out.

SIXTEEN

For once, Dane didn't say a thing about Gibby's driving as they sped up the trail toward Stoney Point. He was too busy loading his Winchester with Silvertips. He considered chambering a round and putting it on half-cock, but there was no sense in taking chances on the bumpy road. There'd be plenty of time when they got there.

"All set?" Gibby sounded anxious.

"Yup." Dane put his carbine in the rack behind the seat. "I'd better load yours, too."

"Can't hurt. I brought a box of rifled slugs, just in case."

Dane loaded Gibby's old double-barreled shotgun with rifled slugs, snapped on the safety, and stuck it in the gun rack. Then he leaned forward and watched out the windshield as Gibby drove. He prayed that they'd find Caitlyn around the next bend, safe and sound in her Explorer, with something as minor as a flat tire.

"Almost there." Gibby's knuckles were white as he held onto the wheel. "She's gonna be all right. I can feel it in my bones."

"Yup," Dane agreed, but there was a lump of worry in his throat and his heart was thudding hard in his chest. He was sure that Caitlyn was in trouble. He'd had a sick feeling in his gut ever since he'd read her note, and he only hoped that they'd get there in time.

Caitlyn's hand shook as she added the last bit of wood to her fire. The only things left were the pinecones, and she added those, too. Then she picked up the sharp rock she'd found at the back of the ledge. It was shaped a little like a spear and it weighed about five pounds. If the cougar leaped down here when her fire went out, she wouldn't go down without a fight.

"Dane. Please hurry." Caitlyn whispered the words into the still night air. And then she heard something that gave her hope. It sounded like an engine, far away in the distance, coming closer and closer with each passing second. Dane was coming to save her. All she had to do was hang on a little longer and he'd be here.

"There's her car." Gibby pointed at the Explorer parked at the edge of the clearing. "She must be here."

Dane nodded. "Unless something's wrong with it and she decided to walk out."

"But then we would've seen her comin' down the road."

"Right," Dane said, but he wasn't as confident as Gibby. Anything could have happened to Caitlyn if she'd decided to walk back to the ranch. The cougar was still out there.

Gibby grabbed Dane's arm, interrupting his dire thoughts. "What's that? I saw something over there by the edge of the cliff."

"Cut your lights." Dane grabbed his rifle and chambered a round. "I'm getting out. You stay here and keep your shotgun handy."

Gibby didn't waste time asking questions. He grabbed his shotgun and clicked off the safety as their eyes searched the darkness at the edge of the cliff. There was a faint glow coming from below the lip of the ridge. A fire. Caitlyn was down there and she'd started a fire. Smart girl!

As Dane got out of the Jeep and moved forward, the glow disappeared. In the shadows cast by the waning moon, he made out a dim shape at the very edge of the cliff. It was the cougar, and it was poised to leap. Dane didn't hesitate. He lifted his rifle, took aim, and pulled the trigger.

* * *

Caitlyn gasped as the shot rang out. It was followed by an eerie scream, and then she saw the cougar twist in midair, falling, hurtling straight down at her. She stepped back instinctively, huddling tightly against the wall as it hit the edge of her ledge with a terrible force that sent part of the ledge crumbling. She kicked out at it, holding onto a protruding rock for balance, and then it was gone, tumbling down into the darkness below.

"Caitlyn? Are you hurt?"

It was Dane's voice and she gave a shaky nod. But he couldn't see her and she had to force the words past her trembling lips. "I'm . . . I'm okay. I just twisted my ankle when I fell."

"Is it broken?"

"No, at least I don't think it is. But I'm stuck down here and part . . . part of the ledge crumbled away when the cougar hit it."

"Just stay put. Don't move a muscle. I'm coming down there to get you."

They were the sweetest words Caitlyn had ever heard.

"Fire up the Jeep, Gibby." Dane's heart was pounding frantically in his chest as he ran back to the Jeep. She was alive and she'd said she was okay. "Caitlyn's on a ledge about sixty feet down. We've got to get her out of there. Angle in as close as you can to the edge. We'll use the winch."

Gibby pulled the Jeep almost to the lip of the ridge. Then he jumped out and got out the harness from the back. "Does she know how to walk up the rocks when we haul her up?"

"I'm not going to chance it. The wall curves out right under the lip, and she's got a bum ankle. She'll get cut up pretty bad if it gives out on her and she can't hold herself away from the rocks. I'm going down there to bring her up."

"But—" Gibby looked as if he wanted to argue, but he stared at Dane for a second and then he nodded again. "Okay. What do you want me to do?"

"Run the winch." Dane grabbed the harness and put it on, adjusting the straps and buckling up tight. It was one of the first things he'd ordered when he'd come on as head wrangler, and they'd used it a couple of times to haul up lambs and other live-stock that had wandered too close to the cliffs.

"Wish we had another harness." Gibby looked worried. "How're you planning to do it?"

Dane shrugged. "She doesn't weigh much. I'll just tie her up to my harness and hold her away from the rocks."

"Okay. Tie her up tight." Gibby walked to the front of the Jeep and loosened the cable on the winch, hooking it to Dane's har-ness. "I'll bring you up real slow. No sense you gettin' cut up on those rocks, either."

"Good. I'll yell out when I get down there. You keep the cable taut. I'll have to work fast. That ledge isn't stable, and I don't want to put my full weight on it."

Gibby powered up the winch. "I'm ready if you are."

"Yup." Dane gave him a tight smile. "Let's get this thing done, Gibby. I've got to get down there before she takes it into her head to move around."

Gibby turned back to the winch, but Dane saw his worried frown. They'd been watching the ledge for a couple of years now, and it was crumbling more every winter. Would it hold long enough to get Caitlyn off and back up here to safety?

Caitlyn watched Dane as he climbed over the lip of the ridge. She'd never seen a more beautiful sight. She held her breath and tried not to move as he walked down, holding himself away from the sharp, jutting rocks with his feet. The winch screeched loudly in the still night, but it was a welcome sound. Dane was coming to rescue her.

"Don't move."

His voice was sharp and Caitlyn's eyes widened. He sounded very worried. Was there something she didn't know? "I won't. Just tell me what to do."

"When I get down to you, grab me around the neck and hang on. And don't let go. Can you do that?"

"Yes." Caitlyn would have grinned if she hadn't been so ner-vous. She'd been dreaming of doing precisely that since the day they'd met.

"Hold up, Gibby!" Dane shouted out and then he turned to face her, his legs spread out against the rocks. "Now, Caitlyn. Reach up and grab me. Lock your arms around my neck and hold on."

Caitlyn complied willingly. Why was he so worried? she wondered. They were perfectly safe, weren't they? And just as she decided that they must be, the ledge gave way beneath her feet.

"Hook your legs around my waist. Come on, Caitlyn. You can do it. Just throw your legs up and climb on me. I've got you. Don't worry."

Caitlyn didn't stop to think about the danger they were in. She lifted her legs, clamped them around his waist, and winced as she hooked her ankles together.

"Haul us up, Gibby." His voice was loud in her ear and she started to tremble, but then he spoke to her again. "Just concentrate on me, Caitlyn. We're gonna make it. I have to kick off against the rocks, and it's gonna be a bumpy ride. Just hang on tight and don't let go."

"I . . . I won't." She gasped as they bounced toward the rocks, but she didn't let go. She clung to him and shut her eyes, pretending that this was just an amusement park ride. It wasn't. She knew that. But pretending helped. Her ankle was throbbing; her wrists felt as if they were going to break, but somehow she managed to hang on.

"Faster, Gibby!"

The winch screamed louder, and she forced herself to breathe. The louder it was, the closer they were to the top. Any moment now, they'd come over the edge and she would be safe on solid ground.

Her grip was starting to loosen slightly. Dane glanced up and took a deep breath. They were about halfway there. His arms tightened around her and he prayed that she wouldn't lose consciousness, becoming a dead weight in his arms. She just had to hang on. There hadn't been time to secure her with the cable. The ledge had crumbled away the moment his feet had touched it. It was a miracle she'd been able to grab him the way she had and lift her legs to secure them around his waist.

"Just a little farther, Caitlyn. We're almost there. Hold onto me, honey. Hold on."

Caitlyn felt the night begin to close in, darker and darker in her mind. He was talking to her and she heard his words dimly. Something seemed to be happening to her. She felt loose and relaxed, and that wasn't good. And there was a buzzing in her ears that had nothing to do with the noise of the winch. If she passed out, she'd lose her grip. She couldn't let that happen. And then she remembered his words and she blinked, startled back to full awareness. He'd called her *honey.* He'd said, *Hold onto me, honey.* She'd heard him right through the buzzing in her ears. He wanted her to hold on, and she couldn't disappoint him. How could she disappoint the man she loved?

But she was slipping again, down into a warm place where she didn't have to think about anything. He wanted her to stay awake, but she just couldn't. She was so sleepy, her eyes had to close and she had to turn over and plump up her pillow and sink into the deepest sleep she'd ever known.

"Caitlyn! Stay awake."

His voice roused her a bit, helping her fight the lassitude, and then there was another jolt as he pushed off from the sheer rock wall. Something grazed her back, right below her shoulder blades. It didn't really hurt; she was too numb with fright for that, but it did startle her into full awareness again. The winch was so loud, she wished she could loosen her grip to cover her ears; but she couldn't. She had to hold on. He'd told her that she had to hold on.

"Almost there. Just a little longer. Only a couple of yards to go. Don't let me down now!"

No, she wouldn't let him down. She loved him and she'd never let him down. Wasn't that what love was? She had to be there for him. She couldn't let him down.

"I'm okay." Her voice was loud in her own ears and it gave

her courage. And then they were up, over the lip of the ridge, and he was shouting for Gibby to shut off the winch.

The silence was blessed, and tears streamed from her eyes. It didn't matter that they were on the ground, her arms still around his neck. She couldn't move, didn't *want* to move. She wanted to stay like this forever.

"You'd better oil that winch when we get back." Caitlyn knew that Dane was talking to Gibby, but his words sounded strange and far off. And then he turned to her. "It's okay, Caitlyn. We made it. You can let go now."

She tried, but her arms didn't seem to work. Would they be locked around him forever? Somehow, that didn't seem like such a terrible fate. "I'm trying, but I can't let go."

"Your muscles are locked up." He grinned down at her. "Here. I'll help you."

And then he was rubbing her arms, kneading the muscles and bringing some life back to her numb cold limbs. Gradually, her fingers loosened and let go and she noticed that he looked pleased with her. "Was that what they call a death grip?"

"Nope. Just muscle fatigue. And we're not dead; we're alive."

Oh, yes. She was definitely alive. Caitlyn smiled up at him. She'd never felt more beautifully, wonderfully, exquisitely alive.

"I'll drive her back in her car," he called out to Gibby. "It'll be warmer. Throw me one of those blankets, will you?"

Caitlyn watched as he caught the blanket. Then he was wrapping it around her and she tried to thank him, but he was talking to Gibby again.

"You go on ahead with the Jeep. We'll come up here tomorrow and take a look at that cat."

Cat? For a moment she was puzzled, but then she remembered the cougar that had stalked her. She wanted to ask whether it was dead, but she couldn't seem to find the words.

"I'd better carry you." He picked her up in his arms and carried her to the Explorer, opening the passenger door. "I'd say you had a pretty rough day."

She nodded. She didn't seem to be able to do anything else. Somewhere between the lip of the ridge and her car, she'd lost her voice.

"Let's get you warmed up." He placed her in the seat and tucked the blanket around her. "I'll take you back."

"I . . . I . . ." She stopped. Her voice sounded rusty and she had the insane urge to cry, or maybe to laugh. She wasn't sure which. "I never even thanked you for saving my life."

He grinned, walking around the Explorer and sliding in under the wheel. "Why shucks, ma'am. T'warn't nothin'."

"Gary Cooper again." She giggled, the sound floating out in a wave that was almost impossible to control. The hot tears ran down her cheeks as her giggles turned into a sob. "You . . . you're being so nice to me."

He plucked a tissue from the box she kept between the seats and handed it to her. "All in a day's work. Besides, I always wanted to shoot a cougar and drive a brand new Explorer, all in one night."

SEVENTEEN

"Mission accomplished." Dane walked into Caitlyn's bedroom and sat down on the edge of the bed. "Joan was happy to get her watch back, and George wants you to know that it was above and beyond."

"She *told* George?"

" 'Course she did," Dane said.

"But she shouldn't have. That was the whole idea. I went up there because she didn't want George to find out."

"She said she just panicked. Then she told George the whole story right after you left. Both of them were worried sick when you didn't show up for the barbecue."

"So it was all for nothing?"

"Nope." Dane reached out and took her hand, rubbing his thumb over the incredible softness in the center of her palm. "You turned out to be great cougar bait. And now that I bagged her, the guests can go out on their day trips again."

Caitlyn shivered and Dane wished he knew if it was because he was holding her hand or if she was still afraid of the cougar. "I certainly didn't go up there with the intention of luring a cougar. I was scared to death."

"Maybe so, but you did the right thing, lighting that fire and all."

She blushed, and it was clear that she was pleased by his compliment. "I'm just glad I thought of it. Do you think the cougar would have . . . have jumped down to the ledge?"

"That's not very likely." Dane shook his head. "Animals have an instinct about things like that. They don't usually jump onto something that won't hold their weight."

"Not even if she got . . . hungry?"

She shivered again, and Dane pressed her hand a little tighter. "She wasn't hungry. She'd just killed three of our sheep. I'd say you were in more danger from the ledge than you were from the cougar."

"Whatever." She gave him a brave little smile that tugged at his heart. "I'm just glad that I'm not still down there. I won't forget what you did for me, Dane. You bailed me out of trouble."

She had such a sweet, grateful look on her beautiful face that Dane knew he'd better change the subject. It took all the self-control he possessed to keep from pulling her into his arms and kissing her trembling lips. He cleared his throat and assumed what he hoped was a neutral tone. "How's that ankle doing?"

"It doesn't hurt anymore and the swelling's down." She pulled back the covers so he could see. "And whatever you put in the water dissolved most of the nail polish."

He glanced down at her delicate foot. "Maybe you should use it on the other foot, too, unless you like that polish."

"I hate it. I told you before, it was a stupid idea in the first place, but I guess it served its purpose."

"And what purpose was that?" Dane held his breath. Would she finally begin to confide in him?

"Well . . . it's kind of complicated, but I guess I can tell you. After all, I owe you one."

"Yup." Dane gave her an encouraging glance and reached out for her foot, massaging it gently. "Tell me."

Her words were halting as she told him about her divorce and that she blamed herself for their problems. She cried as the words tumbled out, and Dane held her, stroking her back and forcing down his anger at the man who had hurt her. She hadn't told him much, but Spencer Sinclair sounded like a spoiled little rich kid who'd always gotten his way. Dane found himself hating the man who'd made Caitlyn doubt herself.

"The polish?" Dane prodded her gently, instinctively knowing that telling him about it would drive away the clouds of self-doubt and depression.

"Oh, that." She looked horribly embarrassed. "It was childish, really. Spencer hated nail polish. Before we got married, he made me promise never to use it. So I bought a bottle of the brightest pink I could find and I painted my toenails the night before I went in to sign the divorce papers. I guess it was just a silly way to get back at him. And I was wearing shoes, so he didn't even know. Do you think I'm crazy for doing it?"

Dane shook his head. "It worked, didn't it?"

"Yes, it did. It gave me confidence, just knowing that my toenails were pink, even though nobody saw them. It was almost like I . . . I had an edge."

"An edge is good, but you don't need it anymore." Dane stood up and pulled the bottle of nail polish remover from his pocket. "I picked this up for you."

Her eyes widened, and Dane felt as if he'd just presented her with the perfect gift. "Thank you. But when did you go into town?"

"I didn't. Ida keeps a couple of bottles in the laundry. She says it's the only thing that takes pine tar off clothes."

Caitlyn's face glowed with pleasure, and Dane prodded himself to leave. If she kept smiling that way, he'd just have to kiss her. "If you're okay, I'd better get going. I need to get an early start in the morning."

"But can't you stay for just a little while? I . . . I'm still a little nervous."

"Sure. I guess." He took a deep breath and told himself not to meet her incredible green eyes. "Do you want me to get you some coffee or something?"

"No," she said. "I just want some company. Otherwise, I'm likely to lie here contemplating what would've happened if you hadn't come searching for me."

"That's understandable," Dane granted, more than ready to offer reassurance. "But probably nothing would have happened. The ledge only collapsed after the cougar hit it. And then again when I stepped on it. I don't really think that your weight would have caused it to give way."

She sighed. "I'm really lucky the shelf didn't crumble out from under me when I kicked the cougar."

"You kicked the cougar?" Dane's eyebrows shot up in surprise. "When did *that* happen?"

"Right after you shot her. She fell on the ledge and she was still twitching. So I . . . I hung onto a big rock and I kicked her over the edge."

Dane stared at her in utter amazement. "You got close enough to kick the cougar and you're just now telling me about it?"

"I . . . yes. You hit her. I saw the blood. But I thought she still might get up and come after me. I really didn't think about how dangerous it was. I just figured it was her or me."

"Remind me never to get into a fight with you." Dane grinned at the expression of determination on her face.

She gave a little laugh and then asked earnestly, "You *really* don't think that she would have jumped down to the ledge and eaten me for dinner?"

"Nope." He shrugged, trying to be casual. "She would have stayed there for a while, flicking her tail and staring at you. And then she would have gone away to find some easier prey."

"Prey?" Her face turned pale, and he wished he hadn't used that particular word.

"Interest," he amended. "She would have gone away to find some other interest. But all that's immaterial. She's dead and you're alive. It all worked out fine in the end."

"Yes, you're right. I am alive." She brightened appreciably.

Dane was impressed. Most people he knew would have gone into hysterics if they'd found themselves in her position. She hadn't panicked. She'd started a fire, and she'd kicked the cougar when it had landed on the ledge. And even though she'd been frightened and exhausted, she'd managed to hang on as Gibby had hoisted them up to firm ground.

"Why are you looking at me that way?" she questioned sharply.

"What way?"

"Like I'm some sort of human oddity."

"Because you are," Dane replied honestly. "I was just trying to figure out why you're not hysterical, that's all."

"Maybe I am. I'm afraid to be alone, and my hands are still shaking. And every time I think about the cougar, my heart starts pounding and I feel as cold as ice. And . . . and I just want to hold onto you and never let go. That means I'm hysterical, doesn't it?"

Either that or it means that you want me as much as I want you. The words popped into his mind, but he bit them back before he could say them. "Just try to relax and remember where you are. You're home in your own bed. Everything turned out all right. You're safe."

"I'd feel a lot safer if you'd hold me."

She looked up at him with pleading eyes and Dane couldn't stand it any longer. He pulled her into his arms and nestled her against his chest. "Is that better?"

"Oh, yes." She gave a soft sigh that made the blood in his veins start to sing. "It's much better. But I'm still cold. Can we . . . can we get under the covers?"

He should go. Right now. She was too tempting and he wasn't made of steel. How much longer could he resist her? The feel of her soft curves against him was driving him crazy.

"Please?"

He groaned and fell back on the pillows, holding her full length against him. She was trembling again, but she couldn't be cold. The heat from her body was radiating to his, making every nerve ending beg for release. It was wrong. She was his partner. It was insane to even think of her naked beneath him, writhing against the sheets, clawing at his back as she shuddered with completion.

"What are you thinking about?"

Her voice was soft, a whisper against his ear, and he shivered with longing. "Nothing. I'm not thinking about anything at all."

"That's impossible." She flicked out her tongue and licked his ear. "I know what you're thinking about. I'm thinking about it, too. Please kiss me, Dane. I want you to kiss me again. I want you to make me feel that I'm really alive."

Dane groaned in surrender. It was impossible to resist her when she was right here, in his arms. He reached out to brush back her glorious hair, nuzzled the side of her smooth silken neck, and then he claimed her lips with his own. They were so sweet, crushing against his mouth like the petals of an exotic flower. And soft. And willing. She kissed him back until he felt his mind spin. And her lovely body was pressing so eagerly against his, it drove all the caution from his mind.

"More." She sounded like a hungry child as he tried to break their kiss. "Kiss me again. And again. And again. Kiss me until I can't think of anything else but you."

She was seducing him and Caitlyn didn't care. She wanted to celebrate the life she'd almost lost. He'd attempted to reassure her about the ledge and the cougar, but she knew the truth. She would have died if he hadn't saved her. And now he was saving her again. Every nuance of pressure from his lips, every touch of his fingers, every breath he breathed into her mouth made her feel that much more alive.

This was how it should be, this wanting, this needing, this compulsion to press even closer to him. She reached down to loosen the buttons on his shirt, glorying in the feel of his warm bare skin. She wanted to feel every part of him, stoking and touching and tasting until her mind was swimming with pure sensation.

"Caitlyn. Honey. We have to . . ."

She hushed him with another kiss, probing his mouth with her tongue. He groaned and met her thrust with his own, exploring her mouth until she was breathless and then reaching up to bury his hands in her hair. She kissed the side of his neck, nibbling with her lips and tasting his salty sweat. It made her ache deep inside with a throbbing loneliness that only he could fill. She wanted to be closer. She wanted all of him. She wanted to pull him inside her body and own him heart and soul.

His hands slid up, under her flannel nightshirt, and she began to shake as if with a fever. His touch sent blazing currents through her trembling body and warmed her to her very core. She lifted the heavy fabric, rolling it up and pulling it off with one sweep of her arms. And then, with her heart pounding frantically and desire surging through her trembling body, she looked deeply into his eyes.

"Make love to me, Dane." Her voice was so low and so husky,

she barely recognized it. She had thought it wasn't possible, that it was just a figure of speech, but he was driving her mad with lust. "Please."

He pulled her to him and kissed her again, driving all rational thought from her head. His hands reached out to grasp her breasts, and she quivered with the hot pleasure that surged through her. His fingers were like fire on her skin, blazing over her nipples and making her cry out with a hunger she'd never felt before. And then she opened to him, willing him to come to her, to share in the passion that was threatening to consume her.

"Are you sure?" His voice was thick with need.

"Yes." Caitlyn reached out for him, not willing to let him go for an instant. "I'm sure. Please, Dane."

He groaned as he pulled off his clothes; and it made her feel powerful, and sexy, and desirable, just knowing that he wanted her as much as she wanted him.

"Wait, Caitlyn . . . honey . . . we need . . ."

"No." Caitlyn knew what he was going to say and she shook her head. "It's all right. I told you before. Nothing can happen."

And then his hard body was lowering to hers and she couldn't stop shaking with the pleasure. He was hot and hard, and she wanted him more than she'd ever wanted anyone before. But there was no need to tell him, no need for any more words. This was what Amy had tried to tell her, what love between a man and a woman should be. She wrapped her arms around Dane's neck, the same way she had when he'd pulled her to safety, and welcomed him into her body with a cry of exquisite pleasure.

EIGHTEEN

Dane lifted her arm and rolled over on his back, gently moving from her sleeping embrace. He wanted to stay in bed with her, to pull her into his arms again and wake her with kisses, but the sky was beginning to lighten and it was time for him to get to work.

He moved slowly, rolling to the edge of the bed and sitting up. My God, what a night! Caitlyn had been tireless and so had he. He grinned as he thought about the way she'd reached for him, again and again, and how he'd somehow managed to have the stamina of a teenager.

Caitlyn moved in her sleep, reaching out for him, and he almost went back into her arms. But he couldn't. There was work to do; and as much as he'd like to stay here with her, the boys were depending on him. He also didn't want anyone to know where he'd spent the night, and that meant he'd have to get back to his own quarters in a hurry. There was her reputation to consider. Their guests and the whole Double B staff would start to gossip if they suspected anything.

She reached for him again, and Dane pulled the pillow into position and let her snuggle up to that. Sweet. She was so sweet. And she was the most passionate lover he'd ever had. He really wanted more, but this wasn't the time.

Slowly, so he wouldn't jounce her awake, Dane sat up and put his feet on the floor. It was as cold as ice and it banished the last vestiges of sleep from his mind. She needed a rug by her bed, something soft and furry so her feet wouldn't get cold when she got up in the morning. He'd look around and find her something nice, maybe a sheepskin.

Dane picked up his clothes, finally locating his shirt draped over her lamp, and got dressed as quietly as he could. He waited until he had gone out into the hallway to pull on his boots. Then he remembered that she might be confused and anxious when she found him gone and he walked back in to leave her a note on the pad by her bed.

What should he say? Dane discarded the idea of writing *You're the greatest* or *Thanks for a wonderful night* and settled on something simple. He penned the words *Went to work—See you later* and signed his name. Signing his name was pretty corny, too, now that he thought about it. She would know who'd left her the note. But he didn't want to risk waking her by tearing off the page and starting another, so he left it and went back out into the hall.

Miracle of miracles, no one was up yet. Dane made it to his rooms without being spotted. He stripped off his clothes and got into the shower, soaping himself and feeling on top of the world. He felt so good, he had the urge to break into song—and he *never* sang in the shower. He hadn't done that since . . .

Dane drew a deep breath and cranked the water to cold. This wasn't the time to think about Beth and the showers they'd taken together, how they'd laughed and played like kids in the old metal shower stall in their tiny bathroom. They'd squirted each other with the removable showerhead he'd installed and lathered each other until they'd both been wild with hunger. And then Beth had thrown the largest towel they'd owned over the bed and they'd . . .

He grabbed the shampoo and washed his hair, trying to rinse out the memories with the suds. Beth had been gone for five years, but he could still see her face etched sharply in his mind.

Wasn't it time to let her go? Dane knew it was, but he just couldn't seem to do it. He didn't feel guilty for going to bed with another woman. That wasn't a problem. He hadn't exactly lived like a monk during his four years at the Double B. He'd enjoyed nights with other women, and that hadn't ever made him feel disloyal to Beth's memory.

But there was a difference between Caitlyn and the other

women he'd taken to his bed. Dane hadn't been serious about any of them, and they'd known it. And they hadn't been serious about him, either. The attraction had been sex, pure and simple. They'd enjoyed making love and then they'd said goodbye. It was different with Caitlyn. She got under his skin in a way that no other woman had. He didn't want to tell her goodbye and say he'd be sure to look her up the next time he wanted to have a little fun. Caitlyn was more like . . . Beth.

That thought scared him, and Dane put it out of his mind. He wasn't looking to fall in love again and he didn't want Caitlyn to fall in love with him. He wasn't ready for another commitment and maybe he'd never be. He had to make that clear to Caitlyn. He was almost sure she wasn't the type to sleep around, and she was bound to expect much more than he could give her. He had to talk to her, to get things straight between them. He'd do it tonight.

Dane shut off the shower, stepped out and dried off, and grabbed clean clothes. Once he was shaved and dressed, he headed for the door. He was about to leave when he caught sight of his bed. The covers were pulled taut, the pillowcases weren't creased, and the sheets were as fresh as they'd been when the maids had left. They'd know that he hadn't slept in his own bed if he left it that way.

Feeling a bit like a fool, Dane walked back and pulled down the covers. He climbed into bed, rolling around a little to rumple the sheets, and gave the pillows a couple of thumps. Once he was sure that his bed looked the same as it did every other morning, he headed for the kitchen with a smile on his face.

Caitlyn woke up hugging the pillow. She felt wonderful, soft and feminine and unbelievably satisfied. She hadn't felt this kind of joyous euphoria since she'd been a child and she'd hopped out of bed on Christmas morning to see what Santa had brought her.

It was strange and Caitlyn frowned. Was she losing her mind? What could be so special about this morning?

Dane. Caitlyn's eyes widened and she sat up, blinking at the sun that was streaming through her curtains. Dane. Dane was why she felt this way. She'd spent the night with Dane!

A heated blush rose to cover her cheeks as she remembered some of the things they'd done, things she'd known about but she hadn't dared mention to Spencer. Her sex life as Spencer's wife hadn't been very adventuresome, but that hadn't mattered to her at the time.

But with Dane, everything had changed. There was a freedom she'd never felt before, an urge to please him in ways he'd hadn't been pleased before. It had brought out the wanton in her, a side of her that she hadn't known existed, and she wasn't willing to bury it out of sight again. Dane had told her that she was wild, and that was a compliment. And then he'd driven her to further heights by making her rediscover her own body. He'd found new places, new depths to caress and tease and touch and kiss.

It had been so perfect, Caitlyn had never wanted it to stop, but finally exhaustion had overtaken them both and they'd slept. And now he was gone without waking her, without telling her that everything would be all right, without saying that he loved her as much as she loved him.

Caitlyn glanced around the room, blinking back tears. She must be a manic-depressive. She'd felt that she was on top of the world when she'd first opened her eyes and now she was crying because Dane had left her without . . .

There was a note on the pad by her bed. Caitlyn was so excited, her hand shook as she reached out for it. She felt like a teenager reading a note that her boyfriend had left in her locker. Even the simple words, no mention of love or fun or anything, pleased her.

Caitlyn bounded out of bed. She felt wonderful and her ankle didn't even twinge. Maybe it was silly, but she wanted to save Dane's first note to her. She'd put it in the bottom of her jewelry box, where none of the maids would spot it. She unlocked the box with the small gold key she kept in the bottom of her dresser drawer and lifted out the tray that held her earrings.

She placed Dane's note on the blue velvet that lined the bottom of her jewelry box and replaced the tray. Then she locked it up tight and hid the key in its usual spot.

Caitlyn stared at the jewelry box. She'd never saved a single note from Spencer. He'd written her countless inter-office memos, little messages asking her to join him for dinner or go to a charity function or meet him somewhere for drinks. Over the years, from the time she was a little girl, she had saved notes from other men in her life, but never Spencer. Why hadn't she saved Spencer's notes? Could Amy be right? Had she never really loved Spencer at all?

They'd decided to keep the guests at the ranch house for one more day, just to be on the safe side. Gibby explained it to her when Caitlyn arrived in the kitchen for a tardy breakfast. Billy had organized a rousing game of horseshoes in the pit behind the horse barn, and Sam had taken a group of guests out to the edge of the pine trees for archery practice. Even Jessie, who was noticeably shy, had agreed to show several couples how he'd trained the ranch dogs to catch Frisbees, and everyone seemed to be having a good time.

Caitlyn had just settled down in a lawn chair to watch four couples play croquet when Joan Henderson came rushing up to her.

"Caitlyn. I really have to talk to you." Joan looked very serious. "Dane told us what happened, and George and I are just sick about the whole thing. Why, you could have been killed, for a . . . a *watch!*"

"But I wasn't. I shouldn't have gone up there alone, Joan. That was my fault. I'm just glad that you got your watch back."

"So am I, but I never meant to cause so much trouble." Joan gave her a tentative grin. "I guess you must be all right. You look fabulous."

"I do?" Caitlyn glanced down at her clothes. Though Ida and Marilyn had done their best to shrink them, Aunt Bella's blue jeans were still much too large. Her blouse, patterned with blue and white checks, hung loosely on her body, and she'd needed to wear three pairs of socks to fill out Aunt Bella's boots.

"If almost getting killed does that to a woman, maybe I'd better try it." Joan laughed. "You really do look radiant. Is it Dane?"

Caitlyn drew in her breath sharply and hoped she wasn't blushing. "Dane?"

"Dane." Joan repeated his name. "You look to me like a woman in love." Caitlyn didn't say anything, and Joan went on. "He's certainly wild about you. Even George noticed that, and he's not the most observant person in the world."

"What makes you think that Dane is . . . uh . . . *wild* about me?" Caitlyn couldn't help asking.

"He searches for you the minute he comes into the room. And if you're not there, he gets a big disappointed look in his eyes. He has incredible eyes, hasn't he?"

"Dane? Or George?"

"Actually, both of them." Joan giggled. "George's eyes are that lovely soft brown with little flecks of gold. And Dane's are so blue, it makes you catch your breath. Haven't you noticed?"

"Mmm." Caitlyn tried for a noncommittal air.

"Anyway, George thinks that Dane looks at you like he wants to gobble you up."

"He does?" Caitlyn couldn't help the grin that began to spread across her face.

"Absolutely. And I just think you two make a perfect couple. A person would have to be blind not to see *that.*"

Joan hurried off to join her husband, and Caitlyn gave a relieved sigh. She liked Joan Henderson a lot, but she really hadn't wanted to talk about Dane.

Five minutes later, at the horseshoe pit, another guest told her that she looked absolutely radiant. And when she stopped to check on the archery practice, two more guests came up to compliment her on her appearance. Even the dogs left Jessie's side and licked her hands, wagging their tails and sporting their canine smiles.

Caitlyn wandered off, bewildered. She knew she didn't look her best today. Aunt Bella's clothes were too big for her; her hair felt lank and sticky because she hadn't had time to wash and dry it, and there was a purplish bruise on her arm where she'd scraped it on the rocks. Though she'd slept late, she'd only gotten about three hours of rest and she was sure there were dark smudges under her eyes. Why was everyone telling her that she looked radiant?

Ida and Marilyn caught her as she was about to check with Gibby in the kitchen. As usual, Ida was in the lead, her younger sister trailing along behind her.

"We're leaving for the day, Miz Bradford," Ida informed her. "But Marilyn and I wanted to see how Bella's clothes had worked out for you."

Caitlyn twirled around like a model to show them her outfit. "They're still too big, but that's all right. It's better that way. I don't want any of the male guests to get ideas. And I certainly don't want the wives to think I'm dressing up to attract their husbands."

"Nope." Ida looked thoughtful as she turned to Marilyn. "What do you think?"

Marilyn laughed. "You're a goner, Miz Bradford."

"A goner?"

" 'Fraid so." Marilyn's eyes twinkled behind her wire-rimmed glasses. "Bella's things might keep the guests from making passes at you, but there's nothin' you can do to hide it."

"Hide it?" Caitlyn wished she could stop repeating every other thing that Marilyn said, but she really didn't know what she meant.

"Marilyn's right." Ida chuckled. "Even if you put on a feed sack, it wouldn't change the way that he looks at you."

Caitlyn didn't want to ask, but she had to know. "He? Which *he* are you talking about?"

"Dane." Marilyn grinned. "You must have noticed. It's plain as the nose on your face."

"You think that Dane . . . uh . . . *likes* me?"

"He surely does!" Ida exchanged a wink with her sister. "And you like him, too. Anybody can see that."

"Of course I like Dane. He's my partner." Caitlyn tried for a little damage control. Ida and Marilyn could all too easily spark rumors with their candid observations.

Ida leaned closer, even though no one was near enough to overhear. "This must be what Bella had in mind when she threw you two together. She'd be as happy as a cat in a vat of cream if she could see you right now."

"I think she'd be happy, too." Caitlyn tried not to blush as she attempted to brazen it out. "Dane and I are working very hard to keep the Double B on its feet."

Marilyn giggled. "That's not what Ida meant, and you know it. Dane's smitten with you. And you're smitten with him. All you have to do is look in the mirror to see that."

"I . . . I . . . You're imagining things." Caitlyn's face felt hot and she dropped her eyes."

"Maybe." Ida patted her shoulder. "Doesn't matter anyway. It's your private business, and we probably shouldn't have brought it up. But I wouldn't wait too long to get things started if I was you. There's more than one woman around these parts who's waiting to climb in your boots."

"You think about it, you hear?" Marilyn chimed in. "And don't you worry about us spreading tales. Whatever happens is between you and him."

"That's right." Ida stepped back. "And you just come and see us if you want to talk or you need us to help, all right?"

"Uh . . . yes. I'll do that. Thank you." Caitlyn watched them go with raised eyebrows. She'd never said a word about Dane to them, but somehow they'd guessed how she felt. They'd only gotten one thing wrong. The attraction she felt for Dane was sex, not love. She still didn't understand Marilyn's comment about looking in the mirror. She looked just the same as she always did. Didn't she?

Caitlyn turned on her heel and headed down the path toward the ranch house. Everyone had complimented her on her appearance today, and that was unusual. And Joan Henderson had said that she looked like a woman in love. What was different about her? She had to find out.

When she got to the ranch house, Caitlyn opened the door and went straight to the living room. She took up a position in front of the mirror that hung over the fireplace and stared at her reflection with critical eyes. What she saw shocked her. She *did* look different. Her green eyes were sparkling, her color was high, and her skin was glowing. And though her clothing was as loose as it could be without falling off, there was a new air of sensuality about her when she reached up to brush back a strand of hair that had escaped her thick braid.

Caitlyn sighed. She'd thought that the compelling attraction she felt for Dane could be explained away in purely biological terms. She'd really believed that once she'd indulged her passions, it would be over. But it wasn't. She thought of Dane and watched her reaction. Her eyes begin to shine with a deep glow and her lips trembled slightly. She looked soft and willing and eager to repeat everything they'd done last night—and then some. Her passions weren't sated. They were blazing again, even hotter than before.

What was happening to her? Caitlyn stared at her reflection, but she found no answers. And then she remembered the questions that Amy had asked her on the eve of her wedding. *When Spencer's not with you, do you feel like a part of yourself is missing? Do you long to be together night and day? When he kisses you, do your knees turn weak? And when he makes love to you, do you see the heavens open up before your eyes?*

Caitlyn remembered nodding and saying yes to them all, but she'd been lying. She'd thought that Amy was just being a hopeless romantic. But now she looked at Amy's questions in a new light, thinking of Dane instead of Spencer. Yes, she felt like a part of her was missing when he wasn't with her. It wasn't that she was dependent on him; she could get along just fine when he was gone. But several times, during the afternoon, she'd wanted to talk to him, to share something funny or to ask a question. And when she'd realized that he wasn't there, she'd felt a little stab of loneliness, nothing that couldn't be handled, but there just the same.

Did she long to be with him night and day? Caitlyn didn't even have to think about that one. Yes, most definitely she did. She'd always enjoyed sleeping late, but she'd found herself eager to get up in the morning just so she could join him for coffee before the guests arrived for breakfast. And at night, when their activities were over and the guests had gone up to their rooms, she wanted Dane to be with her, to love her all night long.

When Caitlyn thought about Amy's last two questions, she

began to blush at the memories that flowed through her mind. Yes, her knees turned weak when Dane kissed her and her mind spun around in circles and she trembled all over. And when he made love to her, it *did* feel like the heavens opened up and whirled her away in a starry glow of pleasure so deep and so fine, she wanted to stay right there in his arms for all eternity.

As the realization sank in, Caitlyn stared at her reflection with awe. She was a woman in love and she loved Dane. He was unlike any other man she'd ever known, and she felt like a complete fool for doubting that this kind of deep, all-consuming love existed. And now that she knew it did, she was going to do everything in her power to make sure that it lasted for a lifetime.

What was happening to her? Caitlyn stared at her reflection, but she came up blank. And then she remembered the quiet phone call Amy had asked her on the eve of her wedding. Well. Sweeney's low, soft murmur. You feel like a fool of yourself or message. Do you want to be sensible, might mind itself. When he kissed you, do your knees turn weak? And I know he really liked it, you could not focus it again for maybe a very emphatic that Caitlyn remembered nodding and saying yes to their slight shift. Her clearly. She'd thought that Amy was just being overeager. Just something. Not now she looked at Amy's question in a new light, thinking of Dane instead of Sheldon. Was she not like a part of her was missing when he wasn't with her? It was when she was away from him, she could get along just fine. When he was gone. But several days, during that afternoon, she'd wanted to talk to him, to share something funny or to ask a question. And when she'd realize that he wasn't there, she'd felt a sense of loneliness, nothing that couldn't be mended, but there just the same.

Did she long to be with him night and day? Caitlyn didn't even have to think about that one. Yes, most definitely, she did. She'd always enjoyed sleeping late, but she'd found herself eager to rising in the morning, just so she could join him for coffee before the guests arrived for breakfast. And at night, when their activities were over and the guests had gone up to their rooms

she wanted Dane to be with her to love her for all night long.

When Caitlyn thought about Amy's last two questions, she

NINETEEN

Something was wrong. Dane had come back right before the barbecue, and he had avoided her. She wasn't imagining it. She was sure of that. She'd caught him watching her several times; but the moment she'd raised her eyes to his, he'd looked away. What was wrong? Was he regretting the night they'd shared together?

Finally, after the guests had eaten their fill and taken another square dance lesson to prepare for the farewell party on Saturday night, they'd gone up to their rooms. Caitlyn had spent long minutes straightening up the living room, hoping that Dane would come to find her, but he hadn't. When the grandfather clock had struck midnight, she'd walked down the hallway to her room and despondently pushed open the door. And then she'd seen it, the note that was propped up on the table by her bed.

Caitlyn had crossed the room at a run and grabbed up the note. *Come to my quarters when you get through. We have to talk.* There had been no signature, but none had been needed. Caitlyn had known that there was only one person who could have left her the note.

And now she was walking down the hallway again, her heart pounding frantically with each step. She felt like a kid who'd been summoned to the principal's office. There was definitely something amiss, and she dreaded finding out what it was.

She was here. Caitlyn took a deep breath for courage and raised her hand to knock. But just as her fingers were about to touch the door, it opened and threw her off balance.

"Caitlyn." He caught her as she stumbled forward, and she

took hope as his arms tightened around her. But he released her the instant she'd righted herself and motioned her inside. "Come in. I've been waiting for you."

Caitlyn worked to keep her voice even. "Sorry. I just found your note. What did you want to talk to me about?"

"Last night. We've got to get some things straight between us."

That comment, coming from any other man, would have amused her, but Dane wasn't any other man. He sounded upset, and her legs trembled as she sat down on his old, leather couch. "What things?"

"Last night was a mistake. It was my fault and I don't want you to get the wrong idea. I'm not looking for a permanent relationship. It's just . . . not an option for me."

Caitlyn's eyes widened. He was really nervous, and she had to set him at ease. She took a deep breath, put on her brightest smile, and said what he obviously wanted to hear. "You can relax, Dane. This isn't the old West, and I don't have a father or a bunch of brothers with shotguns."

"That's a relief."

His words belied a persistent uneasiness, and she felt she had to say more. "Look, Dane . . . I'm not looking for anything permanent, either. And last night wasn't your fault. I share the blame if *blame* is the right word. I don't happen to think it is. We wanted each other; we slept together, and we had a wonderful time. Neither of us wants to make a commitment, and that's fine. End of story."

"It's not that simple." He shook his head. "I mean, I know you're not the type of woman to sleep around. I just don't want you to get . . . attached to me."

"You don't want me to fall in love with you?" Caitlyn faced him squarely. Dane had been hurt. She could see it on his face. And he was afraid he'd be hurt again.

"Yeah," he admitted reluctantly. "That's it. I don't want you to fall in love with me."

Caitlyn shrugged, adopting what she hoped was a carefree attitude. "Okay. I won't."

"But what if you do?"

"Then that'll be my problem, not yours," she assured him amiably. "You're making this whole thing a lot more complicated than it has to be. We like each other. We like to go to bed together. What's wrong with that?"

"I don't know. Nothing, when you put it that way."

Caitlyn stared into his eyes. "And you admit that you had a good time?"

"Of course I do." He stared at her as if she'd just said something ridiculous, and Caitlyn felt a thrill of pleasure. "But that's as far as it can go, Caitlyn."

Caitlyn took a deep breath and fought to keep her tone light. "That's fine with me. We'll just have a good time and leave it at that. It couldn't be simpler."

"It's not that simple for me." He refused to meet her gaze. "I asked you to come here so that I could apologize. I made a mistake and I'm sorry if you thought that it was the beginning of something between us. It wasn't. Can we just forget that it happened and stay friends?"

Caitlyn nodded mutely. There was nothing else she could do. It wouldn't work to argue with him. He'd already made up his mind. He'd decided that their brief affair was over and that was that. And she had to get out of here before she broke down in tears.

"Hey . . . it's not that I didn't enjoy it, Caitlyn. I did. That's what makes it so hard. But it can't go anywhere, and I just think it's better if we call it quits right now, before either one of us gets more involved."

"You've got a point." Caitlyn forced her lips to curve up in a smile as she got up and headed toward the door. "Okay. It was fun while it lasted. See you tomorrow at breakfast?"

"Sure." He reached out to put his hand on her arm before she could open the door. "That cougar last night? She was the one that killed our livestock. We can take the guests out on day trips again."

"Good." Caitlyn opened the door, forcing him to drop his hand. "Goodnight, Dane."

Caitlyn heard his voice answer as she closed the door and she walked down the hallway with the fake smile on her face. Her eyes were filled with tears, but she fought them back. She couldn't let them fall until she got back to her room. Someone might see her.

It seemed to take forever to reach the safety of her room. Once Caitlyn got there, she threw herself on the bed and gave way to sobs of bitter disappointment. Dane didn't love her. The Hendersons had been wrong. And Ida and Marilyn had been wrong, too. But they'd all been right about her. She was a woman who was desperately in love with a man who just wanted to be her friend.

Dane had never been so miserable in his life. Avoiding Caitlyn was pure hell. Every time he'd run into her during the past few days, he'd had to fight down the urge to take her in his arms and kiss her. Was he being a fool by not taking the option she'd offered him? She'd seemed to think that they could sleep together without getting emotionally involved. But he couldn't. He knew it was impossible. He was already involved much more than he wanted to admit.

"What's wrong, Dane?"

Dane turned to stare at Gibby, who'd just finished flipping the last of the pancakes and was stacking them on a plate. "Nothin'. What makes you think something's wrong?"

"You've been pacing the floor like a caged bear. And you've been snapping everybody's head off. Did you have a fight with Miz Bradford?"

"She's got nothing to do with this." Dane turned on him angrily and just managed to control himself. He forced himself to take a deep breath and then he shook his head. "No, Gibby. I didn't have a fight with Caitlyn. Everything's fine."

Gibby shrugged and handed him the plate. "Well, something's sure eatin' at you. You haven't said a civil word to anybody since the day after you shot that cougar."

"I . . . uh . . . I've just got a lot on my mind. Have I really been snapping at the boys?"

"Yup. You've been chewin' on yourself for near to ten days now, and the boys're gettin' real tired of the whole thing. Maybe it's time to take stock and fix whatever's wrong."

"Maybe," Dane granted grudgingly. "Tell the boys I've just got some . . . personal problems. I'll work 'em out; don't worry."

Gibby nodded. "Work 'em out soon. And do me a favor and carry that stack of cakes to the table before they get stone cold. I'll bring the sausage and the bacon."

Dane turned around and headed for the breakfast buffet. Caitlyn wasn't there. She'd been coming in to breakfast late for nine days running, and it was clear that she was avoiding him, too. Gibby was right. He had to work out his problems, but he didn't know what else he could do. When he'd broken off the affair with Caitlyn, he'd felt like an animal forced to chew off his own leg to escape the steel jaws of a trap. It wasn't that he thought of love as a trap, not exactly. But he wasn't free to love Caitlyn the way she deserved to be loved. She would want all of him, and he couldn't give her that. Even though he'd fought it, he still loved Beth, and it wouldn't be fair to Caitlyn to give her only part of his affections.

There were the lies, too, and the secrets no one knew about him. Caitlyn could never really know him, not the way he really was. His whole life for the past four years had been a lie. The only person he'd trusted with the truth was Bella. She had been his salvation, the only one to truly understand his agony and his sorrow. And now Bella was gone and he was completely alone.

Dane's brows knit together and he sighed deeply. He'd tried to solve the problem with Caitlyn, but his solution hadn't worked. They were partners, and he couldn't completely avoid her. He had to see her, to work with her at running the Double B, and the tension between them was affecting his job.

There were plenty of rumors and speculations. Gibby had told him that. And it wouldn't be long before the boys would ask questions. If he didn't give them some honest answers, they'd start thinking about quitting and going to work at a place where the boss wasn't snapping at them all the time. He had to do something, but he didn't have the foggiest idea what it should be.

" 'Course he loves you. He's just too stubborn to admit it." Ida draped her arm around Caitlyn's shoulder. "You just got to nudge him a little. Isn't that right, Marilyn?"

"That's right." Marilyn's head bobbed up and down in agreement. "Maybe you ought to take up with somebody else. A little jealousy might just make the pot come to a boil."

"But I don't want anyone else." Caitlyn blinked back tears. She hadn't intended to confide in Ida and Marilyn, but they'd been so sympathetic, she hadn't been able to resist.

" 'Course you don't, but he doesn't know that," Marilyn explained. "The way I see it, you got to make him decide whether he wants to fish or cut bait."

"Fish or cut bait?" Caitlyn smiled in spite of herself.

"There's other things she could have said that would've burned your ears," Ida said drily. "But give it a thought. Makin' Dane jealous is the only thing that might work."

"I really don't want to do that," Caitlyn objected. "It's just not fair."

"Life ain't fair, honey," Marilyn retorted. "And the way I see it, you gotta fight for your man."

"Find someone to dance with at the party on Saturday night," Ida suggested. "That should spur him into action. The whole town of Little Fork is comin', and there'll be plenty of men to pick from."

"But I don't know anyone from Little Fork," Caitlyn reminded her. "What do you want me to do? Just pick someone and grab him?"

"Nope," Marilyn said quickly. "Don't do that. You gotta plan it out so you don't step on any toes."

"Okay," Caitlyn agreed. "But you'll have to help me. Who should I pick?"

"There's Jerry Campbell." Ida snapped her fingers, pleased with herself. "He's been dragging his feet about getting engaged to Nancy; and as far as I know, he's still footloose and fancy free."

"And there's always Mayor Wellesby," Marilyn added. "His wife died two years ago last Christmas. And then there's Teague Conners."

"Not Teague." Ida rejected her sister's suggestion out of hand. "You can't trust that one any further than you can throw him. He'll have you up in the hayloft so fast, it'll make your eyes cross. How about Bo Wilson or his brother Owen? They're what they call confirmed bachelors, but they still like to look. And you wouldn't be foolish if you picked Jordy Ewing. He's back from that pipeline job he took up in Alaska, and he looks real good now that he's gotten his teeth fixed."

"But I've never even met any of these men," Caitlyn remonstrated. "Maybe they won't want to dance with me."

The two sisters hooted, and Marilyn patted her shoulder. "Any one of 'em will dance with you. You don't need to worry your pretty head about that. You just got to be careful about goin' up to someone before you know who he is."

"You come check with us," Ida told her. "We'll tell you if he's spoken for. You could wind up in a world of hurt if you make a mistake about that. Ranch women get mighty possessive about their men."

"You'll be at the party?" Caitlyn felt much better when the two women nodded. "I won't do anything without asking you first. But there's one name you didn't mention. How about Jake?"

Marilyn's eyes widened. "Jake Wheeler?"

"Yes. He . . . uh . . . he got a little too friendly with me when I first got here. And . . . and Dane didn't like it."

"Just how much didn't he like it?" Ida probed.

"Well . . ." Caitlyn hesitated. It was embarrassing. But Marilyn and Ida really wanted to help her. "Gibby told me that Dane had to have a talk with Jake to straighten him out."

"I wondered why Jake gave up on you all of a sudden," Ida said. "What do you think, Marilyn?"

"I think Miz Bradford's got her man." Marilyn turned to Caitlyn with a huge smile. "You just concentrate on Jake and dancing with him real sexy like. Dane'll take one look and come right around, you'll see."

TWENTY

It was the night of the dance, and Caitlyn was nervous. All the preparations were in place, and everything was set up and ready for the party-goers, who would be arriving in less than two hours. The guests had eaten a light snack about an hour ago. They'd have what Gibby called a "real big feed" later on in the evening.

Caitlyn sniffed the air as she walked toward the chuck wagon. The menu tonight was pure Western, and the three open-pit barbecues had been started last night. She had watched as Gibby and the boys had attached the meat to the spits. There was a half-a-cow revolving slowly over the coals in one pit, a whole pig in another, and lamb in a third. There would also be chicken, but it took less time to cook and Gibby would start that later.

As she remembered the other items on the menu, Caitlyn's mouth watered. There would be corn-on-the-cob, barbecued beans, gallons of coleslaw, Gibby's wonderful biscuits, and apple pie for dessert.

She'd helped Gibby mix the coleslaw last night and she had to admit that it had been fun to bury her squeaky-clean hands in the twenty-gallon drums filled with shredded cabbage. It had reminded her of playing in the sandbox as a child and making mud pies. She'd giggled like a kid as she'd dived into the drum with her fingers and tossed the cabbage with Gibby's homemade dressing. She had been having a wonderful time until Dane had stuck his head into the kitchen. Just the sight of him had reminded her of what she had lost, and she'd had all she could do to keep the friendly smile on her face.

"How's it coming, Gibby?" Caitlyn spotted Gibby by one of the pits, and she walked over to join him.

Gibby shoved the heavy screen over the pit again. "Everything's fine. I figure we're gonna get over two hundred, countin' the guests and our boys."

"That many?" Caitlyn was surprised. Gibby had told her all about the barbecue and dance, but she'd had no idea it would be this big. The annual party had been Aunt Bella's way of thanking the town of Little Fork and the people who lived on the neighboring ranches for helping her to make the Double B Ranch a success. When Dane had asked if she wanted to continue the tradition, Caitlyn had agreed immediately. There was no reason to change things just because Aunt Bella wasn't here. They still relied on the good will of their neighbors and the folks from Little Fork.

"How about the fiddlers? Did they come in yet?" Gibby asked.

"They're already setting up," Caitlyn said. "Are they any good?"

"They're the best this side of the Rockies." Gibby flashed her a grin. "Maybe on both sides of the Rockies, for all I know. Folks around here just love 'em. Bella drew up a contract, and we hire 'em for this big shindig every year."

"Is there anything I can do to help you?"

Gibby shook his head. "I got everythin' under control out here. You should go find Lisa. She just came by here lookin' for you, and I told her you were probably inside gettin' spiffied up."

"I'd better go find her." Caitlyn scanned the yard. "Did she say what she wanted?"

"Nope, but she was totin' a big box and she said it was for you. I asked her, but she wouldn't tell me what was inside."

With a wave, Caitlyn headed back to the ranch house. She knew that some of the neighboring women brought food to the party, even though it wasn't potluck. It was just their way of contributing something, and Gibby said he always got jars of homemade pickles and other preserves. But if Lisa's mother had sent her here with food, she would have left it with Gibby.

Perhaps it was something for the tables. Caitlyn pushed open the back door to her quarters. Lisa had said that her mother always planted a big flower garden. They'd ordered flowers from the florist in Laramie, but they could always use more.

"Miz Bradford? Wait up a minute." Lisa came around the corner. "I'm glad I caught you." The pretty teenager thrust a large, flat box into her arms.

"Is this something for the party?" Caitlyn asked.

"Yes, but it's just for you. You'd better open it. I have to make sure I did everything right."

"Come in." Caitlyn led the way into her rooms. "You didn't have to give me a present, Lisa."

"I know I didn't have to, but I wanted to. And it was Mr. Morrison's idea. Are you going to open it now?"

"I can hardly wait." Caitlyn set the box on her bed, the only surface large enough to hold it. She lifted the lid, folded back the tissue paper, and gasped as she saw the beautiful green-and-white gingham dress that lay inside.

"Lisa!" Caitlyn turned to her in amazement. "It's absolutely gorgeous. But . . ."

"It's for you to wear to the party tonight. I made it. You'd better try it on, though. I had to guess at the size."

Caitlyn didn't need a second invitation. She pulled off her jeans and shirt and let Lisa help her into the dress. It fit perfectly. "You made this?" Caitlyn breathed, running her hand delightedly over the ruffles.

"Yes. Do you really like it, Miz Bradford?"

"I adore it." Caitlyn hugged her. "You just saved my life, Lisa. I thought I'd have to wear that awful blue silk again and stick out like a sore thumb. And now I get to wear the most beautiful dress at the party."

"Mr. Morrison. Wait up."

Dane turned to see Lisa hurrying down the path toward him. He stopped and waited for her to catch up with him, smiling as she ran the last few feet. "Hi, Lisa. All ready for the party?"

"Not yet, Mr. Morrison. Mom's bringing my clothes, and I'm going to dress here. I figured there might be some last minute things I could do if I stayed."

"A dedicated employee!" Dane whistled in admiration. "What did we do to deserve that?"

"Nothing. I like to help, that's all. I just came from Miz Bradford's room."

"Oh?" Dane kept his expression perfectly neutral, but his heart started to thud a lot faster in his chest. He was in big trouble if just hearing Caitlyn's name could do that.

"She just loved it, Mr. Morrison!"

Dane stared down at Lisa with a puzzled look. "Loved what?"

"The dress I made," Lisa explained. "Thanks for thinking of it, Mr. Morrison. It was the best present, ever!"

Dane found her excitement contagious. "It turned out all right, then?"

"Yes. She looks gorgeous in it. Just wait until you see her. She's going to be the prettiest one at the party."

"I expect she might be," Dane affirmed because Lisa seemed to expect it, but what he'd said was true. No one could come close to Caitlyn—not even if she wore her oversized jeans and a sweatshirt.

"Can I do anything for you, Mr. Morrison?"

Lisa looked eager, so Dane gave her something to do. "Sure. Why don't you go see if the band's ready to play."

"Okay. See you later, Mr. Morrison."

Lisa turned, ready to run back the way she'd come, but he stopped her with a hand on her arm. "One other thing, Lisa. Save a dance for me."

"You bet, Mr. Morrison."

Dane found his thoughts returning to Caitlyn. He supposed he should dance with her at the party tonight. It would look strange if he didn't. But how could he bear to hold her in his arms again? Just seeing her in the feminine dress that Lisa had made for her would test every ounce of restraint he possessed. If he held her close for a slow dance, feeling her body press close to his, he'd probably explode from sheer frustration.

Caitlyn had just finished dressing when there was a knock at her door. "Who is it?"

"Jeremy Campbell. I just dropped by to make your acquaintance."

The voice was deep, much deeper than Jerry's, and Caitlyn hurried to open the door. She smiled at the silver-haired man who stood there and motioned for him to come in. "Hello, Mr. Campbell. I'm so glad you came out here for the party."

"I almost didn't. Too many memories." Jeremy walked in and gazed around at the room. "You haven't changed a thing in here. It's just the way Bella left it."

Caitlyn nodded. "She had everything arranged perfectly, and it seemed silly to change it. Does it bother you, seeing it just the way it was when Aunt Bella was alive?"

"No. It's kind of nice, in a way. She was a good lady, your aunt."

"I know. That's what everyone says."

Curious, Caitlyn studied her visitor. Jeremy Campbell was a handsome man, and she could see why her aunt had been attracted to him. Though he was in his late sixties, he had a long lean body and he looked good in blue jeans. His Western-style silk shirt didn't show any extra bulges around his waist, and it was clear that he'd kept in good physical shape. "I just wish I'd known Aunt Bella better."

"She was worth knowing. Every once in a while, I think about what she'd say if she could see me now. She'd laugh her fool head off."

"She would?" Caitlyn felt a bit uncomfortable. Was Mr. Campbell referring to his memory lapses? And did he know that Dane had told her about them?

"Bella always said that if I kept working so hard, I'd wear out the engine and strip a couple of gears. She was right. Has that man of yours told you about the way I go out sometimes and mow my lawn in the middle of the night?"

Caitlyn was in a quandary. Should she admit that she knew about his strange behavior? Or should she lie? Opting for honesty, she nodded. "If you mean Dane, he . . . uh . . . he mentioned it once."

"Good. Then I don't have to explain it to you. Doesn't happen very often, just every couple of weeks or so. I figure the mayor ought to give me some kind of award for the best mowed lawn in town."

Caitlyn felt her tension disappearing. It was wonderful that Mr. Campbell could laugh at himself. "How's the refrigerator doing?"

"Fine, now that your man told Jerry to glue that dial in place. It was the strangest thing. I'd turn it off and not even remember that I'd done it. I guess things like this happen when a person gets older. I'm just sitting around waiting for the next strange thing to happen."

"At least your life's not boring."

Caitlyn regretted the words the moment they'd left her mouth. What if he didn't know that she was joking? But Mr. Campbell slapped his knee, delighted by her witticism.

"That's exactly what Bella would've said. You don't look anything like her, but you've got her sense of humor. That's good. Bella was never the type to cry over things that couldn't be helped. You know what she said to me on the night that she died?"

"No." Caitlyn held her breath. She hoped it wouldn't be sad.

"You need a little background before I can tell you. Otherwise, you won't catch the joke."

Caitlyn nodded. "Okay."

"We used to run a lot of races when we were kids, and everybody beat Bella. She was younger and her legs were shorter, so she'd always wind up as the rotten egg. She just hated being the rotten egg."

"The rotten egg?"

"Yes. That's what we called it in those days. One of us would yell out *The last one to the fence is a rotten egg* or *The last one in the water is a rotten egg.* Bella was always the rotten egg."

Caitlyn nodded again. "I understand."

"Well, right before she died, Bella squeezed my hand and said, *I'm getting there first, Jerry. This time you're the rotten egg.* I think that's a real nice way to go out, don't you?"

"Yes. Yes it is." Caitlyn blinked back a tear, but she was smiling. "I hope that she wasn't in much pain."

"Dane made sure that she wasn't. Bella didn't suffer once *he* took over. I just wish you'd been here for the shouting match he had with old Doc Henley."

"Dane had a fight with the doctor?"

"He sure did. They didn't exchange punches or anything like that, but I've never seen Dane so fired up."

Caitlyn frowned. "What did they fight about?"

"Drug addiction. You've got to understand that Doc Henley's from the old school. You must know the type. He refused to prescribe too many painkillers because he didn't want Bella to become addicted."

"But that's crazy!" Caitlyn objected. "Aunt Bella was dying."

"The doctors at the hospital said that she had terminal cancer with no possibility of a remission. Doc Henley saw the tests, but he still wouldn't change his mind."

"What did Dane do?" Caitlyn's voice was shaking. She'd always thought such a close-minded attitude was barbaric.

"He drove into the hospital and had a meeting with the doctor who'd diagnosed Bella. He must have been pretty persuasive, because he came back with all the drugs and equipment he needed to take care of Bella by himself. Then Bella told Doc Henley to stop coming out and Dane took care of her until the day she died."

"But isn't that illegal?" Caitlyn winced as she realized what she'd asked. Mr. Campbell was a lawyer.

"No, it's not. The doctor signed off on all the drugs. And Dane didn't do anything to hasten Bella's death; he just made damn sure that she didn't suffer. That makes it right in my book."

"Mine too," Caitlyn agreed. "I'm really glad that Dane was here and Aunt Bella didn't have to rely on Dr. Henley."

"Me, too. And that's enough talk for now." Mr. Campbell gave her what Caitlyn could only describe as a wolfish grin. "Come with me, missy. I'll walk you down to the party—if you promise to save me a dance."

Caitlyn grinned right back. "My pleasure. You can even have the first dance, if you want. Nobody else has asked me."

"They will." Jeremy was smiling as he took her arm. "Once the boys get a look at the likes of you, you'll be lucky if you don't wear the leather right off your shoes."

TWENTY-ONE

Caitlyn had seen the look of naked longing in Dane's eyes when he'd spotted her, and it had sent shivers up and down her spine. He still wanted her. There was no doubt in her mind about that. But Ida and Marilyn had been right. Dane was too stubborn to admit that he needed her. He was trying to tough it out, to ignore his feelings for her, and she would have to do something to make him react.

"You look as pretty as a picture tonight." Marilyn said approvingly as Caitlyn approached her. "Is that the dress that Lisa made for you?"

"Yes. Isn't it beautiful?" Caitlyn turned around so they could see how the skirt whirled out.

"It surely is," Ida declared. "And someone else noticed—in case you missed it. Dane's been watchin' you like a hawk on a mouse. You'd better do something fast before he decides to crawl off under the nearest bush and lick his wounds."

"I will." Caitlyn ignored the mixed metaphors and exchanged grins with the two ranch women. "Wish me luck."

"You won't need it," Marilyn teased. "You already got him roped. Now all you got to do is wrestle him down and tie him up good."

Caitlyn took a deep breath and set out across the dance floor. Jake had just finished dancing and he was leaning against the wall, talking to Jessie and Sam.

"Hi, Jake." Caitlyn arrived at his side slightly breathless. "I haven't danced with you yet. How about it?"

"Uh . . . sure, Miz Bradford."

It was clear that he didn't want to dance with her, and Caitlyn almost took back her invitation. But then she saw him glancing toward Dane and she understood his reluctance.

"Come here, Jake." Caitlyn pulled him away from the other ranch hands and found a deserted spot by one of the tables. "I know why you don't want to dance with me and I don't blame you. But that's also the reason why I really need your help."

Jake's brown eyes widened in surprise. "How's that, Miz Bradford?"

"I need to make Dane jealous. He's just sitting on the fence when it comes to me, and I've got to make him decide whether he wants to fish or cut bait." Caitlyn winced. Mixed metaphors again. She must be catching it from Ida and Marilyn. "You understand, don't you, Jake?"

Jake nodded. "Yup. We all know he's got a problem when it comes to you. But makin' Dane jealous might be playin' with fire. Are you dead sure you know what you're doing?"

"No, I'm not. But it's the only thing I can think of to do." Caitlyn sighed deeply. "He's miserable. And I'm miserable, too. I've got to do something."

"Guess you do, at that," Jake conceded. "Okay, I'll help you out. But you got to make sure he doesn't up and fire me for hittin' on his gal."

"He can't fire you. We've both got to agree before we fire anyone. And I'll never agree to fire you."

"Okay." Jake flashed her a grin. "Are you sure the insurance is paid up?"

"Insurance? What insurance?" Caitlyn was confused.

"The medical insurance." Jake's grin grew wider. "If I make this look the way you want it to look, he's likely to break my jaw."

Dane's mouth dropped open in shock. What was she doing with Jake? He couldn't believe that Caitlyn was dancing with Jake . . . after he'd warned her. She was asking for trouble, and he sure wouldn't be the one to bail her out. Not this time. She was on her own, and he sure as hell hoped she knew what she was doing.

"Hey, Dane. How about a dance?"

Dane whirled and came face-to-face with Shawna, Mayor Wellesby's only daughter. She was dressed in a low-cut red dress that looked as if it had been sewn on her. He'd gone out with Shawna a few times, between her second and her third marriage. They'd had an understanding. Neither one of them had wanted to get serious. They'd had a lot of fun before Shawna had found a rich man to marry and they'd called it quits, no hard feelings on either side. "Don't tell me you're divorced again, Shawna!"

"Okay. I won't tell you." She glanced up at him in that sexy way she had, and Dane was surprised to find that it didn't affect him anymore. He'd always experienced an instant heat when she'd smiled like that in the past.

"So? You want to dance?"

Dane led her onto the floor—even though he didn't really want to waste his time with Shawna Wellesby. "Okay. One dance and then I've got some things I have to do."

He was dancing with the most desirable woman she had ever seen, a sexy brunette in a red dress that clung to her curves like a second skin. Caitlyn moved a little closer to Jake and whispered in his ear. "Who's that?"

"Shawna. She's Mayor Wellesby's daughter. Dane went out with her a couple of years back, before she got married."

Caitlyn glared at the stunning brunette. She was dancing so close to Dane, a paper plate couldn't have fit between their bodies. "Where's her husband?"

"Oh, she's probably divorced by now." Jake shrugged. "Shawna never stays married to any of her husbands for more than a year. Most of the folks around here think she wears them out."

Caitlyn's eyes turned to green icicles. "And Dane dated a woman like that?"

"Well, not exactly. Maybe *dated* isn't the right word."

"I see," Caitlyn fumed. She didn't have to be a rocket scientist to read the meaning behind Jake's words. "Hold me closer, Jake. And put your hand a little lower."

"But Miz Bradford . . . I'm no coward, but don't you think that's kinda dangerous? I mean, Dane's been starin' at us and all, and his face is beginnin' to get red."

"Good. That's the general idea. Dance me a little closer to them."

Jake gave in with obvious reluctance. "You're the boss, Miz Bradford. You promise to spring for some flowers for my funeral?"

"There isn't going to be any funeral"—Caitlyn's eyes glittered—"unless it's hers. Come on, Jake. You promised to help me."

Jake hesitated a moment longer and then he gave her a grin. "Okay, Miz Bradford. Here goes nothin'."

"What's the matter with you, Dane? You're positively glowering."

Dane tore his eyes away from Jake and Caitlyn and looked down at Shawna. "Sorry. I've just got something else on my mind, that's all."

"Does it have anything to do with the redhead in the green-and-white dress?"

Dane shook his head, but he felt the red beginning to creep up the back of his neck. Jake should know better than to put his hand *there*.

"So that's the way the wind blows." Shawna held him even closer. "Okay, hot shot. Let's cut in on them."

"What?" Dane turned his attention to the woman in his arms. What was she suggesting?

"I've known you too long to play games with you, Dane." Shawna gave him her sexiest smile. "Haven't you learned anything from me? If you want something, you've got to get out there and grab it."

Dane took a deep, shuddering breath. "I don't . . . uh . . . that's not such a good idea, Shawna."

"What's wrong with you, Dane? I've never seen you act shy before. It must be love. Nothing else can do that to a man."

"No. Of course it isn't. It's just that . . . what are you doing, Shawna?"

Shawna took several quick steps to the side, reaching out to grab Jake's arm before Dane could stop her. "Hey, Jake. You look mighty handsome tonight. Let's switch partners so I can teach you all those things you never learned in school."

Caitlyn gasped as Jake shoved her into Dane's arms and danced off with Shawna. "Dane! I . . . I guess we should go and sit down or something."

"Nope. Everybody's watching to see what we're going to do."

Dane's arms closed around her, and Caitlyn felt a moment of panic. He made her want to snuggle up to him, to pull his face down and force him to kiss her, to . . .

"I think we'd better dance."

His voice interrupted her train of thought, and Caitlyn gave a grateful sigh. "Yes. I guess it would look strange if we didn't."

And then they were dancing, moving to the slow beat of the music, their bodies barely touching. His eyes were hard as he stared down at her, and Caitlyn felt miserable. Being in Dane's arms like this was almost worse than not dancing with him at all.

"What the hell were you doing with Jake?"

His voice was sharp, and Caitlyn felt a surge of elation. She'd succeeded in making him jealous. But he wasn't giving an inch, and she had to do something to make him really look at her. He was staring at a point about six inches over her head.

"I was just dancing." Caitlyn was proud of herself. Her voice was steady and she'd actually managed to sound casual. "Jake's a very attractive guy."

"He's wrong for you."

Yes, he was definitely jealous. And now she had to use his jealousy to her advantage. Caitlyn tried to look much more self-assured than she felt. It wouldn't do to let him know that she was melting inside just from the touch of his arm around her waist. "Would you rather that I danced with someone else?"

"Yes."

Caitlyn shivered. He really was irate. She hoped she hadn't carried things too far. "Okay. Who would you suggest?"

He was silent, as tightly wound as a spring and as unreachable as the peaks of the mountains. And the music was ending. She had to do something fast. Without a thought about how it would look or whether or not he'd catch her, Caitlyn stumbled, lurching to the side. "Ouch!"

"What's wrong?"

His arms tightened around her, and Caitlyn knew she had the advantage. "It's my ankle. I think I sprained it."

"Just lean on me." His voice was softer now, more caring. "Let's get you over to a chair and have a look at it."

Caitlyn shook her head. He'd be able to tell that there was nothing wrong with her ankle. "No. Please, Dane, will you just help me back to my room? I don't want to spoil the party when everybody's having such a good time. I'll put on an ice pack and it'll be just fine."

"Okay. Sure." Solicitous, he helped her from the dance floor. "Can you put any weight on it at all?"

Caitlyn pretended to wince as she stepped down. "No. I don't think I can. You don't suppose I broke it, do you?"

"I doubt it, but sprains can be painful. I'd better carry you."

"Yes." That was exactly what she'd been hoping he'd say. Caitlyn averted her gaze as he lifted her up into his strong arms. Snuggling up to him, she sighed, hooking her arms around his neck. "I'm terribly sorry, Dane."

"That's all right. You didn't hurt yourself on purpose. Just hang on, and I'll have you in bed before you know it."

I'll have you in bed before you know it? Why had he said that? Dane sighed as he carried her up the path to the ranch house, her body so sweet in his arms. His shrink friends would have called it a Freudian slip and he supposed it was. All he'd been thinking of was taking her to bed and quenching the fires she'd awakened in him. How could he possibly remain cool and aloof when her delightfully warm body was pressing against his?

"Am I too heavy?"

Her voice was trembling and he smiled down at her. "Nope. You're not heavy at all. Did you lock your back door?"

"No." She shook her head, her hair brushing against his cheek like perfumed silk. "I couldn't have. I left that way, and it's a deadbolt from the inside. And I left the light on. I'm sure of that."

Dane didn't say any more. He just held her, carrying her forward in the moonlight. There was a hint of autumn in the wind, and the air smelled clean and fresh. A wolf howled in the distance, and there was an answering cry, much closer. She shivered, and he looked down to find that her eyes were wide. "Are you cold?"

"No. I just heard the wolves."

"The wolves won't hurt you. There's never been a recorded instance of a wolf attacking a person."

"I know, but they sound so eerie, out there in the dark."

Was she crying? Dane glanced down and saw a trail of glistening tears on her cheeks. "Caitlyn. Is your ankle that bad?"

"No."

He gazed down at her with worried eyes. Caitlyn wasn't the type to cry. He'd seen her thrown from a horse, pulled into the lake, and almost attacked by a cougar. And through it all, she hadn't cried. "What's wrong, Caitlyn?"

"I don't know. Everything, I guess." Her voice was shaking as he reached her back door and opened it. "It's just that everything is so . . . so awful!"

Dane carried her to the bed and sat down on the edge, still holding her in his arms. He was on dangerous ground. He wanted to protect her, to dry her tears and comfort her. Every instinct told him to leave her and run before he got any more involved than he already was. But he couldn't do that. She looked too vulnerable and she needed him.

He took a deep breath and smoothed back her hair, holding her as he would hold a frightened child. And then he said the words that might seal his fate and bind him to her forever. "Please don't cry, honey. Maybe it'll help if you tell me about it."

TWENTY-TWO

He'd called her *honey,* and Caitlyn felt so guilty, she couldn't stand it anymore. Everything she'd done tonight had been a lie. She'd practically forced Jake into helping her make Dane jealous; she'd pretended to hurt her ankle so that he would carry her away from the crowd and back to her room, and now she was pretending that the wolves had frightened her. The wolves hadn't alarmed her at all. She thought their howls in the night were wild and beautiful. But she *was* frightened. That wasn't a lie. She was frightened of the person that she had become, the scheming and deceptive woman who'd tried to trap Dane into loving her.

"Honey?"

He looked down at her, and Caitlyn lost every bit of her resolve. She couldn't lie to the man she loved, even if telling the truth meant she'd lose him. She took a deep breath and blurted it out, all of it, not even caring that her words were jumbled and might not make sense.

"It was Ida and Marilyn's idea. They saw how miserable I was and they wanted to help me. Jake, too. He was only trying to help and he said that you were miserable, too. I can't live this way any longer. It's just not right. I can't leave and I can't stay. I don't know what to do."

"You didn't hurt your ankle?"

Was his voice still soft, or had she imagined it? Caitlyn wasn't sure. But it didn't matter whether he ended up hating her. She couldn't deceive him any longer. "My ankle's fine. And I wasn't afraid of the wolves. I was just afraid that I'd lose you and . . . and that's all."

"I make that much difference to you?"

"Yes." Caitlyn took a deep shuddering breath. "When you see me and you look away, I want to scream. And I want you all the time—here, like this, with me. I don't care if you don't love me. I just want you anyway."

He held her even tighter; and when he spoke, his voice was strangled, as if he were forcing out the words. "I want you, too. Ida and Marilyn were right. I'm just as miserable as you are. What are we going to do about it, honey? I'm not free to love you. There's someone else, and I can't get her out of my mind."

"You . . . you love someone else?" Caitlyn shivered. She was suddenly as cold as ice, even though he was still holding her.

"Yes. She's gone. I lost her five years ago."

"Will she . . . is there any chance that she'll . . . come back?"

"No." He shook his head, and Caitlyn saw the despair in his eyes. "But I still love her. I can't stop loving her. Can you understand that?"

Caitlyn nodded. "Yes. I understand. And I don't care. Do you . . . do you love me a little?"

"I love you a lot, but I can never give you everything you want. That's why it's not fair to you if we—"

"The hell with fair!" Caitlyn interrupted him before he could say more. "I don't care about fair. We can't be here together and stay apart like two strangers. It just doesn't work . . . for either one of us."

He nodded. "I know. But I can never marry you, Caitlyn. Or give you what you want."

"Then I'll take what you can give me." Caitlyn reached up to wrap her arms around his neck. "And it'll be enough, I promise."

"Dane . . . please?"

Her voice was soft, pleading with him, and he wanted her with every fiber of his being. They had a right to grab what happiness they could. Life was bleak without her. With her, it could be warm and loving, sustaining them both.

Dane groaned deep in his throat and lowered his lips to hers, thrusting his tongue into her mouth with a promise of things to come. And he felt as if she'd given him a precious gift as her lips and tongue welcomed him home, where he belonged.

"Again?" Caitlyn laughed; and as she reached out to touch him, she noticed that the sky was lightening. Morning already. And they hadn't slept. But she needed him more than sleep. She could sleep some other time. The moments they had together were priceless, and she didn't want to waste them in sleep.

She tried to roll over, to mold her body to his, but he held her captive. "No. Stay there, baby. I want to love you this way."

And then he was in her, hard and demanding, holding her tightly and driving himself so deeply inside her that he touched her very core. She cried out, thrusting herself back against the part of him that gave her so much pleasure. There was a moment when she thought that she would die, trembling on the brink of an abyss. But he held her so tightly, she couldn't fall; and with a mighty thrust his life poured into her, blazing with white heat until she exploded from pure joy.

They slept then, his arms still around her, his body still pressed to hers, until the bright rays of sun turned her red curtains to fire and the birds sang their morning songs in a cacophony of sound that would have roused even the soundest of sleepers. She heard his deep breathing change, almost imperceptibly, and she knew that he was awake. He was still inside her and she squeezed herself tightly around him, a tightening that brought an immediate response. And then he was moving inside her—slowly, at first, and then faster with smooth strokes of soft morning love that brought tears of happiness to her eyes. She felt languid, soft, utterly feminine as he caressed her tenderly. She sighed, floating on a warm wet wave in a current that carried her farther and farther from the bed, the room, even their place in time. It was endless pleasure, lapping against a golden shore, until they reached nirvana. She gloried in the sensation, opening herself to him completely and loving him with every shuddering breath she took.

"Caitlyn. Darling." His words were soft against her ear. "It's morning."

She smiled, reaching back to touch his dear face. "I know."

"You don't have to get up. I'll handle breakfast."

"Without me?" Her grin grew wider. "No way. I love the mornings with you. I'll get up, too."

There was a pause, and then he chuckled. "I thought you hated mornings."

"I did." She rolled away from him, the hardest thing she'd ever done, and sat up to greet the day. "You changed my mind. If every day can start like this, I'm going to love getting up in the morning."

Of course everyone knew. Caitlyn lowered her eyes as she sat down at the table with her morning cup of coffee. Gibby was whistling, Jake was grinning, and even Jessie was staring at them with a curious but approving smile on his face.

"You think they know?" Dane pulled out a chair and sat down next to her, slipping his arm around her shoulders.

"Yup." Caitlyn grinned up at him. "And I think it's okay."

As the guests began to come in, it was clear they noticed that something was different. Several of the women remarked that it was good to see Caitlyn looking so happy, and a businessman from Phoenix came up to clap Dane on the shoulder and say it was good to see him smiling for a change. The breakfast was fun; and when it was over and the guests had gone back to their rooms to pack their belongings, Caitlyn slipped down to the laundry to see Ida and Marilyn.

"It must've worked." Ida greeted her with a grin. "Just look at you!"

Marilyn nodded. "Haven't seen you smile like that in a long while."

"Like what?" Caitlyn's smile grew wider.

"Like a woman who's just had a whole lot of a good thing." Marilyn surveyed her, winking at Ida. "Did you work out your differences?"

"Yes. We did."

"We saw you leaving with him," Ida spoke up. "Looked like your ankle was hurtin' real bad."

"It wasn't too bad."

"I get it," Marilyn said in a loud aside to her sister. "She was fakin' so she could get him back to her room."

Ida raised her brows. "And it worked?"

"Perfectly."

"Well, he must've cured what ailed you, 'cause you sure ain't limpin' now," Ida remarked. "And he didn't even get into it with Jake. I saw him this mornin' and he was still walkin'. You want to give us the details?"

Caitlyn shook her head, grinning all the while. "I think I'll keep them to myself."

"That's even better," Marilyn deemed. "It must've been somthin' if you don't even want to talk about it."

"It was. And thanks for helping me."

Caitlyn gave each of the women a hug and then she walked out of the laundry. The sun was golden, the sky was blue, the clouds were fleecy white, and she knew she'd never seen such a perfect day in her whole life.

"So are you gonna marry that gal, or what?" Gibby hoisted himself up on the fence beside Dane.

"She's not asking for anything like that."

"Doesn't matter. I figure you ought to marry her anyway, and so do the boys. None of us ever saw you this happy before, not even when you used to come back from seein' Shawna. You can't let a good thing like this get away from you."

"She's not going anywhere, and neither am I," Dane said good-humoredly.

"Better keep an eye on her then. She's a mighty pretty woman, and you might have some competition on your hands."

"From you?" Dane gave Gibby a teasing grin.

"Me?" Gibby looked so shocked, Dane laughed. "Not on your life! I'm a bachelor and I'm proud of it. But twenty years ago, I might've given you a run for your money."

"She's something, isn't she?" Dane couldn't help but ask. "You don't think the boys will treat her any different, now that we're together, do you?"

"No." Gibby shook his head and then he laughed. "They're all just glad you're back to normal again. Ain't none of 'em gonna interfere with that."

It had been a long day, and Caitlyn was tired. Her lack of sleep was beginning to catch up with her, and she noticed that Dane looked tired, too. When the last of the new guests had gone up to their rooms, she turned to him with a smile. "Are you ready to turn in, Mr. Morrison?"

"Yup. How about you?"

Caitlyn nodded. "I can hardly wait to get into bed."

"Me, either."

The grin he gave her made Caitlyn blush. How could he have so much energy? Between the two of them, they couldn't have gotten more than an hour's sleep.

"Your place or mine?"

He was still grinning, and Caitlyn felt a warm rush of pleasure. He wanted to spend the night with her. Again. "Mine, I guess. My bed's bigger than yours, isn't it?"

"Yours is a double. Mine's just a single."

Caitlyn pushed down the urge to ask him about the other women in his life. Had he always gone to their place? Then she decided that she really didn't want to know. That was then. This was now. "Do you think we should get a larger bed?"

Why had she asked that? Caitlyn mentally berated herself. What if he thought that buying furniture together was some type of commitment? He might think that she was pushing him into a closer, more intimate relationship. But he was still grinning and she felt that he'd given her a reprieve.

"That's a great idea. We'll send Jake out with the guests and drive into Laramie tomorrow. Do you like waterbeds?"

Caitlyn shrugged. "I don't know. I've never slept in one. Aren't they really . . . uh . . . bouncy?"

"They used to be. I haven't slept in a waterbed since I was in medi . . . uh . . . Medina, Kansas."

She noticed his hesitation and wondered what he'd been about to say. Somehow she didn't think he wanted her to ask, so she didn't. "Is there a waterbed store in Laramie?"

"Probably. Do you want to go?"

"Sure," she responded promptly. "It'll be fun."

"We'll leave as soon as the guests are gone. It shouldn't take long, and we can stop off at the cafe in Little Fork on the way back. I need to make sure you eat right. You're losing weight on me again."

"Just a couple of pounds. What's the matter? Are you afraid I'll get sick on you?"

The expression on his face made her wish she hadn't asked that question. It was so sad, it nearly brought tears to her eyes. "Yeah. Maybe I am."

"Well, I won't." She longed to erase the unhappiness that lurked in the depths of his blue eyes. "I'm as healthy as a horse, maybe even as healthy as Warrior."

"Good." He changed the subject back abruptly. "About the bed—do you want queen-sized or king-sized?"

"King. Definitely king." She contemplated all the room they'd have for . . .

"More room for fun?"

He finished her thought before she could say it. "Right. You must have read my mind."

"That's impossible. We were just thinking along the same lines. Come on, honey, I'm plumb tuckered out. I might even fall asleep the minute my head hits the pillow."

"Really?" She looked up at him with a teasing expression and licked her lips.

"Then again, maybe not." He grabbed her around the waist and lifted her up into his arms. "I like the way this worked out last night. What do you say we make a practice of it?"

"That's fine with me." Caitlyn raised her arms and hooked them around his neck. And then she cuddled up and kissed the hollow below his throat. As he walked down the hall, carrying her in his strong arms, she felt like the happiest, the luckiest, and the most cherished woman in the world.

TWENTY-THREE

The past three weeks had been heaven on earth. Caitlyn studied her reflection in the mirror with satisfaction. She'd gained some weight—not much, just a couple of pounds, but he'd been so pleased with her. Weight loss was a red flag with him for some reason. He equated it with serious sickness. Jeremy Campbell had said that Aunt Bella had lost a lot of weight when she'd gotten sick, and perhaps that was the reason why Dane was so touchy about it.

Illness was another one of his buttons, and Caitlyn was careful not to push it. One morning when she awakened with a headache, she'd asked him to get her some aspirin. He'd been so worried and he'd asked her so many questions, she'd decided then and there that she'd have to be plenty sick before she'd mention it to him. She hadn't said a word about the flu she'd caught a couple of days ago. It hadn't lasted long—a little queasiness in the mornings and then it had gone away. That hadn't surprised her. She'd always had marvelous resistance to the minor epidemics that had gone through the office. The people around her could be sniffling and coughing, but usually she'd escaped with no symptoms at all.

This morning was no different. She felt wonderful, on top of the world. She tied a green ribbon around her braid, giving her outfit a perky touch to match her carefree demeanor.

Dane had gotten up early, something about checking on one of the horses who'd come up lame on the trail. He was the Double B's unofficial veterinarian. The boys called him in whenever one of the animals had a problem. If Dane couldn't fix them up, they had to call in the vet from Laramie; but that didn't happen very often. He'd told her that he had been raised on a ranch and he'd learned how to doctor livestock from his father.

Caitlyn swallowed the lump that suddenly rose to her throat. She felt queasy again for the fifth day running, and she was glad that Dane had left early. Her stomach churned at the thought of strong black coffee, and she reached into her dresser drawer for the stash of crackers that she kept there. Munching on one seemed to settle her stomach.

A couple of minutes later, she felt much better and the thought of coffee was palatable again. She straightened the quilt on the king-sized waterbed they'd bought in Laramie and went out the back door to find Dane. It was Sunday morning. She had to say goodbye to the guests that were leaving and enjoy one more breakfast with them. Then, if they were lucky and no crisis reared its ugly head, she'd have several hours to be alone with Dane before the new bunch of guests arrived.

Dane leaned back against the padded headboard. "I feel like a slacker, being here in bed in the middle of the day."

"I don't think anybody could call you a slacker," Caitlyn protested as she rolled over next to him. "I'm so content, I don't ever want to get up."

"But it's time and we have to." Dane pulled her close for one more kiss before sitting on the edge of the bed. Then he got to his feet and came around the bed to pull Caitlyn up. "Come on, honey. We have to get dressed. Our guests will be here in less than an hour."

Caitlyn slipped into his arms. "Is there time for a shower?"

"Only if you take it alone. If we get into the shower together, we won't get downstairs tonight."

"You got that right, cowboy."

Caitlyn dashed for the shower, making short work of it. When she came out, Dane went in, and less than twenty minutes later, they were both dressed and ready to go out.

"You know what I love about you?" Dane stared down at her.

"No. What?" Caitlyn held her breath, hoping he wouldn't realize that he'd used the word *love*. It was another of his touchy subjects, and she'd learned not to ask him anything about love.

"You can get ready in two shakes of a lamb's tail," he replied proudly.

"I'm fast. And so are you, cowboy, except for the times when I don't want you to hurry."

"And when would that be?"

"I think you know." Caitlyn giggled softly. "But if you don't, I'll show you tonight, after the new guests go to bed."

Caitlyn's best welcoming smile vanished in an instant when a beautiful woman with shining blond hair hurtled herself into Dane's arms.

"Oh, Dane! It's so good to see you."

"It's good to see you, too, Julia." Dane kissed the woman's cheek and gave her a hug before he turned to introduce them. "Caitlyn, this is Julia McAlister. She's a friend of mine."

Caitlyn shook the woman's hand. "It's good to meet you. Welcome to the Double B Ranch, Mrs. McAlister."

"Oh, please call me Julia. I took my maiden name back after the divorce, and Ms. McAlister is too much of a mouthful. I'm so sorry about your aunt. Dane called right after it happened. Bella was such a wonderful woman."

Caitlyn nodded. "Yes, she was. You've been here before . . . Julia?"

"I've been coming out here every year since Dane took this job."

"Julia and I are like family," Dane explained.

"Then I'm very glad you're here." Caitlyn remained polite despite her unanswered questions. What was going on? Dane looked guilty and he wasn't meeting her eyes. Was Julia an old girlfriend? She and Dane were certainly affectionate. Determined to show Dane she trusted him, Caitlyn forced herself not to appear jealous. "I'll let the two of you catch up," she suggested, moving in the direction of another newly arrived guest. "Why don't you show Julia to her room, Dane?"

Dane's eyebrows shot up, but he took her up on her offer. "Good idea," he said. "I'll be back in a minute."

"There's no hurry." Caitlyn felt a surge of pride at how confident she sounded. "I can take care of things down here."

As Caitlyn walked down the steps, she couldn't help glancing back. And she felt a current of jealousy flow through her whole body as Dane put his arm around Julia's shoulders and led her into the ranch house.

"The new guests seem nice."

"I think it's a good group." Dane felt a moment's uneasiness as he climbed into bed with Caitlyn. There was tension in her voice that he'd never heard before.

"You said that Julia was like family. Have you known her long?"

There it was again, that underlying nuance that put him on the alert. "I met Julia when I started first grade. She lived on a neighboring ranch."

"Then she's your age?"

Dane nodded. The nuance was gone, and he breathed a sigh of relief.

"She mentioned that she was divorced."

"That's right." Dane frowned. What would happen if he told Caitlyn the truth, just laid it all out and bared his heart for the first time since he'd told Bella? But he couldn't do that. It was a secret that he'd kept for too long. Maybe he could tell her someday, but not now. "Julia just got divorced. Her marriage didn't last long, a little over a year."

"Oh. That's too bad."

"I guess you could say that Julia's the closest thing to a sister I ever had." There. That ought to relieve her mind. If she knew that he thought of Julia as a sister, she wouldn't be as concerned.

"You never talk much about your family."

"There's not much to say." This new subject still dredged up painful memories, but it put them on safer ground. "I had one brother, but Mom died giving birth to him and he only lived for a week. Congenital heart failure. For a long time, it was just Hank and me. And then Hank died right after I started my junior year in high school."

"So you were all alone?

"Yes." Dane pushed aside the memory of how lonely he'd felt. There had been only one time that was worse, and that was after Beth died.

"What did you do?"

Her voice was soft with sympathy, and it made Dane feel better. She really cared about what had happened to him all those years ago. "The McAlisters took me in so I could finish high school. There was a little money left after we sold the ranch and paid off Hank's bills, but they wouldn't take a penny of it. They just told me to help out while I lived with them and save it for college."

"And you did?"

"Yes. It was enough for tuition and books. I worked full time and I got by."

"I guess I had a free ride, compared to you." She nestled closer to him. "My parents paid for everything—tuition, books, my dorm. I didn't *have* to work at all."

"But you did?" Dane was curious.

"Yes. I wanted to help out, to pay them back somehow. I sent them part of my paycheck every month."

"And the rest?"

"I blew it on movies. There was an old movie theater right around the corner from the dorm that showed nothing but Westerns. My roommate Amy and I were crazy about them. We saw *The Searchers* so many times, we could say the dialogue right along with John Wayne, but our favorite was *Butch Cassidy and the Sundance Kid*. Amy was wild about Robert Redford. She had posters of him all over our room."

"How about you?" Dane pressed.

"Redford was okay, but I preferred Paul Newman. I've always been partial to men with dark hair and blue eyes."

A smile tugged at the corners of Dane's mouth. He had dark hair and blue eyes. "How about your ex-husband? Did he have dark hair?"

"No." She sounded surprised. "His hair was light."

"You made an exception in his case?"

"I guess so. It's really strange. I never thought about it before."

"Well, how about that?" Dane gave her an easy grin. "I guess you're in luck, because I always preferred women with red hair. There's something very sexy about a redhead."

She giggled. "You mean you don't have a wife out there with blond hair?"

"Actually . . ." Dane paused, gearing himself up for a partial confession. "I did. Once."

"You were married?"

"Yes." She pulled away slightly so she could see his face, and Dane almost groaned. Why had he even brought up the subject? But he had, and he owed her the truth. "My wife was blond."

"And she's the woman that you still love?"

Bingo. He should have known she'd zero in on that. "Yes."

"You don't want to talk about it, though."

"No. Not now." Dane pulled her into his arms and buried his face against her neck. At first he thought she was going to resist him, to ask more questions. But she didn't. She just snuggled closer and reached up to stroke his hair.

"How about if I take your mind off anybody but me?"

Her tone was light and teasing, and Dane gave a grateful sigh. That was one thing he really loved about her. She knew when to keep quiet. "You think you can?"

"Yes."

She laughed and then she slid down the length of him, blazing a trail with her lips. And all his painful memories of Beth disappeared with the magic of her tongue and her lips.

Caitlyn and Julia rode back into the corral together. All her fears had been laid to rest, and now she couldn't understand why she'd ever been jealous. Julia was friendly and very nice. Caitlyn actually liked her. And over the past three days, she'd never treated Dane like anything other than a loving brother.

"That was fun." Julia dismounted expertly and handed the reins to one of the ranch hands. "What do we do tonight, Caitlyn?"

Caitlyn grinned as she slid off Nanny's back, a little less gracefully than Julia, who'd admitted that she'd learned to ride almost as soon as she'd learned to walk. "There's a big barbecue and then we're going to have square dance lessons."

"For the party on Saturday night?"

"That's right." Caitlyn led Julia down the path to the ranch house. "How do you feel about barbecued ribs, barbecued beans, and corn-on-the-cob?"

"Sounds great," Julia enthused. "Forget the calories. I'm on vacation. I'll go on a diet when I get back."

"But you're not too heavy," Caitlyn observed. Julia's figure was perfect.

"That's what Dane always says. He told me my hipbones were too sharp. He's spent years trying to convince me that I should put a little meat on my bones."

Caitlyn felt a moment's unease. That was the very thing that Dane had said to her. Exactly how did Dane know that Julia's hipbones were too sharp?

"Is Gibby making those incredible biscuits of his, just dripping with butter?"

"Of course." Caitlyn forced a smile. "It wouldn't be a barbecue without them."

Julia grinned. "Good. I'm starving and I can hardly wait. What time is dinner?"

"Six." Caitlyn couldn't help the sharp note that crept into her voice, but Julia didn't seem to notice.

"I've been meaning to ask you. Are you in love with Dane?"

Julia was staring at her with a perfectly innocent expression, and Caitlyn wasn't sure how she should answer. Of course she was in love with Dane. But should she admit it to the woman he said he thought of as a sister? "Actually, things haven't really gone that far yet. I'd really rather not answer that."

"Okay." Julia didn't take offense. Instead, she leaned toward Caitlyn and offered advice. "If you are, I wouldn't tell him. Dane tends to run from any kind of commitment. Believe me, I know."

They were nearing the ranch house, and there wasn't any time for further conversation. Once they'd entered and walked toward the stairs, Julia turned to her again. "I'm going to go up to my room to take a shower. I'd invite you to come up, but I really feel like just being alone and relaxing for a while."

"Okay. I'll see you later, when you come down for the barbecue." Caitlyn found herself even more confused about Julia than ever. How had Julia known that Dane tended to run away from commitment? There was one way that occurred to her immediately, but Caitlyn didn't even want to think about that.

"Where's Julia?" Dane looked around at the crowded tables.

"She's here somewhere," Caitlyn said casually. "She was sitting with Jake just a couple of minutes ago. They were sharing a beer."

Dane began to frown. "Julia was *drinking?*"

"Yes. And they were flirting a little, but they're both single and they seem to like each other. What's wrong with that?"

"Plenty! Jake's got no brains when it comes to women, and it's a sure bet he won't take care of Julia."

Caitlyn tried to be reasonable. "But surely Julia knows how to take care of herself. And I can't believe that Jake would force her to do something she didn't want to do. Why are you so upset?"

"You don't understand. I told you that Julia and I go way back. It's up to me to look out for her. And drinking with Jake is the worst possible thing she could do."

"Okay," Caitlyn said reasonably. "I know that she's like your sister. You told me that. But I still think that you're making a mountain out of a mole—"

"I've got to find Jake." Dane interrupted her, shoving back his chair. "I need to set him straight."

"About what?"

"About Julia. She could be in real danger if she's been drinking with Jake."

Caitlyn stared after him as he strode through the crowd. His steps were determined, and there was a fierce expression on his face. One of Ida's favorite phrases flashed through Caitlyn's mind. Dane looked as mad as a wet hen. But why was he so upset that Julia and Jake had been having a little innocent fun together?

Jake wasn't married, and neither was Julia. Perhaps Dane was just being overprotective of his *sister,* but Caitlyn had the sinking feeling that he was jealous of Julia's little flirtation with Jake.

"Caitlyn? What's a *do-si-do?"* Claire Benson, a first-time guest, came up to her table with her husband in tow. "Howard says it's like a swing, but I don't think that's it."

Caitlyn spent several minutes explaining square dance terms to Claire and her husband, promising that they'd practice once the barbecue was over. Then another guest came up with a question about horseshoes and she answered that, too. She was so busy, she didn't even notice when Dane came back. When he reached out to touch her arm, she looked up and frowned when she saw his grim expression.

"I can't find either one of them. Can you handle the square dance practice alone? I'm going up to check Julia's room."

Caitlyn was about to say yes. What else could she do? But Dane didn't even stop to wait for her answer. He just headed for the ranch house at a lope, confirming all of Caitlyn's suspicions and making her feel as helpless as a woman who'd just lost her man to an old rival she hadn't even known she had.

TWENTY-FOUR

Dane sat on the edge of Julia's bed and held her hand. She hadn't been with Jake, after all, but she asked him to help her up to her room because she hadn't felt well. That was no surprise. The moment Dane had heard that she'd shared a beer with Jake, he'd known that they were in for trouble. Julia couldn't drink. Even the tiniest sip of alcohol always made her as sick as a dog.

"I'm better now, Dane. You should go back to Caitlyn." Julia gave him a wan smile.

"I still don't understand why you drank that beer." Dane tried to keep the censure out of his voice. It was the last thing Julia needed. She'd already been punished enough for her lapse in judgment. "You know alcohol always makes you sick."

"I know. I just thought that a couple of sips wouldn't hurt. And I was so depressed, I had to do something."

"You were depressed?"

"Yes. You know what today is, don't you? You couldn't have forgotten."

He *had* forgotten, the first time in four years. "I know what date it is, Julia. But dwelling on it isn't going to do either one of us any good. And drinking is the worst possible thing you could have done."

"You're right." Julia dropped her eyes and looked as guilty as a kid with her hand caught in the cookie jar. "I guess I was just hoping that I'd outgrown it."

"You can't outgrow it, Julia. It's hereditary and it'll be with you all your life. Beth couldn't drink, either. And neither could your mother."

"It's just that it makes me feel like such a freak. Everyone else can enjoy a glass of wine or a beer. People look at me as if I'm some sort of Carrie Nation type because I always order club soda or a soft drink, or—oh no! Not again."

"Hold on." Dane grabbed the plastic wastebasket they'd been using as a basin and held it up to her lips. In a minute it was over and Julia leaned back, her face as white as the pillowcase.

"It's a lot worse this time, and I know I only had three or four sips." Julia looked frightened. Her eyes were wide and her hands were shaking. "I've never had it this bad before, not even the time I had a whole glass of champagne."

Dane nodded. He'd nursed her through a couple of her reactions, and she was right—this one was much worse. "Are you sure you only had three or four sips?"

"I'm positive. I really feel awful, Dane. Do you think there could be something else wrong?"

"I doubt it, but I'm going to keep an eye on you." Dane reached out and put his hand to her forehead. "It feels like you're running a little fever."

Julia roused herself enough to give a shaky laugh. "It *feels* like I am? Shame on you, Dr. Morrison. Don't you carry a thermometer around in your pocket?"

"Not anymore. I'm just a simple cowboy now, remember? And be careful about saying things like that. I don't want anyone out here to know."

"I wouldn't dream of blowing your cover, but I still think you should tell Cait—oh, Dane! I'm going to—"

Dane grabbed the wastebasket again and held it in position. Julia was right. There must be something else wrong. She was much too ill for a simple reaction to alcohol. "Can you handle this while I run down and get my medical bag?"

"Yes, but . . . what do you suspect?"

"We won't know until I examine you. Just take it easy, honey. It won't take me more than a minute or two."

"Okay," she acquiesced. "But hurry back. I'm really scared."

"I know you are. Just close your eyes and try to get a little rest. I'll be back before you can miss me."

Dane headed down the hall at a run. The grandfather clock at the head of the stairs was chiming as he passed it, and he glanced at the time. Midnight. All the guests were asleep. He thought about dashing down to Caitlyn's quarters to tell her what was the matter, but she was probably asleep by now. And he really should get back to Julia as fast as he could. He wished he'd taken the time to phone Caitlyn earlier, or to send someone with a message for her. Now he'd have to explain it all later, once this crisis was over, but Caitlyn was bound to understand.

Lightning flashed as Dane passed the hall window. Another storm was rolling in, and it looked like a bad one. He dashed inside his quarters and grabbed his bag and a jacket. The Medivac helicopter would be grounded in weather like this. If he discovered that Julia needed more medical attention than he could give her, he'd have to drive her to the hospital himself.

There was no way that she could sleep. Caitlyn paced the floor, growing angrier with each step that she took. Dane hadn't come back and she didn't know where he was. He'd never done this sort of thing before, and she hoped he wasn't out there somewhere, searching for Jake so that he could punch him out for trying to pick up on his woman.

Julia was Dane's woman. Caitlyn was certain of that now. Nothing else made sense. All the little things Julia had said, the things she'd known about Dane, all pointed to that fact. Dane had been angry when he'd stalked off to look for Jake. Angry and anxious and worried when he'd left her so abruptly to race up to Julia's room.

Was that where he was now? In Julia's room, holding her in his arms? Caitlyn couldn't bear to think about that. She'd assured Dane that their relationship would be simple, just two people who liked each other and enjoyed each other in bed. But it was more complicated than that. She'd lied about her feelings for Dane. She'd never told him that she loved him more than she'd ever loved anyone else. And now he was leaving her for another woman and she didn't know what to do.

Ida and Marilyn would say that she should fight for her man. They'd told her that ranch women were possessive. They didn't cotton to another woman moving in on their husbands or their lovers. Ida and Marilyn would encourage her to march right up to Julia's room and find out if Dane was there. But what would she do if she found him in bed with Julia?

Perhaps he wasn't with Julia at all. It was possible that there had been some crisis she hadn't known about, a sick horse or another rogue cougar or bear. She'd feel like a fool if she barged into Julia's room and found her sleeping peacefully, all alone. But she couldn't just sit here and wait. She had to do something and she had to do it now.

Caitlyn picked up her flashlight and headed for the door. She'd take a walk through the halls. If she met anyone, she'd just say she'd heard a noise and was checking it out.

As she opened the door, Caitlyn *did* hear a noise and it sent shivers up and down her spine. She'd been much too upset to notice before, but thunder was growling overhead, giving every indication of the onslaught of a really bad storm.

Caitlyn ran back to grab her box of matches. If the power went out again, she'd be prepared. As much as she hated electrical storms, the sound of rain pelting against the roof made her glad. Dane could be out calming the horses. Or he could be lighting the hurricane lamps on the walls.

As she stepped into the hallway, Caitlyn took a deep breath and squared her shoulders. The storm had given her an excuse to patrol the ranch house. She had to be there to reassure the guests if the storm woke them. And if the power went out, it would give her the perfect reason to knock on Julia's door to ask if she knew how to light her lamp.

"Okay, I'll have to drive her in. Tell Dr. Wexler to get ready for a hot one." Dane was frowning as he hung up the phone. Now that he knew what was wrong with Julia, he had to take action. There wasn't time to wait for the storm to pass, and the Medivac helicopter couldn't fly in this weather. Julia's appendix was about to rupture, and he had to get her to the hospital in Laramie immediately.

"We're going to take a little trip, honey." Dane gathered her up into his arms. Julia was still conscious and he'd given her something for the pain, but she was still wide-eyed and frightened.

"Tell me the truth, Dane. Am I going to die? Like Beth?"

"No way." Dane gave her a reassuring smile. It was incredibly bad timing that her appendix had flared up on the anniversary of Beth's death. Julia, who was normally an intelligent woman, really believed that twins were linked in some psychic way. She'd confessed that she'd taken a few sips of beer to calm her anxiety about this particular date, and the effects of the alcohol had effectively masked her other, more dangerous symptoms. He hadn't discovered that her appendix was enlarged until he'd examined her. And from what he'd learned of her condition, there was no time to waste. He had to save her. He couldn't lose Julia, too. She was all he had left of Beth.

"You won't leave me, will you, Dane? Tell me you won't leave me."

Caitlyn ducked into the alcove at the end of the hall as the door opened and Dane came out. He was carrying Julia in his arms, and Caitlyn gasped in dismay.

"I won't leave you, baby, I promise."

There was a tenderness in Dane's voice that brought tears to Caitlyn's eyes. He was holding Julia gently, and she was clinging to him, her arms around his neck. What were they doing? What was going on?

"It's going to be all right, honey. Trust me. Once we get there, I'll stay with you."

Caitlyn sagged weakly against the wall. Dane was leaving with Julia. And he was calling her *honey* and *baby*. She'd been a fool not to realize that Dane loved Julia.

"But what about Caitlyn?" Julia sounded worried.

"Don't worry about her." Dane's voice was deep and it carried over the noise of the storm. "I'll call and explain everything. She'll understand."

Caitlyn stepped out of the alcove and followed them to the landing, hugging the wall so she wouldn't be seen.

She could hear Julia's voice as they hurried down the stairs.

"You're the only one who ever really loved me, Dane," Caitlyn could hear Julia say as Dane carried her down the stairs. "Parker was wrong for me. I know that now. How could I have ever made such a terrible mistake?"

Caitlyn drew in her breath sharply and reached out to grab the newel post. Her knees felt weak, and fear rippled through her.

"You were lonely when I left, Julia. I should have stayed in New York with you."

"You won't leave me again, will you?"

Caitlyn's lips parted in a soundless scream as she waited for Dane's answer. But somehow, she knew what it would be.

"I won't leave you, Julia. I promise. Everything's going to be fine. Just hang on and trust me."

The front door banged closed behind them, and Caitlyn sank to her knees at the top of the stairs. Dane was going away with Julia. The man she loved was leaving her for another woman. She knelt there for what seemed like hours, and then she crept back through the darkened hallways to the sanctuary of her room. Dane didn't love her. He loved Julia. And all her dreams and hopes and plans for a loving future had turned to ashes.

She must have slept. The sun was streaming through Aunt Bella's red curtains when Caitlyn opened her eyes. It was a beautiful day, and all traces of the storm were gone. She dressed with leaden fingers, pulling on the first things that came to hand. She didn't care what she wore. Dane was gone, and nothing else mattered. She'd lost him forever.

But she had a job to do and she would do it. Caitlyn stepped out her back door, squinting in the strong sunlight despite the dark sunglasses she'd put on to hide her reddened eyes. The guests would think it was strange if she didn't join them for breakfast; but she wouldn't go on the day trip, not today when just thinking about the trails she'd ridden with Dane brought new tears to her eyes.

Gibby caught her the moment she entered the kitchen. "I got

a message for you, Caitlyn. Dane called early this morning. He's gonna be gone for a couple of days on family business."

Caitlyn didn't say anything. She just nodded, not trusting her voice. Family business? That was appropriate when he'd lied and told her that he thought of Julia as his *sister*.

"He said it was some kind of emergency. He didn't have time to go into detail, but he'll explain everything when he gets back."

Dane was coming back? Caitlyn's eyes widened in shock. Then she remembered that he owned half of the Double B, and she nodded in sudden understanding. Of course Dane wouldn't leave the ranch. He had too much at stake. He'd probably find Julia a place somewhere in Little Fork and waltz right back as if nothing had happened.

"He left the roster of new guests on the table in his room. You're supposed to call them today and confirm their reservations."

"Okay." Caitlyn nodded again, proud that her voice hadn't betrayed her. "Is there any coffee?"

"I just filled the urn. Do you want me to get it for you?"

"No, I'll get it myself." Caitlyn forced a smile. Gibby was being very sweet.

"I hope nothin' bad is wrong," Gibby said worriedly. "It ain't like Dane to take off like this. He's never done it before. It's gotta be somethin' pretty serious."

"I'm sure it is." Caitlyn's eyes snapped behind her dark glasses. It was serious, all right! And if Dane thought he could jolly her around with some cock-and-bull story when he got back, he was dead wrong.

Once the guests had left on their day trip, Caitlyn walked down the hall to Dane's quarters. She had to get the roster to confirm reservations for their new batch of guests. She pushed open the door and shuddered. Dane's room brought back painful memories. They'd slept here once, laughing at the way they didn't dare turn over on his narrow bed.

Forget him. He lied to you about Julia. You were a fool to trust him. He's no better than Spencer with his sleazy little affair with Ardis.

"I know I'm a fool. You don't have to rub it in." Caitlyn answered the voice in her head and then, the moment she realized that she'd spoken out loud, she gave a bitter laugh. Not only had Dane broken her heart, he'd also driven her to talking to herself! She had to stop this sort of behavior right away.

She was about to turn and leave when a photograph in a silver frame caught her eye. It was sitting on Dane's dresser, and she was certain it hadn't been there before. As she walked over for a closer look, she found herself gasping for air. It was a wedding picture.

Caitlyn didn't dare reach out to pick up the photograph. Her hands were trembling too much. She just stared and then she gave a cry of shock. It was Dane's wedding picture. He was younger, but she still recognized his dark good looks and his sexy, almost-lopsided grin. His beautiful bride was staring straight at the photographer with a gloriously happy expression on her face and she was . . .

Caitlyn caught herself on the edge of the dresser as her knees buckled. Dane's bride was a few years younger and a little heavier, but there was no mistaking her features. Suddenly everything fell into place with painful clarity. Dane had warned her that he was still in love with his former wife.

And his former wife was Julia.

TWENTY-FIVE

Dane was whistling as he drove up the long driveway to the Double B Ranch. Home at last. And everything had turned out all right. It had been touch-and-go for two days. By the time he'd gotten Julia to the hospital, her appendix had ruptured, just as he'd feared it would. But Dr. Wexler was competent and the whole hospital staff had been standing by. Dane had gone into surgery with Julia, calming her fears and holding her hand until the anesthesiologist had taken over. And then he'd waited, pacing the floor and praying that he wouldn't lose Julia the way he'd lost Beth.

It was clear to him now that Julia had been a lost soul since Beth had died. Of course, he'd expected her to be grief-stricken, but the twins had gone their separate ways when he'd married Beth. He hadn't thought it would hit Julia quite that hard, but he supposed he'd been blinded by his own grief.

Julia and Beth had been close. Julia had even moved to New York when they had, accepting a teaching position there. But Julia and Beth hadn't really seen that much of each other. They'd gotten together at holidays and enjoyed an occasional lunch together, but that was all. Now he knew that it had been enough for Julia just knowing that Beth was close. And when Beth had died, it had crumbled the foundation on which she'd built her life.

When Julia had come to him for help right after he'd moved in at the Double B, Dane had given her a pep talk. He'd encouraged her to get on with her life, to move past the sorrow of her twin's death, and to find a place for herself independent of Beth.

He'd thought that had happened when she married Parker, but it hadn't.

Julia had brought the cheerful, easy-going teacher to the Double B, and Dane had liked Parker a lot. He'd been happy and relieved when they'd married, assuming that Julia was taking his advice and getting on with her life. The things he'd learned about Julia in the past three days had told him a much different story. She'd admitted that she'd expected Parker to fill the aching void that Beth had left in her life, to take her twin's place. When that hadn't happened, she'd left Parker.

She'd been on the verge of a serious breakdown when she'd arrived at the Double B. Julia had called in for a last-minute reservation and Dane hadn't even realized she was coming to the ranch.

Things would improve for Julia now that she realized she needed help. And once he'd explained the situation to Caitlyn, he was sure she'd be supportive. Julia needed to start over, to leave New York and the failing support system she'd built up around Beth. It was the only way she could become whole again and learn to rely on herself. If Caitlyn agreed, Julia would move out to the Double B and become a part of their extended family.

He had to see Caitlyn right away, to explain where he had been. He was going to tell her everything and ask for her help. Once Caitlyn learned the truth about his background and what had happened with Beth, he was sure she'd welcome Julia with open arms.

Just thinking about their extended family made Dane grin. He was going to ask Caitlyn to marry him. He loved her. He'd realized that as he'd waited with Julia in the recovery room. He loved Caitlyn more than life itself, and it was time to tell her that. He knew she loved him, and at last they could start a new life together with no pretences and no deceptions. Perhaps she'd be upset with him at first for leaving without an explanation, but he'd bring her around in no time at all. Caitlyn had a generous and forgiving heart.

There was a wide smile on Dane's face as he walked up the steps of the ranch house. It was Tuesday morning, and the new guests would be out on a day trip. He hoped that Caitlyn hadn't gone with them. He needed to pull her into his arms and hug her hard, promising her that they'd never be apart again.

The past three days without Caitlyn had been torture for him. When Dane hadn't been worrying about Julia, he'd been worried about Caitlyn. He knew she wouldn't have trouble running the ranch. The boys would take care of that. But she would be anxious about him and where he'd gone and he hadn't been able to contact her on the phone. There was something wrong with the extension in her room. Every time Dane had called her, she'd answered and then, before he could tell her what had happened, the line had gone dead. But he was here now, and he'd explain in person. And then he'd hold her close, kiss her sweet lips, and tell her how much he'd missed her. Just thinking about the happy reunion they'd have made Dane fairly run down the hall to Caitlyn's rooms.

She knew he was coming and she knew he'd want to talk to her. Caitlyn had seen him pull up beside the ranch house and she'd rushed back to her quarters. Their meeting would be private. It was no one's business except theirs. And once she'd said her piece, Dane would be out of her love life for good!

"Caitlyn! I'm back."

He was knocking, and Caitlyn took a deep breath. She would be strong and refuse to listen to his explanation. It would be a pack of lies anyway. She'd tell him exactly what she'd decided, and then she'd close the door in his face. She wouldn't give herself the chance to think twice, to admit how she had missed him. He was a liar and he was a cheat. There was no place for a man like Dane in her heart.

She opened the door and stared at him. He looked so good. But this wasn't the time for weak-kneed gazing. It was the time to be firm. She gathered all her courage and held up her hand. "Don't come in. I don't want to hear what you have to say."

"But, Caitlyn"—he took a step back, reading the anger in her face—"I need to tell you what—"

She interrupted him before he could go further. "It's too late for explanations or anything else. I've decided that our relationship isn't working. From now on, we're business partners and nothing else. I don't want to see you or talk to you privately. At all."

"That's ridiculous, Caitlyn. If you'll just listen, I can explain everything."

He looked as if he might barge in through the door, so Caitlyn kept it in place between them. "I'm not interested in any explanations. Whatever they are, they won't make any difference. Just go. I'm sure you have work to do. And . . . and leave me alone."

Caitlyn slammed the door shut and locked it. And then she dissolved into tears. It had been awful, seeing him again, and she'd almost given in to the urge to listen to him. But she had her pride and she wouldn't let him make a fool of her again. Not Dane. Not any man. She'd do her job, speak to him only when other people were there, and stay in her room with her door locked during the long and lonely nights. She'd made up her mind. She'd done exactly what she'd intended to do. But she still felt horrible about it.

Dane stood there for long minutes, not believing what had happened right before his eyes. She hadn't come into his arms, saying how glad she was that he was back. She hadn't kissed him or welcomed him in any way. She'd looked at him as if he were some kind of intruder. And she'd refused to even listen to him.

He turned away from her door with disbelief written all over his face. He'd intended to ask her to marry him. He'd thought about it all the way home. He'd thought she'd be delighted, that she'd be so glad to see him. Caitlyn wasn't who he'd thought she was if she could turn her back on him like that. He didn't want a wife who'd fly off the handle at the slightest provocation and not even give him the benefit of the doubt. It was clear that Caitlyn didn't trust him. And if she didn't trust him, she didn't love him, either. Trust and love were all wound up together and they couldn't be untangled. One was no good without the other. And a marriage without trust didn't have a prayer of making it.

Dane's eyes turned hard as he strode down the hall toward his own quarters. It was good he'd found out about Caitlyn now, before he'd gotten in any deeper.

TWENTY-SIX

The past ten days had been awful, and only the arrival of the children had saved her from total despair. Caitlyn forced a smile as she left Jessie and went off to find Michael Williams and his parents. Michael was her favorite of all the recent guests who had arrived at the ranch. Caitlyn felt close to him, almost like a loving aunt—or even a mother—and that was surprising in itself. She'd never really felt comfortable around children before, but Michael tugged at her heartstrings.

It was Camp Week at the Double B Ranch, a tradition Aunt Bella had instituted ten years ago. At the end of every summer, right before school started, Aunt Bella had taken in twelve children and their parents for a free vacation. The children and their parents came from Cheyenne, recommended by teachers and various social organizations. They were families that couldn't afford the luxury of taking a vacation, and Aunt Bella had felt that these special children should have at least one week of happy memories.

The children seemed to love the life at the ranch. Most of them were from the city and they'd never seen this much open space before. Caitlyn had organized outdoor activities for them, things they'd never had the chance to experience in the city. They'd fished with their parents, learned to ride the ranch ponies, and gone swimming in the shallows at the edge of a mountain stream. They'd enjoyed an exhibition of trick riding and roping, watched a roundup, and gone camping up in the mountains to learn the stories of the night stars. There had been crafts, parties, games, and lots of good food from Gibby's chuck wagon over the past six days. And now it was time to say goodbye to the little boy Caitlyn had grown to love.

Caitlyn brushed back a tear as she saw Michael waiting by the bus with his parents. Her heart had gone out to him the moment he'd arrived, the only child who couldn't speak. His parents had told her about it on their first night at the Double B. Michael had stopped speaking when his older brother had been killed in a bicycle accident last year. He hadn't said a word for over ten months, and Vanessa and Peter Williams were very worried about their little boy. At five years of age, Michael, who had always been outgoing and friendly, had become withdrawn and almost unsociable.

But he hadn't been unsociable with Caitlyn. Michael had formed an immediate bond with her on his first full day at the ranch. She'd seen how his eyes had followed the ranch dogs and she'd asked Jessie to put on a Frisbee demonstration just for him. It was clear that Michael loved animals, and he'd watched with wide eyes as Jessie had thrown the Frisbee and he'd even come out of his shell enough to try it once himself. His favorite dog was the little cocker spaniel named Lady, and both Caitlyn and Jessie had noticed how attached he'd grown to her.

Lady was a dog that Jessie had rescued as a puppy. He'd found her, cowering and frightened, under a truck that had been parked in front of the cafe in Little Fork. When no one had claimed her, Jessie had brought her out to the Double B to join their other ranch dogs. But Lady had never really adjusted to life at the ranch. It was clear she preferred small spaces and would be happier in a home or an apartment setting.

From the first day on, Michael and Lady had been inseparable. Vanessa Williams had confided that Michael had taken Lady up to his room and the little cocker spaniel had slept on the foot of Michael's bed. She'd even heard Michael laugh once in the middle of the night when Lady had crawled up on the pillow to lick his face, and it was the first time that Michael had laughed since his brother had been killed. Vanessa had thanked Caitlyn for letting Lady sleep in their room. Perhaps, she'd confided, they should get a dog.

That had given Caitlyn the obvious solution, and she'd discussed it with Michael's parents. Vanessa and Peter had told her that they loved dogs. They'd just never thought of adopting one before. Caitlyn had made her suggestion and Michael's parents had eagerly agreed. And now it was time to see if the plan they'd hatched would be successful.

"Hi, Michael." Caitlyn reached down to give him a hug, and Michael hugged her back. "Are you all ready to go home?"

Michael stared up at her with solemn eyes. He didn't look happy about leaving the Double B, but Caitlyn had a big surprise in store for him.

"I need to ask you for a favor, Michael." Caitlyn led him away from the group of other children, his parents following closely behind. "It's very important, and you're the only one who can do it."

Michael's eyebrows shot up and he looked at her inquiringly. He didn't speak, but Caitlyn hadn't expected him to.

"We've got a real problem with Lady." Caitlyn sighed deeply. "You want to help her, don't you?"

Michael nodded quickly. He looked very concerned, and Caitlyn smiled to reassure him.

"Jessie and I think that Lady will be very lonely when you go home. We're worried about her."

Michael nodded again, and a tear appeared in the corner of his eye. It was clear that he loved the little cocker spaniel.

"I think Lady wants to go home with you, and your parents say that's okay with them. But Lady's never lived in Cheyenne before and you have to be able to call her if she wanders away. Do you think you could work very hard to say her name so she'll stay close to you?"

Michael nodded. And then he smiled. And then Jessie appeared with Lady in his arms, right on schedule.

"Just try it, Michael," Caitlyn urged him. "It doesn't have to be perfect. Just try to say Lady's name."

Michael took one look at Lady and then he spoke for the first time in ten long months. "Lady? Do you want to go home with me, Lady?"

Lady jumped out of Jessie's arms and raced to Michael. The little boy sat down, and Lady climbed right up onto his lap.

"You can sleep in my bed, Lady." Michael turned to his parents. "She can do that, can't she, Dad?"

Peter Williams nodded, and Caitlyn saw that he was fighting back tears. "Of course she can, son. When we get home, I'll teach you to take Lady for a walk. We'll do that together every day."

Michael turned to look up at his mother. "Can Lady eat some of my food, Mom?"

"Yes. I'm sure she'd like some table scraps." Vanessa's voice was trembling. "But we'll get Lady her own food, too. You'll have to fill her bowls every morning, before you go off to school. Lady has to have plenty of food and water."

"I will. I'll take good care of Lady, Mom. She's not going to die if I watch out for her. And I'll . . . I'll never let her go on a bicycle, not ever."

Caitlyn exchanged glances with Michael's parents. They'd guessed that Michael felt guilty over his brother's death, and this confirmed it.

"What happened to Davey wasn't your fault, Michael." Caitlyn sat down next to him. "It was an accident. You couldn't have stopped Davey from riding his bicycle. And you couldn't have stopped the car that hit him."

"I . . . I guess not."

Caitlyn put her arm around Michael and hugged him tightly. "So there's really nothing you could have done. I know you're sad about Davey, and your Mom and Dad are sad, too. But they have you, and they love you very much. And now they have Lady, too. I think you can all be happy again."

"Maybe." Michael stroked Lady's soft fur and he began to smile. "We can try. Isn't that right, Caitlyn?"

"That's exactly right," Caitlyn assured him. "And Lady will help. Why don't you run along with Jessie? I think he has a collar and a leash all ready for you down at the horse barn."

"Okay." Michael got to his feet, still holding Lady. "Come on, Jessie. Let's go!"

When Michael had left with Jessie, Vanessa reached out to hug Caitlyn. "It's a miracle. I don't know how to thank you enough, Caitlyn."

"I didn't do anything. It was Lady. Michael just needed a friend, someone he could take care of and love."

Peter shook his head. "No, you said exactly the right things to him. We tried, but he didn't listen to us."

"You're wonderful with children, Caitlyn." Vanessa smiled at her. "You should think about having some of your own. You'd make such a wonderful mother."

Caitlyn's eyes widened with surprise. No one had ever told her that before. She'd wanted a baby when she had been married to Spencer, but she'd felt insecure about parenting. "Do you really think so?"

"Absolutely," Peter declared firmly. "You have all the right instincts. Michael could tell you really cared about him, right from the beginning."

"You're a natural-born mother," Vanessa said. "Just make up with that nice man of yours and get married. And then have lots of kids. He'd be a good father, too. I watched him when he taught Michael to ride. He's perfect daddy material."

Dane moved away from the other side of the bus and headed out to the corral. He'd heard everything and he wished he hadn't. Caitlyn *would* make a wonderful mother. And she'd make a fine wife, too, except for one small failing. Should he have tried harder to make her listen to him when he'd attempted to explain about Julia?

"Hey, Dane." Gibby rushed up, holding a clipboard. "I got the roster of the new guests."

"Thanks." Dane took the list and glanced down at it. Usually he enjoyed the prospect of new guests, new people who'd arrive and might turn out to be friends. But today, he couldn't have cared less. All the excitement he used to feel had disappeared.

"Look, Dane . . ." Gibby looked very nervous. "I really hate to bring up a sore subject, but—"

"What?" Dane interrupted him.

"You got to do something about her. The boys and me, we can't stand this pussyfooting around anymore."

"What are you talking about?" Dane's eyes were cold. He

knew Gibby was referring to Caitlyn, but he didn't want to discuss her.

"I know. It's your business. That's what you've been tellin' me for ten days. But this thing with Caitlyn is really gettin' to you. You've been snappy with all of us, and downright rude when we try to talk to you. You're behavin' like a bear that's been rousted out in the middle of the winter, and that makes it our business, too."

"Fine." Dane glared at him. He knew Gibby spoke the truth, but he simply couldn't keep a civil tongue in his head. "What do you expect me to do about it?"

Gibby shrugged. "I don't know. You got to make up your own mind about that, but we can't go on like this. If you don't get things straightened out with Caitlyn pretty soon, all the boys're gonna quit . . . me included."

Caitlyn grabbed her designer blue jeans. She had several hours before the new guests arrived, but there were preparations to make. She had to check the rooms to make sure that they had been properly cleaned and go over the inventory and see that everything they'd ordered had arrived. She should also find Gibby and double-check that he had all the food he needed for the barbecue tonight.

Even though Gibby's menu was always the same for the first night of the guests' arrival, she hadn't grown tired of the food. His barbecued beef was delicious, and she loved the beans he made. There would be biscuits—and homemade pies and ice cream for dessert. She'd smelled apple pie baking this morning and she could hardly wait. Perhaps, if she went out to the kitchen, she could have a piece right now.

Caitlyn pulled up her jeans and frowned. Ida and Marilyn had shrunk them. They were two inches too small around the waist and there was no way she could pull them together tightly enough to snap them. She'd have to wear a pair of Aunt Bella's oversized jeans.

Shrugging, Caitlyn pulled out her dresser drawer and grabbed a pair of her aunt's jeans. She put them on, and her frown deepened as she snapped them at the waist. They were tight, too—uncomfortably tight. Had Ida and Marilyn been using boiling water in the laundry? She tried another pair, and then another, but they were all too tight for comfort.

She was gaining weight. Caitlyn sighed as she remembered the three cinnamon rolls she'd wolfed down for breakfast, along with bacon and eggs and a huge glass of orange juice. If she didn't stop eating like a pig, she'd start to look like one.

Caitlyn's stomach growled with hunger and she tried to remember what she'd eaten lately. She'd had two huge sandwiches for lunch, even though she usually didn't care for egg salad. And last night at the party, she'd gone back for a second helping and she'd eaten a chocolate sundae and two pieces of Gibby's fudge cake for dessert. Why was she so hungry? She'd never had a weight problem, but lately she'd been eating enough for . . .

The moment she thought of it, Caitlyn's face paled and she rushed to her calendar to check the dates. No, it was impossible. She'd tried for two long years with Spencer, and nothing had happened. She couldn't be pregnant now! It was just a freak hormonal thing; there was nothing to worry about. She was infertile. She had to be. Spencer certainly wasn't. She'd talked to Bitsy on the phone just last week, and she'd said that Ardis was getting as big as a cow.

Caitlyn took a deep breath and forced herself to stay calm. That she'd missed twice in a row didn't mean anything at all. It was merely an imbalance in her system. Emotional stress could affect a woman's body in all sorts of ways. She was upset over Dane, and that was bound to take its toll. Even the thought of any other explanation was completely absurd.

But she *had* been sick in the mornings. Caitlyn sank down on the edge of the waterbed she'd shared with Dane and groaned. It had started over a month ago, and she'd thought that she'd caught a touch of the flu. What if it hadn't been the flu? What if her slight queasiness in the morning had been the first sign of pregnancy? What if she were carrying Dane's baby?

No, it couldn't be. There was some other explanation. But just to put her mind at rest, she'd drive into Laramie before the new guests arrived and buy a home pregnancy test. It would be negative. Caitlyn was sure of that. But she'd do it anyway and she'd do it now, before she could get any more worried about something that was probably just a figment of her imagination.

Dane squared his shoulders and walked to the ranch house. Gibby was right. He had to talk to Caitlyn. This time he wouldn't take no for an answer. He'd march right into her room and force her to listen to him. If she didn't believe him, that was fine. Then he'd know for sure that she wasn't right for him. He didn't handle rejection well. He never had. But if she rejected him after he'd poured out his heart to her, he could put her out of his mind for good.

She'd been so good with Michael. Dane sighed as he thought about how Caitlyn had talked to him, telling him that it wasn't his fault when bad things happened, that people just had to put them behind them and try to be happy. It was exactly what his friends and colleagues had told him when Beth had died. He could still remember the platitudes and the words they'd used to console him. *Her suffering is over. You have to put it behind you. It's not your fault. There's nothing that you could have done.* Instead of soothing him, their words had made him burn with a white-hot rage. Yes, Beth's suffering was over, but that didn't make up for the fact that she *had* suffered. He'd seen the pain deep in her eyes, and he'd insisted that they increase her morphine. They hadn't wanted to do it, citing the same reasons as old Doc Henley. She could die of an overdose. She could become addicted. And he'd had the same response. Did it really matter? Beth was dying. There wasn't any cure or even any way to delay the inevitable. And though the hospital had fought with him, they'd had to comply when he'd accepted full responsibility for his decision.

The other pat phrases they'd used had irritated him beyond belief. How could he put Beth's death behind him? She was his wife, and he loved her. Death couldn't change that. And it *was* his fault. He'd been the best diagnostician in New York and he'd been too busy to recognize Beth's symptoms. Of course there was something he could have done. If he'd caught her cancer in the early stages, Beth might have had a fighting chance.

It was something Julia had said in the recovery room that had brought him up short. She'd told him that she'd had a throbbing pain in her side all day and she just hadn't wanted to mention it. And then she'd said, *Beth and I were raised to think of illness as a sign of weakness. We used to walk around with a fever when we were kids and never say a word about it. It was a badge of courage for us. We always waited until we were so sick, somebody else had to notice.*

That had got him to thinking about Beth, and how she'd made all those excuses for her weight loss. She hadn't complained, and by not complaining, she'd failed to alert him that something was wrong. He'd mentioned it to Julia and she'd just sighed. And then she'd said, *Beth was even worse than I was. There's no way you could have known she was sick when she decided to hide all her symptoms from you. She didn't even tell me, her own twin. It was selfish of her, and sometimes I hate her for doing this to us.*

Sitting there by Julia's hospital bed, Dane had felt a great weight slip from his shoulders. Beth hadn't wanted him to know and she'd protected her secret until it had been too late. It had been her decision, and there really was nothing he could have done. Even if he'd spent more time with her, he wouldn't have suspected that she was ill. Julia hadn't even guessed and she had known Beth better than anyone else ever could.

He'd thought he'd made the right decision when he'd sold his practice and started another life. He'd told himself that a good doctor wouldn't have let his wife die and Beth's death proved that he wasn't a good doctor. Now, he wasn't so sure. No doctor, no matter how brilliant a diagnostician, would have ordered tests on a patient who presented no symptoms. It would be like jerking a bystander off the street and examining him for no reason, without his consent.

Dane guessed he'd made his peace with Beth's memory that night in the hospital. He'd held Julia's hand while she'd slept, and he'd made some decisions. Caitlyn's rejection of him had caused him to back off, but now he was filled with new determination. He owed it to himself, and to Caitlyn, to talk it all out and see if there was still a chance for them.

Her Explorer was gone. Dane stared at the place where it should have been parked. It seemed that the minute he made up his mind about something, there was an obstacle in his way. Now Caitlyn was gone and he couldn't confront her, but he wouldn't let that stop him. She'd be back and when she was, he'd march to her room and force her to listen to him.

"Dane!" Jake shouted at him, barreling up in the ranch Jeep. "Come with me. We got a problem."

Dane hurried up to the Jeep. Jake looked worried. "What is it?"

"Tommy Purdy and Clay Lathrop hiked up Elbow Ridge last night. They were gonna camp out and come back in the morning, but they're not back yet. Sheriff Blayne just called and asked us to go up and take a look."

Dane climbed hurriedly into the passenger seat. "Got the rifles?"

"In the rack. Extra ammo's on the seat." Jake pulled the Jeep around and headed for the trail.

"Harness and ropes?"

"I packed up before I came to get you," Jake said. "Got the medical kit, too. You don't suppose they tried to climb up Devil's Peak, do you?"

"Yup." Dane knew it as surely as if they'd left a map. Tommy and Clay had been practicing on the smaller ridges all summer. The boys were adventuresome, and it stood to reason that they'd want to put all that practice to the test before school opened tomorrow morning. "My guess is they're sitting on that ledge right below Devil's Peak."

Jake still looked worried. "Do you think they fell?"

"I doubt it. They both went off to climbing school at the beginning of the summer and they're not stupid. I figure they're stuck, that's all. They'll be cold, and hungry and scared half out of their wits. And they'll be mighty grateful to see us."

TWENTY-SEVEN

Caitlyn stared dumbly at the indicator. It was clearly a plus sign, not a minus. There was no longer any doubt in Caitlyn's mind that she was going to have Dane's baby.

What could she do? Where could she go? Would she have to tell Dane? The questions that bombarded her made Caitlyn so dizzy, she flopped down on the edge of the bed. She couldn't ignore this, hoping it would go away. It wouldn't. She was carrying Dane's baby and she needed to decide what to do.

Caitlyn stared out the window, gazing at the sun as it lowered behind the peak of the mountains. The rugged terrain stretched out as far as she could see, bathed in the golden sunset. The Double B Ranch would be such a wonderful place to raise a child. Her baby could run and play, make friends with the ranch hands and all the ranch dogs, and attend the wonderful school in Little Fork. But she couldn't stay here, not a moment longer. Someone would be sure to guess that she was pregnant. And everyone would guess that Dane was her baby's father.

Could she say that she'd been pregnant when she'd come out West, but hadn't known about it? Caitlyn felt her hopes rising. She really wanted to stay here and raise her child at the Double B. Everyone else might believe her, but Dane would know the truth.

What would he do if she told him? Tears sprang to Caitlyn's eyes. He'd marry her. She was certain of that. She'd seen the soft light in his eyes when he'd played with the children who had been their guests. Dane loved children and he'd marry her to give his baby a father.

For just a moment, Caitlyn gave herself the luxury of thinking about marriage to Dane. They'd be together for her whole pregnancy. Dane would protect her, make sure she ate right and did the proper things. He'd hold her hand when she went into labor and drive her to the hospital and tell her not to worry, that he was there. And after the birth, Dane would be there to see their baby's first steps, to experience all the precious moments that parents share over the years until their children are grown. She'd be able to go to bed with him every night and wake up with him every morning. They'd be a couple with a child. Their life would be full and rich and . . .

Impossible. She loved Dane, but he didn't love her. How could she spend the rest of her life with a man who loved someone else? Waking up next to him every morning, knowing that he longed for Julia would be more than she could bear.

Dane would be a wonderful father. But Caitlyn couldn't beg him to marry her just for the sake of the baby. He didn't love her. He loved Julia. If they got married, they'd both be miserable.

She had to leave. There was no other choice. Mentally, Caitlyn reviewed her finances. She'd find a job now and work hard. She had excellent references, and she was sure that another advertising agency would hire her. She'd kept up her medical insurance, and paying the premiums would be no problem. She'd save every cent she could and then, a few weeks before the baby was due, she'd quit and devote herself to her child. She'd have enough money to last for a while, and perhaps she could find free-lance work so that she could stay at home until the baby was old enough for school. There was the money from the Double B to consider, too. The ranch turned a profit, and part of it would be hers. Dane was honest and she was sure he'd mail her share of the profits to her new address, when she had one.

Caitlyn squared her shoulders. It would be hard, but she could do it. She'd make a new life for herself and her child. Single mothers could make it. She'd known several single women who had juggled work and motherhood. She'd never lacked courage or conviction and she was determined to be a good mother and raise a happy child.

It didn't take long to pack. Caitlyn filled her suitcases and lugged them out to the Explorer, making sure that no one saw her. The new guests would be arriving in less than an hour, and she had just enough time to leave a note for Dane before she left.

But when Caitlyn sat down at her aunt's desk, tears filled her eyes. She couldn't cry now. She had to hurry. She had to go before Dane realized that she was leaving.

The words didn't come easily, but Caitlyn forced her hand to move, writing out a message to the man she loved. She felt her heart breaking as she penned the lines to let Dane know that she was leaving for good. She wrote that she'd decided to accept his offer of running the ranch without her. Things weren't working between them, and it was better this way. She promised to call the ranch office with her new address just as soon as she got settled and asked if he would please send her a check for her share of the profits at the end of the season.

There were tears on the note. Caitlyn stared down at it in dismay. But there wasn't time to write it over; she had to leave now before the new batch of guests arrived. With trembling hands, she folded the note, wrote Dane's name on the outside, and propped it up against her pillow, where he would be sure to see it when he came to look for her.

It was time to leave. Caitlyn took one last look at the room she'd come to think of as home. The dresser where she'd learned to braid her long hair. The closet where she'd hung the lovely square dance dress that Lisa had made for her. The waterbed that she'd chosen with Dane, exchanging secret smiles as the salesman had promised them that it wouldn't bounce too much for a good night's sleep. She'd snuggled under Aunt Bella's patchwork quilt with Dane, feeling safe and cherished in his arms, as if nothing could ever hurt her again.

Caitlyn gave a bitter laugh. She'd been so naïve, so trusting, so wrong. And Dane had broken her heart. But her baby had been conceived in one of those moments of perfect happiness, and she'd always cherish that memory.

She couldn't stay any longer. There was no time to linger and think about what might have been. Caitlyn picked up her last two suitcases and walked out of the room, blinking back tears and closing the door on all her dreams.

* * *

Dane felt a sense of relief as the Jeep pulled away. Jake was taking Tommy and Clay back home to their anxious parents. They'd found the two boys on the ledge, right where Dane had thought they'd be. With the help of the harness and the winch, they'd managed to hoist them up with no problem. Neither boy had been injured, just stuck between a rock and hard place.

A wry grin crossed Dane's face. That was probably the origin of the old expression. He had been stuck between a rock and a hard place, too. His stubborn pride was the rock. He'd thought it was important to him, but it wasn't. And the hard place was where he'd be for the rest of his life if he didn't get things settled with Caitlyn. But there was no one to hoist him up to safe ground. He had to get there by himself.

As Dane walked down the path to the back of the ranch house, he pulled Bella's key out of his pocket. He'd been carrying it on his key chain since the day Bella had been confined to bed. It unlocked the dead bolt on the back door. He'd intended to give it to Caitlyn, but it had slipped his mind. And now he was glad that he'd kept it. Caitlyn couldn't refuse to see him if he suddenly appeared in her room.

The dead bolt slid back with a well-oiled click, and Dane opened the door. As he crossed the threshold, he sighed deeply, remembering how many times he'd come in this door before, carrying her in his arms to the bed they'd shared together. It just couldn't end like this. He wouldn't let go of his one chance at happiness. He'd been miserable without Caitlyn and he knew she'd been every bit as miserable without him.

"I love you, damn it!" Dane whispered the words to the empty room. "And you love me, too. I know you do."

The shower door was open, and Dane could smell the sweet scent of the soap she used. It reminded him of newly mown grass and the wildflowers that grew at the grassy spot on top of Devil's Ridge. Just being in this room again made his breath catch in his throat.

Dane walked into the bedroom and swallowed hard, remembering the nights they'd spent together. Caitlyn had been so eager, and so sweet. He'd never experienced that kind of giving before. She had a way of gazing up at him, her green eyes filled with growing passion, that made his hands start to shake at just the thought. How could he let that sweetness go without putting up a fight?

Her closet door was open. Dane blinked and then he took a quick step forward to stare at the empty hangers. Caitlyn's clothes were gone. He rushed to the dresser and pulled out a drawer. It was empty.

Panic began to rise in Dane's body as he realized that all the pictures of Bella were gone. The room had been stripped of all Caitlyn's belongings. Then he turned to the bed and gasped as he saw a note propped up on her pillow, a page torn from the yellow legal pad she'd always kept on her desk.

His name was written on the front of the note, and Dane grabbed it, unfolding it with a sinking feeling in his stomach. As he read the words, his hands began to shake. Caitlyn was gone.

Dane stared down at the note with shock. Caitlyn had left him. For good. Before he'd even had the chance to talk to her. He stood frozen, feeling an emptiness inside him that was as cold as ice. But then his mind kicked into gear and he noticed that her note was still wet with splotches of tears. She hadn't been gone for long. He had to catch her.

The suitcases had presented more of a problem than she'd thought they would. She had more things now, and the Explorer was packed. She'd finally managed to find room for the last of them, on the passenger seat, and she'd just climbed behind the wheel when the ranch house door banged open.

Caitlyn looked up, her eyes widening in surprise as she saw Dane running down the steps. He looked worried—and determined. He'd read her note and now he was coming after her.

He seemed desperate, almost crazy, and Caitlyn felt a moment of doubt. Was she truly doing the right thing? But she had to leave. Staying with Dane, knowing that he didn't love her, would be unbearable. She couldn't live a lie, not even to give their baby a father.

Tears filled her eyes as she stared at the man she loved. But then her reflexes took over and she started the engine with a roar. Her fingers trembled as she pressed the button that rolled up all the windows. She didn't want to hear what he had to say. She couldn't hear it. She might be swayed from her decision, if only for a little while; but then her good sense would take over and it would be even harder for her to leave.

"Caitlyn! Wait. I have to talk to you."

She heard his words even through the closed windows, but it was too late to talk things over. She'd made her decision, and it had to be the right one. She stomped on the accelerator, and the Explorer shot forward. And then she was roaring down the driveway, sending the gravel flying and leaving the man she loved with all her heart in a cloud of gritty dust.

He couldn't let her get away. Dane jumped into the ranch pickup and started the engine, thanking his lucky stars that they had a policy of leaving keys in the ranch vehicles. He slammed the truck into gear and peeled off down the driveway after Caitlyn. He loved her, and she was going to listen to him.

Dane peered uneasily at the road. She was ahead of him, but he couldn't see her. The dust was too thick. He had to catch up with her before she reached the freeway. Once she hit the asphalt, she'd pull ahead and he wouldn't be able to keep up with her. The Explorer could outperform the old ranch truck, and he'd be left behind.

There was only one thing to do. Dane tromped on the gas pedal and almost flew over the gravel. He'd pass her once she turned onto the country road that ran past the ranch and he'd force her to stop. It was the only way to settle this whole mess they'd gotten themselves into. He couldn't lose Caitlyn now, not when he'd finally realized that his pride didn't matter. Nothing mattered except telling her that he loved her and being with her for the rest of his life.

* * *

As she turned onto the country road, Caitlyn glanced in the rearview mirror. What she saw made her hands start to shake and her heart pound frantically in her chest. Dane was chasing her in the ranch truck! She couldn't let him catch her. She had to get away from him. Nothing he could say would make any difference, and it would destroy her if she had to see him again.

Caitlyn pressed down hard on the accelerator, frenzied with the desire to escape the man she loved. She wouldn't let him catch her. She couldn't. If she had to look into his dear face again, she'd die!

And then Caitlyn saw it, the sharp curve ahead that everyone called Dead Man's Drop-off. She was going much too fast. She'd never make it.

She hit the brakes, pumping them hard, and went into a squealing, wrenching skid. She tried frantically to steer her way out of the skid, but her speed was too great and the Explorer was fishtailing, hurtling toward the sheer rock wall on the left side of the road. Her front bumper glanced off the rocks, and the vehicle straightened slightly from the impact. For one brief moment, Caitlyn thought that she'd made it, that she was safe. But then her forward momentum changed abruptly as her front tire blew out. A second later, the Explorer was careening across the width of the road, straight toward the metal guardrail on the opposite side.

Caitlyn screamed, a shrill sound of panic, as she crashed into the guardrail. And then the Explorer shot through the barrier and tumbled end over end down the steep ravine.

There was a moment of terrible silence, silence as deep as a grave. Caitlyn's last thought was for her baby, and then everything—her panic, her pain, her despair for the future, even her mind—went hurtling and spiraling down into the darkness.

TWENTY-EIGHT

She had to open her eyes. Caitlyn tried, but nothing happened. What was wrong? Panic overwhelmed her, and then she slipped back down into the quiet darkness where there was no pain or anxiety.

It could have been seconds; it could have been hours. Time was irrelevant in this dark, safe cocoon. It didn't exist. There was only peace. And emptiness that stretched on even past the flimsy borders of understanding. She was secure here, an egg in a soft cradle. But then her mind rose up again, like a giant pendulum on a giant clock, swaying in and out, up and down, despite her wishes.

There was a comforting warmth on her hand. The sun? Only the sun could feel this wonderful. Was she sleeping on a beach in partial shade, with only her hand exposed to the lovely warm of the sun?

She tried to open her eyes to see where she was, but they refused to open. Her eyelids felt as if they were weighted with something heavy and impossible to lift. She wanted to move her hand, the one that felt so warm and cherished, but her muscles wouldn't work. But she could hear and there was a voice. At least, she thought it was a voice. It buzzed at the gates of her mind, pesky and irritating, like a fly buzzing against the screen of the ranch house kitchen, trying to get inside where someone she couldn't remember was baking . . . something that smelled like . . . apples.

It wasn't a fly. It was a voice and it was talking to her. She was beginning to recognize individual sounds and they sounded thick with emotion and tears. They didn't make sense, but that was all right. Nothing made sense. Why should the strangely familiar, buzzing voice be any different?

What had happened to her? Why couldn't she sit up, get off the beach blanket, and pull her hand out of the sun? Why couldn't she go back to the darkness, where she had been so very comfortable?

The voice wouldn't let her go back. It was holding her here against her will. It was trapping her, tethering her, keeping her from leaving. She hated the voice. It was calling her awake when all she wanted to do was sleep.

Dane's voice. The thought flowed through her like warm honey. It was Dane. He was talking to her, but she didn't want to listen. The words slipped through the dark fog that had settled over her mind, and even though she tried to block them out, she heard words. *Love.* That was one word. *Trust.* That was another. He was keeping her here, tying her down with words that hammered at her mind like golden chisels. But Dane wanted something that she couldn't give him. His voice was a lifeline, but she wouldn't take it. She couldn't come back to him. She had to think about something else, someone else. If only she could push back the dark fog long enough to remember who it was . . .

"You really need to rest for a while."

Dane looked up at the nurse with bleary eyes. He knew she meant well, but he couldn't rest, not until Caitlyn came out of her coma. "No. I'm okay. I can't leave her now."

"But you've been here for over thirty hours." The nurse placed a comforting hand on his shoulder. "If you keep this up, we'll have to admit *you* as a patient."

She was concerned about him and Dane appreciated that, but he wasn't the one who mattered. Her concern should be for Caitlyn, not him. "I can't rest. I have to talk to her, to pull her out of this."

"At least let me bring in a cot for you. If you can just catch a few minutes of sleep, you'll feel much better."

Dane sighed, shaking off her comforting hand. "I don't need

to feel better. Caitlyn does. And I can't sleep and talk to her at the same time. Don't you see that I *have* to talk to her? It's her only chance."

"I know it's hard." There was sympathy in the nurse's voice. "But she hasn't responded to any stimuli since you brought her in. You're putting your own health in jeopardy for something that's not helping either of you. Ms. Bradford is in a deep coma and she can't hear you."

Dane raised his head and glared at the nurse. Perhaps she meant well, but well-meaning people were beginning to irritate him. "She *can* hear me. Read the literature, Nurse Fischer, before you make a medical judgment. Patients have come out of deep comas and repeated every word that was said to them. My voice is Caitlyn's only link with reality. If I stop talking to her, she'll sink back down into an even deeper coma."

"But you can't get along with no sleep and no food." She was placating him, and Dane's anger rose. "Please let me help. I can talk to her while you sleep."

"Caitlyn doesn't know you. The sound of your voice would mean less than nothing to her. If you really want to do something to help, bring me a cup of strong, black coffee and then leave me alone."

Dane was right. Caitlyn wished that she could tell him that. She *did* hear him, and the sound of his voice had caused the dark fog to lift slightly. But her lips wouldn't move, even though she told them to, and she couldn't make a sound. She was a prisoner of her own body and she'd never felt so desperately helpless.

"Whatever you say, Dr. Morrison. I'll be right back."

The nurse's words were clipped, and Caitlyn wished that she could smile. Dane had managed to shake her composure and perhaps that was good. And then something that Nurse Fischer had said floated into the active part of her mind, the part that wasn't paralyzed by the dark fog. The nurse had called him *Dr. Morrison*. Dane was a doctor!

Now that Caitlyn thought about it, it made perfect sense. Why hadn't she guessed before? He'd known exactly what to do with her injured ankle and he'd helped Aunt Bella when she'd been so sick. Of course he was a doctor. He knew too much medicine to have picked it up from living on a ranch. But why hadn't he told her? And why didn't he practice medicine anymore?

He was speaking again, and his voice was filled with anguish. Caitlyn listened, his words washing over her like a healing balm. His hand was warm, holding hers, and he was telling her that he loved her.

Had her eyelids flickered slightly? Caitlyn wasn't sure. They felt as if they had, but perhaps that was an illusion. Was all of this an illusion? Was she dying? Were his words just a figment of her fading mind?

No. His words were real. Caitlyn was sure of it. She could never have imagined the strange story that he was telling her . . . about Julia and Beth and giving up his Park Avenue practice when he couldn't save Beth.

Caitlyn held her breath, hoping he'd tell her more. And Dane went on, in his tired but loving voice, telling her everything that had happened on the night of the storm, when he'd left the ranch house with Julia.

It *had* been a family emergency! Caitlyn wanted to tell Dane that she understood, but the words wouldn't form on her lips. And then he told her that he did love Julia; he'd always loved Julia, because she was Beth's sister. She was his last link to Beth, the only family he had left, and he'd always love her as a sister. He'd tell her all about it when she woke up. She *had* to wake up. He couldn't bear it if she didn't.

Tears of remorse filled Caitlyn's eyes, and one slipped out to run down her cheek. She could feel it, hot and wet on her skin. Was that a good sign? Could she wake up if she just tried a little harder? And now Dane was telling her that he loved her and begging her to come back to him. She had to wake up. For him. For their baby.

Her eyelids were too heavy. How could she lift them? But she had to try harder, to let Dane know that she loved him with all her heart. Caitlyn concentrated, willing her eyes to open, forcing them to lift. She saw a small glimmer of light, just a crack. Would it be enough? And then her eyelids fluttered again; she could feel them. And Dane saw them. She heard him gasp, and his hand squeezed hers, hard. And then he was shouting out for someone named Dr. Pierce.

Caitlyn heard the sound of running feet, and then there was a buzz of voices in the room. Nurse Fischer. Caitlyn recognized her voice. And Dane. The third voice, sounding harried and a bit irritated at being summoned, must belong to Dr. Pierce.

And then Dane was pleading with her to open her eyes again, to give them all some sign that she heard him. Trying with all her strength, Caitlyn made her eyelids flutter again.

"There. You see. She's coming out of it."

Dane's voice was joyous, and Caitlyn was glad. She had proved him right in front of Nurse Fischer and Dr. Pierce.

"It's nothing, just an involuntary reaction." Dr. Pierce sounded disdainful, and Caitlyn felt an instant dislike for the man. It was clear he doubted Dane's opinion, but Dane was right. "Patients in deep coma have been known to flutter their eyelids, even cry. It means nothing. You're emotionally involved with the patient, Dr. Morrison. You're simply grasping at straws."

The nerve of the man! Caitlyn felt her anger rise like a red tide, chasing every remaining vestige of the dark fog away. She wished her eyes would fly open and she could shout out that he was wrong. But her eyelids wouldn't open all the way. They would only flutter. She tried moving her hand, and to her shocked surprise, her fingers moved.

"Her fingers just twitched!" She heard Dane sit down in the chair again and she felt him pick up her hand. "Squeeze my hand, honey. Come on, Caitlyn. Squeeze my hand."

Caitlyn tried, but she seemed to have no control over her muscles. Yet just a moment ago, she'd been able to move her fingers. It was frustrating, and anger flowed through her again. She wanted to prove that Dane was right and they were dead wrong.

"Just relax, Dr. Morrison, and try to get some rest. You've been here for too long. We'll bring in a cot for you, if you insist, but I think you'd rest better if you slept in our residents' quarters."

"You don't understand." Dane's voice was low and he sounded so tired, Caitlyn almost wished that he would take Dr. Pierce's advice. "I have to stay here. It's critical. Caitlyn knows the sound of my voice and it's important for me to keep talking to her."

"Nonsense. You're exhausted and you're deluding yourself. If the patient is going to regain consciousness, she'll do it whether you're here at her bedside or not."

Dr. Pierce was really insufferable, and it was up to her to do something about it. Ranch women fought for their men, and she was no exception. Caitlyn made her fingers twitch. It was a little easier this time. And then she concentrated on her eyelids. They fluttered again, opening a bit further this time.

"I'll be right back. Don't leave her alone. I just want to splash some cold water on my face." Caitlyn's heart thudded painfully as she caught sight of Dane. There were dark circles under his eyes, and he looked as if he hadn't slept for a week. And then he was walking to the other side of the room, out of her field of vision, leaving Nurse Fischer and Dr. Pierce standing close to her bed.

Caitlyn eyes opened a bit further, and she noticed that Nurse Fischer was a very pretty woman. She moved slightly, and Caitlyn saw her arm reach up to rest on Dr. Pierce's arm.

"Could he be right, doctor?" Nurse Fischer's voice was low, so Dane couldn't hear her.

"No." The handsome doctor in the white coat shook his head. He had carefully styled gray hair and he looked as if he vacationed every year in the Bahamas. "Dr. Morrison is in denial. I've seen it many times before. His emotions have rendered him incapable of accepting the inevitable. We should have seen the writing on the wall and kept him out. He's a troublemaker, and this isn't doing either of them any good."

"She's not going to make it?" Nurse Fischer sounded anxious, and Caitlyn noticed that she pulled her hand back.

"Patients who sink into a deep coma seldom recover. To put it in layman's terms, I'd say it would take miracle."

Caitlyn eyelids lifted, and she glared at him. He didn't notice. He was too busy trying to impress Nurse Fischer with his expertise. The pompous idiot. If he'd just look at her, he'd see that her eyes were open all the way. She'd like to shock him right out of his complacency.

Could she? Caitlyn's lips moved, shaping and starting to form the word she wanted to say. She had to call Dr. Pierce an idiot for not believing Dane. He was the one who had pulled her back from the brink of death and sustained her with his love. Caitlyn thought about the things that Dr. Pierce had said, how he'd ridiculed Dane, and somehow, she found the courage to test her voice.

"Idiot."

She had thought that she'd shouted, but the word came out in a whisper. That was strange. They hadn't even heard her. Caitlyn gathered herself for a second attempt. They'd hear her this time. She'd tell the world that Dr. Pierce was wrong.

"Too bad you don't believe in miracles, Dr. Pierce!" This time her voice was audible enough to make them gasp, and they whirled to stare at her. She was back. The ranch woman was back. And she was ready to defend the man she loved.

"Caitlyn!" Dane rushed across the room to gather her into his arms, and she felt his body trembling against hers. "Honey?"

Caitlyn felt her lips turn up in a smile. Dane had saved her, and she couldn't wait to shout it from the rooftops. But first there was something that she had to do.

"Dane?" She looked up at him, surprised to see tears falling from his sky-blue eyes. "Tell Dr. Pierce to leave, will you? And Nurse Fischer, too. We don't need them anymore. I just want to be alone with the man who saved me with the miracle of his love."

TWENTY-NINE

The whole town of Little Fork had been invited, and it was what Gibby called *a bang-up shindig*. It hadn't taken much planning. They were used to entertaining crowds at the Double B, and this celebration was no exception.

Caitlyn took one last look at her wedding dress in the mirror as she waited for Lisa and Julia, her two bridesmaids, to lift it up, over her head. Lisa and her mother had made it, and it was a dream of a dress constructed of white ruffled organdy and lace. It was a bit old-fashioned, just the sort of dress a ranch bride would wear, and Caitlyn had worn it proudly as she'd exchanged vows with Dane in the ranch house living room.

Jeremy Campbell had given her away, and he'd looked very proud as he'd walked her up to the makeshift altar in front of the river-rock fireplace. And after the ceremony he'd confided to Caitlyn and Dane that he hoped their wedding would give Jerry a nudge in the right direction.

Jake and Trevor had been the groomsmen, and they'd posed for wedding pictures after the ceremony as Sam and Gibby had clicked away with two of the ranch cameras.

"It was such a beautiful wedding, Miz Bradford." Lisa hung the dress on a hanger, and then she giggled as she realized what she had said. "I guess I should call you *Mrs. Morrison* now."

"Call me *Caitlyn*." Caitlyn grinned at the friendly, outgoing girl she'd come to think of as a friend.

Caitlyn could tell Julia was blinking back happy tears as she asked, "What should I call you?"

"How about *Sis?* I never had a sister and I've always wanted one."

"Sis." Julia tested the word and then she grinned. "I like it. *Sis* is just right for you."

Caitlyn swiped at her own tears of happiness. Julia was here to stay on the Double B Ranch. Dane and Caitlyn had decided that she should have Dane's old quarters and Julia had arrived, bag and baggage, yesterday morning.

"We'd better get you dressed for the party. Your new husband will be wondering what's taking you so long." Lisa took Caitlyn's square dance dress off the hanger, holding it up so Caitlyn could see the waistline. "There was plenty of material, and I altered the waist. It's elastic now, and there's plenty of room for later. I made this sash to go with it. You just tie it around you to cover the elastic."

"That's very clever," Caitlyn said delightedly. "I promise to wear it to every square dance we have, even when I get too big to dance."

It didn't take long to put on the lovely green-and-white dress. Caitlyn stared at her reflection in the mirror with a secret smile. Lisa had told her that Dane suggested she make the dress as a gift for her. In a way, it was from him as well as from Lisa, and Caitlyn knew she'd wear it until it was old and tattered. And when that happened, she'd ask Lisa to make another, just like it. It was a symbol of the love that would grow between husband and wife from this time forward.

There was another symbol of their love for each other, and it sat on her bed—a huge stuffed animal that Dane had given her on the day he'd brought her home from the hospital. It was a toy cougar, comical and cute, not at all like the real cougar that had struck terror into Caitlyn's heart. And Caitlyn knew exactly why Dane had bought it to give to her. Both of them were certain that the night he'd rescued her from the cougar, the night he'd first made love to her, had been the night that she'd conceived their baby.

"Where are you going on your honeymoon?"

Lisa's eyes were shining and Caitlyn smiled at the excited

teenager. "We're going to the most romantic spot on earth, of course."

"Where's that? Hawaii?"

"Nope. We're staying right here. As far as I'm concerned, the Double B Ranch is the most romantic spot on earth."

"Really?" Lisa looked surprised.

"That's right. It's where I met Dane and it was Aunt Bella's dream." Caitlyn felt a bittersweet sadness fill her. If only Aunt Bella could have lived to see the result of her brilliant match-making scheme. "I almost left it once, and that was a big mistake. Now I'll never leave it again."

"I guess it is romantic, now that I think about it," Lisa agreed. "And it's even more romantic because it's the place where you found your true love. Is Mr. Morr—I mean, *Dr.* Morrison really going to set up his practice here?"

"Yes." Caitlyn nodded emphatically, reaching up to brush her long red hair, the hair that Gibby claimed was the color of cinnamon. "We're building a clinic right here on the ranch. Now that Doc Henley is retiring, anyone who needs a doctor can come out here and see Dane."

"The people in Little Fork are really going to appreciate that. We didn't know what we'd do without a doctor. And now we have one. He's been here all along, and we didn't even know it."

Caitlyn thought about what Dane had told her last night. The carpenters would arrive tomorrow to start construction on the small four-bed clinic, and they'd promised him that they'd finish in plenty of time for her delivery. Their baby would be born on the Double B Ranch, and Dane's first clinic patient would be his son or daughter.

"Let's all have a toast to my sister, the bride, on her happy wedding day!"

A cork popped from the vicinity of the dresser, and Caitlyn turned to look. Julia had opened a bottle, and she was pouring its bubbly contents into three fluted glasses. "Julia, please don't," she protested. "Neither one of us should drink."

"Relax. It's sparkling apple juice." Julia handed Caitlyn a glass. "Jake drove all the way into Laramie this morning so I'd have something to use as a toast."

There was a soft look in Julia's eyes when she mentioned Jake's name, and Caitlyn wondered if there was romance in the air. She'd mention it to Dane later to see what he thought of the idea, but she didn't have time to speculate about it now. Dane was waiting for her, and she could hardly wait to go into his arms and begin the rest of her happy life as his wife.

"To my boss, the bride."

Lisa touched her glass to Caitlyn's, and Julia did the same. And just then the door opened and Dane stepped in.

"That better be apple juice, Julia."

"It is, Doc Morrison." Julia laughed and hurried over to pour a glass for Dane. "We were just toasting the bride."

"To my bride." Dane clinked his glass against Caitlyn's and took his place by her side. And then they all linked arms and smiled at their reflection in the mirror.

Caitlyn had a thought then, in that moment of perfect happiness, one that would come back to warm her in years to come. They were three pretty ranch women, one who'd just married her perfect husband, one who might be experiencing the first blush of love, and one who had yet to give her heart. And all three of them truly believed that dreams were possible and that true love was alive and well at the Double B Ranch.

ABOUT THE AUTHOR

Gina Jackson lives with her family in Granada Hills, California. *Caitlyn's Cowboy* is her first contemporary romance, and she is currently working on her second, *Cookies and Kisses*, which will be published in April, 2000. Gina also writes Regency romances under the pseudonym Kathryn Kirkwood. She loves hearing from readers, and you may write to her c/o Zebra Books. Please include a self-addressed stamped envelope if you wish a response. You may also contact her at her E-mail address: yr-writer@aol.com.

BOOK YOUR PLACE ON OUR WEBSITE AND MAKE THE READING CONNECTION!

We've created a customized website just for our very special readers, where you can get the inside scoop on everything that's going on with Zebra, Pinnacle and Kensington books.

When you come online, you'll have the exciting opportunity to:

- View covers of upcoming books

- Read sample chapters

- Learn about our future publishing schedule (listed by publication month *and author*)

- Find out when your favorite authors will be visiting a city near you

- Search for and order backlist books from our online catalog

- Check out author bios and background information

- Send e-mail to your favorite authors

- Meet the Kensington staff online

- Join us in weekly chats with authors, readers and other guests

- Get writing guidelines

- AND MUCH MORE!

**Visit our website at
http://www.zebrabooks.com**

Coming in October 1999 From Bouquet Romances

#13 Loving Max by Wendy Morgan
__(0-8217-6348-2, $3.99) Living under an assumed name, Olivia Halloran cannot afford to call attention to herself. But when she rescues two children from drowning, she suddenly finds herself in the media spotlight. For the twins belong to Max Rothwell, a brooding, reclusive man Olivia finds herself irresistibly attracted to.

#14 Crazy For You by Maddie James
__(0-8217-6349-0, $3.99) Lovely nineties-style flower child, Tasha Smith, has been in a funk over her broken engagement. Determined to shake her blues, she heads down to a resort in Jamaica, and meets the most unlikely companion—a workaholic salesman who has no idea how sexy he looks in his Brooks Brothers suit!

#15 Love Me Tender by Michaila Callan
__(0-8217-6350-4, $3.99) Determined to raise her unborn twins in a wholesome community, Eden Karr leaves behind her career in New York City to open up a clothing boutique in Texas. Unused to her new surroundings, she can't help feeling she's made a mistake. That is, until sexy carpenter Jace Morgan strides into her store.

#16 The Prince's Bride by Tracy Cozzens
__(0-8217-6351-2, $3.99) Society editor Nicole Aldridge knew she was out of her mind to agree to find Prince Rand his ideal queen. No paragon of perfection could possibly fit into Rand's narrow glass slipper—unless love took charge and changed their lives forever.

Call toll free **1-888-345-BOOK** to order by phone or use this coupon to order by mail.

Name_____

Address_____

City_____ State _____Zip _____

Please send me the books I have checked above.

I am enclosing	$_____
Plus postage and handling*	$_____
Sales tax (where applicable)	$_____
Total amount enclosed	$_____

*Add $2.50 for the first book and $.50 for each additional book.

Send check or Money order (no cash or CODs) to:

Kensington Publishing Corp., 850 Third Avenue, New York, NY 10022

Prices and Numbers subject to change without notice. Valid only in the U.S.

All Books will be available 9/1/99. All orders subject to availability.

Check out our web site at **www.kensingtonbooks.com**

Put a Little Romance in Your Life With
Janelle Taylor

__Anything for Love	0-8217-4992-7	$5.99US/$6.99CAN
__Forever Ecstasy	0-8217-5241-3	$5.99US/$6.99CAN
__Fortune's Flames	0-8217-5450-5	$5.99US/$6.99CAN
__Destiny's Temptress	0-8217-5448-3	$5.99US/$6.99CAN
__Love Me With Fury	0-8217-5452-1	$5.99US/$6.99CAN
__First Love, Wild Love	0-8217-5277-4	$5.99US/$6.99CAN
__Kiss of the Night Wind	0-8217-5279-0	$5.99US/$6.99CAN
__Love With a Stranger	0-8217-5416-5	$6.99US/$8.50CAN
__Forbidden Ecstasy	0-8217-5278-2	$5.99US/$6.99CAN
__Defiant Ecstasy	0-8217-5447-5	$5.99US/$6.99CAN
__Follow the Wind	0-8217-5449-1	$5.99US/$6.99CAN
__Wild Winds	0-8217-6026-2	$6.99US/$8.50CAN
__Defiant Hearts	0-8217-5563-1	$6.50US/$8.00CAN
__Golden Torment	0-8217-5451-3	$5.99US/$6.99CAN
__Bittersweet Ecstasy	0-8217-5445-9	$5.99US/$6.99CAN
__Taking Chances	0-8217-4259-0	$4.50US/$5.50CAN
__By Candlelight	0-8217-5703-2	$6.99US/$8.50CAN
__Chase the Wind	0-8217-4740-1	$5.99US/$6.99CAN
__Destiny Mine	0-8217-5185-9	$5.99US/$6.99CAN
__Midnight Secrets	0-8217-5280-4	$5.99US/$6.99CAN
__Sweet Savage Heart	0-8217-5276-6	$5.99US/$6.99CAN
__Moonbeams and Magic	0-7860-0184-4	$5.99US/$6.99CAN
__Brazen Ecstasy	0-8217-5446-7	$5.99US/$6.99CAN

Call toll free **1-888-345-BOOK** to order by phone or use this coupon to order by mail.

Name _____

Address _____

City _____ State _____ Zip _____

Please send me the books I have checked above.

I am enclosing	$_____
Plus postage and handling*	$_____
Sales tax (in New York and Tennessee)	$_____
Total amount enclosed	$_____

*Add $2.50 for the first book and $.50 for each additional book.

Send check or money order (no cash or CODs) to:

Kensington Publishing Corp., 850 Third Avenue, New York, NY 10022

Prices and Numbers subject to change without notice.

All orders subject to availability.

Check out our website at **www.kensingtonbooks.com**

Put a Little Romance in Your Life With
Fern Michaels

__Dear Emily	0-8217-5676-1	$6.99US/$8.50CAN
__Sara's Song	0-8217-5856-X	$6.99US/$8.50CAN
__Wish List	0-8217-5228-6	$6.99US/$7.99CAN
__Vegas Rich	0-8217-5594-3	$6.99US/$8.50CAN
__Vegas Heat	0-8217-5758-X	$6.99US/$8.50CAN
__Vegas Sunrise	1-55817-5983-3	$6.99US/$8.50CAN
__Whitefire	0-8217-5638-9	$6.99US/$8.50CAN

Call toll free **1-888-345-BOOK** to order by phone or use this coupon to order by mail.

Name_____

Address_____

City _____ State _____Zip_____

Please send me the books I have checked above.

I am enclosing	$_____
Plus postage and handling*	$_____
Sales tax (in New York and Tennessee)	$_____
Total amount enclosed	$_____

*Add $2.50 for the first book and $.50 for each additional book.

Send check or money order (no cash or CODs) to:

Kensington Publishing Corp., 850 Third Avenue, New York, NY 10022

Prices and Numbers subject to change without notice.

All orders subject to availability.

Check out our website at **www.kensingtonbooks.com**

Celebrate Romance With Two of Today's Hottest Authors

Meagan McKinney

__The Fortune Hunter	$6.50US/$8.00CAN	0-8217-6037-8
__Gentle from the Night	$5.99US/$7.50CAN	0-8217-5803-9
__A Man to Slay Dragons	$5.99US/$6.99CAN	0-8217-5345-2
__My Wicked Enchantress	$5.99US/$7.50CAN	0-8217-5661-3
__No Choice but Surrender	$5.99US/$7.50CAN	0-8217-5859-4

Meryl Sawyer

__Half Moon Bay	$6.50US/$8.00CAN	0-8217-6144-7
__The Hideaway	$5.99US/$7.50CAN	0-8217-5780-6
__Tempting Fate	$6.50US/$8.00CAN	0-8217-5858-6
__Unforgettable	$6.50US/$8.00CAN	0-8217-5564-1